The Ghosts of Carmen De Santo

Valerie R. Kacian

ISBN: 098830242X
ISBN-13: 978-0988302426

DEDICATION

I dedicate this novel to my beautiful and loving family who have all been so patient during this process. I love you all so much!

CONTENTS

PROLOGUE   1

PART ONE   5

PART TWO   225

EPILOGUE   275

"The work of magic involves transformation, and the first transformation is the shift of perception."

Marion Weinstein.

PROLOGUE

That feeling of unease flooded her veins again. She opened her eyes slightly as an intake of breath made her cough and her eyes burn. Immediately she closed them, turned over, and buried her head deeper into the pillow. It always seemed that the vast depth of a pillow served the specific purpose to block out all feelings, sights, and sensations. After half an hour of dozing she began to hear a high-pitched wail in the next room. What was that? Another wail. Oh, the telephone. She opened one eye intent on sleeping and quite certain she would not get up for the phone. The ringing stopped, then started again. Carmen let out a breath of frustration and rolled out of bed. As soon as she raised her head the room spun around her and it was all she could do to keep herself from falling over. The ringing of the phone seemed to be very distant and she grabbed a chair to keep from falling. The room spun once more then steadied itself enough for Carmen to walk to the bedroom door. She left the room and stumbled to the phone, which was screaming, screaming, screaming like a spoiled baby by now. She lifted the receiver, slumped against the wall, and breathed a hello.

"No, I'm desperately ill, and I'll go to the doctor tomorrow if this doesn't pass." A pause. "I haven't a clue why, but I am on death's door right now." Pause. "No, I really cannot." A pause. "Oh, fuck you, fine," she breathed. "I'll be there at seven, but don't call all day unless it's really serious. I'll be in bed." She hung up the phone, pushed her back against the wall, and closed her eyes for a moment. When she opened them again they

1

stung mercilessly. Carmen shuffled to the bathroom to pee, then hurried back to the bedroom. Once in bed she snuggled back into the pillow desperately wishing she hadn't agreed to head out that evening. "This is ridiculous," she breathed. He always did this to her and it was stupid she fell for it every time. Her head began to spin again, as she drifted back to sleep.

Part One: Discovery

VALERIE R. KACIAN

CHAPTER ONE

Jared tied his shoelaces, then rushed down the stairs to greet his wife in the kitchen. It was a beautiful morning in mid-August and he was excited for a nice, long run while it was still relatively cool. Clarisse looked up from the counter where she was preparing breakfast, her face ashen.

"Is something wrong?" he asked with concern.

"Shhh....shhhh...." She snapped waving her hand in the air. The radio buzzed in the background. "The Emery boy is missing. Everyone's a mess this morning," she breathed. She put her hand up again and they both listened to the broadcast.

"The boy was last seen inside Tom and Annie Emery's home last night at approximately seven o'clock when he was put to bed. Annie Emery discovered the boy missing at six thirty this morning when she went to his bedroom to wake him up for school...."

Clarisse clucked her face etched with worry. "Do you think we're going to find him?" Her eyes widened when she said this.

Jared snatched a piece of toast from the plate in front of her and stuffed it in his mouth. "We'll find him, Clarisse." He chased down the toast with orange juice. "We always find our kids. Remember Gregory Patton? Poor kid was missing an hour and the parents were in hysterics. Remember how he just decided to stay out a little later than his curfew that night? We found him. We'll find the Emery boy."

"Mark," Clarisse said quickly.

"What?" Jared took another swig of orange juice.

"That is his name. Mark Emery." Her eyes were wide.

Jared kissed his wife on the cheek. "We'll find him," he whispered. "Now, I'm out for my jog. Eggs, scrambled this morning, dear." He called over his shoulder and rushed out the front door. Clarisse would worry until they found Mark Emery; she worried about near everyone in town and listened to the local news endlessly as if to fuel her anxiety.

The air was balmy and Jared could tell it would prove to be a sweltering day. There weren't all that many cars driving by as he stepped out onto the sidewalk and stretched out his long, lean muscles. He shook his head to ward off the haze of sleep and ran his fingers through his short hair already damp with sweat. Yes, it was going to be one incredible day. He began to walk slowly down East Street, then picked up the pace until he was at last jogging and beginning to feel the apprehension of the morning melting away. That's what running did for him every morning. It gave him something to wake up for and something to get through the day. Some people had alcohol. Some people had food, or drugs or women; he had running. Sweat began to drip down his forehead and slide down to his nose. He brushed the drip aside as he turned right on East Street to start on Central Street. Already he could feel his breath coming quicker than usual. It had to be the heat. Jared brushed aside another drip of sweat and decided once he was at the end of Central Street, he would take Collins Ave, then head down the dirt path through the wooded area that he always liked – and that remained cool on days like these.

As the jarring, rhythmic motion of his feet began to put him into a near-meditative state, Jared began to contemplate the Emery boy. Missing. He allowed the word and the shocked, desperate look on his wife's face to register. He could feel his heart sink just slightly. Kids shouldn't go missing. That's just the way it was. A mother should never have to wake up one day, check on her son, and find him gone. Just gone. Vanished into thin air as she lay in her bed dreaming of all those sticky, sweet good times. Although a religious man, it was times like these that Jared almost had to question God's true motives with those on Earth. Almost. God was listening.

Jared began down the dirt path and ducked so that a branch would not scratch his face. It scratched his shoulder instead. He turned to look and saw a thin line where the branch had dawdled.

Annie Emery was an odd duck. She kept to herself mostly and spoke quietly with a strained look on her face and a "deer in headlights" appearance to her eyes. Annie always looked in a constant state of anxiety; as if she were just waiting for bad news. She was always warm, loving, and attentive to her son, Mark, however. Never was there a smile upon her face unless she looked upon him. And now this. Jared felt his heart begin to fall to his knees and he had to exhale quickly to make the sorrow he felt for Annie fade away a bit. Neighbors and friends of the family had to be positive and encouraging to families who were experiencing this kind of loss and fear. However, it looked pretty grim. Young boys just don't disappear from their beds. They are taken and generally that means a long road to recovery for the parents and the child should the child ever return. He felt the sinking in his stomach again and had to take another deep breath.

Jared entered an area where the trees thinned out a bit, which would mean there would be fewer branches to scratch and maul him. As the sun shifted through the trees a tiny flash of light caught Jared's eye. He began to slow his pace to a fast walk, then a slower walk. He kept his eye on the area where the light had flashed not because he wanted to, but because he felt compelled to do so. Jared backtracked slightly, then walked in the direction of where the sparkle had been. His breathing was heavy from the run and from the slow trace of fear that was beginning to creep through every cell in his body. Something was very wrong here.

Through the blades of grass that reached up as if exalting the sun lay a necklace. Jared knelt down and picked it up. The necklace consisted of a gold chain with a long amethyst stone hanging from it affixed with a gold cap. It was familiar somehow and the feeling of fear and dread did not dissipate. He turned it over on his hand and the sun licked it just enough to jog Jared's memory.

Carmen. Instantly Jared was at a local cookout. He was walking to the table where drinks were laid out carefully all in a row on a red and white-checkered tablecloth. The sun was in his eyes and he had to furrow his brow so that he could see up ahead. From the corner of his eye he saw a sparkle. He turned to see Carmen De Santo laughing and talking to Kitty Montgomery. Carmen smiled wide, laughed that infectious laugh, and twirled the necklace between her fingers. Carmen's eyes flashed just as the necklace shimmered and her laugh could be heard for miles.

Jared looked back down at the necklace in his hand. Carmen's necklace? He could hear his wife's voice in his mind. "Oh, that Carmen De Santo. Forever with that necklace. Fiddling. Fiddling. I swear she's always so nervous. Does she ever take that thing off? Do you think?" Jared focused his attention back on the necklace. How did it get here? In the middle of the woods?

He put the necklace back where it had been among the blades of grass and stood up. He looked at it a moment longer. All he could think was that perhaps she had taken a walk in the woods, as she was known to do, and it had fallen off and she had not realized it. The nagging doubt he felt could just be the effects of the news that Mark Emery was missing. Nothing more. He took a deep breath, looked to the sky, then tilted his head so his ear touched his shoulder for a deep neck stretch. He switched to the other side, rolled his shoulders back, and felt some of the tension release. There, much better.

Jared took another deep breath, took one last look at the necklace, and began to jog slowly along again. Just ahead the woods could get thick so he decided to run for another minute or two, then turn back on his way home. Finding the necklace had taken a few extra minutes he hadn't meant to spend. As he ran he started thinking about what he would be doing at work that day. Papers on his desk needed to be signed and attended to, calls needed to be made, and he had wanted to talk to his secretary about a personal matter with her family. His feet pounded heavily now and his mind was beginning to clear. Just as he was about to turn around and head back home a surprisingly cool breeze almost-lovingly brushed his body. Although only late August there was already some fallen leaves along the ground that flew up into the air just briefly, then came back down again. He could sense he was approaching a clearing by the way the trees were becoming more and more sparse, however, he could not attest to the coolness of the breeze because he did not remember any body of water in this area of the woods. Despite the strangeness of it, the cool was a comfort in an otherwise deathly warm morning. Jared decided to jog to the edge of the clearing he could see up ahead before heading back home.

Just as the clearing was a few feet in front of him another cool breeze brushed his body, this time a little more insistent and a little more chilling. Jared stopped jogging immediately and stared ahead of him. The clearing was nothing more than a field of grass that had already started to brown from lack of sunlight due to seasonal changes. Despite this a sense of fear and excitement began to trickle through Jared's entire body. In the middle of the clearing lay something he couldn't quite make out. The wind had also brought a scent that was unmistakable to anyone. It was the sweet, syrupy smell of death. Jared's nearly empty stomach turned at the scent, but he continued to stare. An odd sensation of wonder overtook him and he couldn't move. He didn't want to move, but he knew he had to. He knew what was out there.

He took one step further and the object ahead of him was closer, but not by much. Another step. He was holding his breath now. He saw a hint of white embedded into the darkening brown of the grass. He stopped and the world tilted for just a moment as a wave of dizziness rushed over him. He closed his eyes, took a deep breath, and opened them again. Same browning grass. Same sky. Same trees. Same white object in the field. He could feel an odd kind of numbing at the very palms of his hands, and yet somehow he took two more steps closer. The white object was not just a blur of white anymore, but was starting to take on a specific shape. Jared closed his eyes again and his stomach turned nausea overcoming him. He dropped to his knees and watched the brown grass rush up to meet him. With his hands and his forehead on the ground he took deep breaths to ward off the nausea, then looked up. Yes, it was. It very well had to be. In that moment with what little bit of strength and courage he had left, Jared stood up and took a few more steps. His face felt numb, his legs were weak, and he was holding his breath again. But who? Who was it? Curiosity overcame his disgust and fear and he took a couple more steps forward.

Just as he closed his eyes again afraid of whom he would have to see in this condition a cool breeze, not as cold as the previous, caressed his body and a thought came to mind that this would be ok and he would be ok. A calming sensation replaced the breeze and he opened his eyes slowly. His eyes scanned the browning grass, the bright blue sky, and the white object that could only be this woman. The world tilted, but Jared remained at ease.

Her long white hands lay upon the grass palm up as if enjoying the warm sunshine. The tips of her fingers seemed to twitch slightly as if keeping rhythm. Seemed to twitch slightly, they couldn't really be twitching now could they? He scanned up her arm, delicate and white against the grass, to her shoulder also white as porcelain to her neck stained a deep red, trails of the red running down to the grass below and underneath her body. He looked to her face, which was just as white as her body with her cheeks beginning to sink just a bit. Red splashes dusted her cheeks, lips and ears. Her hair, a light, reddish brown was also stained red. On her forehead there was a horrible incision made and Jared did not wish to look close enough to determine what this was. Her eyes were slightly open and looking downward, unseeing, solid, and lifeless. He scanned down her body, which was clad in what looked like a white nightgown. The white of the nightgown and the white of her skin contrasted greatly with the large black and red splashes and scratches at various points on her chest. Her legs and her bare feet lay straight out in front of her and besides dirt and leaves they were perfectly clean. Not a spot of blood on them.

Jared dropped to his knees and began to pray. Rest her soul. God, rest her soul. God what has happened? What was happening to this world? From the corner of his eye Jared thought he saw her hand twitching, twitching, twitching again. Through a haze of tears he stared at her hand wishing it back to life; wishing her entire body back to life.

In his mind he could hear her laughter, infectious and intoxicating. Her bright smile all red with cherry lipstick and brilliant white teeth. Her eyes sparkling and intense, a dynamic greenish blue in color. The lilt in her voice as if she were almost singing all the time. Her mischievous smirk. God help her. God help this poor creature. May God help Carmen De Santo.

CHAPTER TWO

"So, it'll get worse before it gets better, " Special Agent Jill Simko breathed into her cell phone. "That's a relief." Her tone was sarcastic. She rolled her eyes and watched as her partner, Special Agent Jack Pellingworth entered the Boston police archive library. He was holding a manila envelope, which he promptly threw down on the table in front of her. It made a short, slapping sound. "All right....all right. I have to get going. I've got something here....ah...yes, yes, ok, ok, bye." She ended the call on her cell phone and looked up at Jack, again rolling her eyes.

"How's the kid?" he asked her.

"Same. Bad. And all the lovely details to go along with it," she sighed. Jill leaned back in her chair staring at the case file in front of her. The fact that they had been interrupted during their trip to Boston only meant one thing. He had struck again. "Tell me. Is it bad?" Her face was serious and her eyes were tired.

Jack leaned on her desk and picked up the case file. "Well, it's strange that's for sure." He sighed and opened the file. "Not his usual type....anyway, we have to look this over quickly and get to the location ASAP."

Jill rolled her eyes again, "ASAP? Don't they have local authorities that can look at this?" She was nearly whining and began rubbing her eyes.

"They do, but the Bureau believes this is a matter of immediate concern. The wound patterns and positioning of the body are very familiar. This may be our man, and we can't ignore the case." Jack stood up and

11

looked at her with a blank, serious expression. "Besides, we're already here and the scene is maybe forty-five minutes away." He grinned, but only slightly.

Jill stood up and pushed her chair back. "Oh, I know, Jack. I was just hoping to get back home to Virginia to spend a little bit of time with Amanda. I'm worried about her." She grabbed the file from Jack.

Jill opened it and pulled out a picture of Carmen De Santo laying face up in a field of grass. She was wearing all white and the wounds on her chest, neck, and face had turned a dark black. The photo had been snapped by local authorities and e-mailed directly to the Bureau in Virginia. Not only were the local authorities baffled by the severity of the wounds and the degree of her death, but they, too, had recognized the familiar characteristics of a wanted serial killer on the East Coast. "When was she discovered?" She looked up at Jack.

"This morning. Early. I don't have all the details yet. The body is still at the location as far as I know. We should be there as soon as we can, of course."

Jill nodded and closed the file. "I'll look at this closer on the ride over. In the meantime, call the local authorities and ask that they not touch a hair on her precious head until we get there, ok?" Jill began to leave the archives room.

"No problem."

Jill looked back over her shoulder at Jack. "Why do I have a feeling this one is going to take a while?" she asked softly.

CHAPTER THREE

The air was balmy and thick when Jill Simko and Jack Pellingworth stepped out of the Ford sedan onto Lake Shore Drive. A breeze swept up as Jill's feet touched the grass on the outskirts of the wooded area in question. She paused for a moment and looked up. The sky was perfectly clear and suddenly seemed enormous.

Lake Shore, Massachusetts was a very small community, mostly wooded with a small green for a common area and absolutely no significant lake to speak of, which made the name of the town a mystery in and of itself. The first thing Jill had noticed about the town was that it was very silent and there weren't many people walking around despite the fact that the sun was out and that was getting more and more rare in New England. Of course it was also blistering out so that must have been why the town looked nearly deserted. Jill hoped that the crime scene and contact with the local people would give her more insight into this strange, little town.

Jill looked over at Jack, who nodded to her, then proceeded down a path in the woods that had been trampled with the constant traffic to and from the crime scene throughout the day. The area was taped off with crime scene tape. Jill reached into her pocket and pulled out her plastic gloves as she looked closely at the branches, trees, and shrubbery all around her. Aside from the crime scene traffic there did not seem to be much disturbed in this area, which could mean that not many people walked through, nor played in this area of the woods. Near a large tree and a patch of shrubbery a small area had been taped and marked. Without a word both she and Jack headed in that direction.

A wooden stake marked CSI #1 had been driven into the ground next to a gold necklace with what looked like an amethyst stone dangling from it. Jill looked up from the exhibit and took a deep breath. Upon initial observation, there did not appear to be any other signs of distress along the path, however there could be trace evidence that was yet to be found.

"That's the necklace," a voice said behind them.

Jill and Jack turned around and came face-to face with what appeared to be a local police officer and another man in a tan suit. The police officer was a tall, large man with a slightly protruding gut and a kind smile in his eyes. The man in the tan suit had a calmness about him that was slightly disconcerting, and a smug smile.

"Oh, I'm sorry. I'm Lieutenant Copeland, and this is Detective Winsler." He shook both Jack and Jill's hands.

Jill then offered Detective Winsler her hand, "I'm Special Agent Jill Simko, and this is my partner, Special Agent Jack Pellingworth. I assume you are both aware that we have been called in to this case." Both men nodded. "Then I thought we would start with some crime scene review." Her words were steady and secure.

"Ah, yes, we are very happy to have you. As you must know, this kind of thing doesn't always happen in Lake Shore." He let out a soft chuckle, then his eyes turned slightly sad. "Carmen was a good kid." The sadness left his eyes as quickly as it had come. "Detective Winsler is here to help us find the missing Emery boy, however he has done some preliminary questioning of witnesses in this case, as well."

Jill looked quickly at Jack and back at Lieutenant Copeland. "There's a missing child in this town?" She frowned slightly trying to discern why this had not been mentioned in the De Santo file.

Lieutenant Copeland nodded, then turned to Detective Winsler. "Yes, the boy was discovered missing early this morning. We are working to find him, but we currently believe this is a runaway case. The boy's parents are in deep shock right now and have not provided enough information. We believe they will be cooperative enough once this really sets in."

Jill looked at Jack for just a slight moment, then glanced down at the ground. Obviously the local authorities had no idea how to handle cases of this magnitude. A missing child was nothing to sneeze at, runaway or not. However, Jill decided she would consult Jack on this, as well as ask a few casual questions here and there to get a better idea of what authorities were actually doing to find this child. Regardless, they had been sent to investigate the death of Carmen De Santo and that's just what she intended on doing.

"We were checking out your exhibit here," Jack said turning around to point to the necklace. "Got any info on this?"

Lieutenant Copeland nodded. "Ah, yes, Jared Prentice found this just prior to finding Carmen..." He cleared his throat. "I mean, just before discovering the victim."

Jill crouched down and picked up the necklace with a gloved hand. "We'll have to bag this and keep with forensics, if you don't mind," she said looking up at him.

"But of course. Also, we've detained Jared for a bit so he is available for questions if you'd like."

Jill stood up. "Yes, we'll want to speak with him."

Jack chimed in, "He need not be detained, however, Lieutenant, Detective." He nodded at each man. "That is, unless you consider him a suspect."

Lieutenant Copeland let out a short laugh. "Oh, no. Jared's a good guy. He's very shaken up so we took him to the station to relax for a bit. He wanted to fill out some paperwork and be available without anyone coming to his house." He stepped forward and said softly. "His wife is a bit of a busy-body and he would rather all the lurid details stay at the station, if you get my drift."

There was no drift to get. This was confidential information and in a small town like this news traveled fast. Jill nodded, "Certainly. Have forensics bag the necklace and look for trace evidence in a ten-foot radius."

"Yes, ma'am," Detective Winsler winked, nodded and then headed off further into the woods.

Jack pointed to where Detective Winsler had gone. "Is the body that way?"

Lieutenant Copeland nodded. "Yes. She's down there."

Jill paused. "This must be difficult for you. I'm assuming you knew Carmen well?" She took one step closer to him.

"We all knew Carmen well. Her husband is a prominent businessman in Boston. He also holds offices in New York. As a housewife, Carmen spent much of her time helping people in this community. I cannot imagine anyone who would want to hurt her." His eyes clouded over with deep remorse.

"It's ok, Lieutenant. We'll be speaking with people in the community who may have known her so that we can get a better idea of who may have wanted to hurt her. She may have been a victim of someone outside of this community, as well, so there are a lot of factors here." She smiled kindly.

Lieutenant Copeland nodded. "Yes, there are. We are very happy to have you, Special Agent. It's not every day that we have something like this happen."

"Of course," Jill said softly. "We'll proceed to the….to Carmen if that's all right."

"Yes, yes, please do. I will oversee the Forensics Team in this section." It was obvious Lieutenant Copeland wanted a break from the duty of overseeing Carmen's body.

"Excellent, " Jack stated.

As they headed down the path in the woods outlined with crime scene tape, Jill turned to Jack, "Wow. This is like a different world out here."

"I agree. I'm worried about how they've handled the body so far."

"My guess is pretty well since Lieutenant Copeland is still referring to her as if she were alive."

Jack nodded. As they got closer to the crime scene, forensics experts whisked by them heading back up the path presumably to collect the necklace. Jack and Jill approached an enchanting clearing in the woods. The sun in the sky glistened off the tufts of gold and red from the pre-Autumn grasses creating an effect that was nothing short of ethereal. When she stopped to take in the scene she felt a soft, cool breeze brush over her face. Her cheek tingled where the breeze had touched her and a feeling of calm came over her body. It was like nothing she had ever experienced before. She glanced over at Jack who was bending down to duck under the crime scene tape, but he seemed unaffected.

He stood upright and looked back at her his eyes slightly puzzled. "Coming?" he asked.

Although dazed she shook her head in the affirmative and slipped under the crime scene tape. Detective Winsler walked over to them and gave them the same slow, condescending smile as if their very presence were a joke to him. "Will you need time alone with the body?"

Jack's jaw twitched in his irritation. He was no stranger to confrontation when being called in to some cases, and Detective Winsler was just subtle enough about it to get right underneath his skin. Jack held back his annoyance and nodded. "Yes, we'll let the forensics teams take care of most of the evidence collection, but we need to examine the body for a little while."

"Ah, yes, after your examination, the forensics team will continue to canvas the area with your additional instruction, then we would like to bring her to the morgue for autopsy." He smiled again as if he were discussing what he was having for dinner that night, then pointed in the direction of the body. "She's over there. Let me know when you are finished." He turned to leave.

"Detective Winsler?" Jill asked. "Do you know who was first response here?"

Detective Winsler turned back around slowly his eyes twinkling blue as if her question were amusing somehow. "Jennifer Townsend was first response. She is an EMT with Lake Shore. She responded to an emergency call from Jared Prentice."

"Will she be available for questioning later?" Jill asked.

"Absolutely. Is there anything else I can help you with?" His tone was one of impatience, though he smiled after he said it.

"No, I think we are all set. Thank you, Detective," Jack stated. As Detective Winsler turned back around Jack whispered, "Prick." Jill grinned. It was nice to know that at least she and Jack were on the right page.

They proceeded to where the body lay, which was at present surrounded by a huddle of forensics experts. Jack tapped one on the shoulder. "Who's your unit leader?"

A short man with brown hair and a cheery disposition turned to face him. "Oh, I am! Can I help you?"

"I am Special Agent Jack Pellington, and this is Special Agent Jill Simko."

The man's smile broadened. "Ah, yes, we're happy to have you. I am Jon Cutting. I have the team working here, but we can move if you'd like to view her." He wrote something down on his clipboard as he talked.

"Yes, please, that would be great," Jill stated.

"All right, gang!" Jon called in a cheerful way. "Let's take a break. We have federal agents to conduct a brief investigation here!"

Blank faces looked up at both Jack and Jill for a moment, and then with a few grumbles the group began to move away from the body. "Let's go! Let's go!" Jon called like a cheerleading coach. He turned to Jack and Jill. "I think you're all set. Let me know if I can be of any help."

Jill smiled back at Jon Cutting, but said nothing. It was now their turn to take a closer look at Carmen De Santo. They both turned around and looked down. Carmen De Santo lay on her back her arms limply at her sides and her legs out straight. Jack took out a camera and began with preliminary pictures of her body. She wore a long, white dress of some kind, which was hideously stained with dark blood. Her neck bore a deep gash that yawned open slightly exposing the tough tissue underneath. Blood splatter dotted her pale face and smeared around her mouth. Black blood had pooled underneath her body mingling with the dirt and grass. Jill instantly knelt down next to the body to take a look at her forehead, which bore a large incision. Jack leaned in close behind her to take a few pictures of her face and the incision.

"The medical examiner will need to examine this closer. It's not as deep as the others. Not enough blood and tearing." Jill gazed down her neck to her chest and looked closely at what appeared to be stab wounds. "Also, there are four stab wounds here on her chest. Did you get shots of these yet?" Jill looked up at Jack who proceeded to take a few pictures of her chest. Jill stood up and looked down at the body taking in the flow of blood to the ground below and the outline of her body. Then she took a moment to analyze Carmen's face. Despite the blood splatter her features were smooth and clean and her skin pale with death had begun to sink slightly which was to be expected at this point after death and in this degree of heat.

"Jack, look at her face. Her complexion." She paused a moment to look down at Carmen again. Carmen must have been one Hell of a beautiful girl. Her skin even in death was smooth and clean, her lips full, and her hair vibrant and young, although heavily matted. "We'll have to check with forensics, but I think she may not have been dead as long as her case file claims."

Jill took note of this, then proceeded to scan down Carmen's legs, which were set slightly apart under her white dress. "We'll need to make sure forensics runs a rape kit," she muttered more to herself than to Jack. "Oh, Renault. You do keep us guessing don't you?"

Renault, or so he called himself, was the man who had consumed Jill and Jack's lives for nearly two years. It started with a prostitute who had been raped and murdered outside of the DC area and had escalated to high-profile cases all along the East coast. Renault's modus operandi was to slit his victim's throat, make a large incision of a cross on the forehead, and rape just prior to or at the victim's death. Renault had begun conversing with local authorities in the form of in-depth letters describing certain murders approximately six months after the first body was discovered.

Jack Pellington and Jill Simko were handed the case when Lina Musterelle was murdered. Lina was the daughter of an important businessman in DC, who apparently had ties to the President of the United States, and thus her murder became national news. She was not a prostitute, but a wealthy college kid who studied hard and partied harder. One night on the way home from a wild party on the southern end of campus Lina was approached by a man who asked her directions to the Campus Center. Lina stumbled over to the vehicle only to be grabbed and pulled in. Her battered body was found in a field thirty miles away approximately one week later. The intensity and severity of the case forced the FBI to put on more manpower, which meant Jack and Jill were designated the case full time and began the two-year journey that had led them to Carmen De Santo in this sleepy town of Lake Shore, Massachusetts.

"Is this woman important?" Jack asked looking down at her again. "By that I mean is she socially important here?"

Jill nodded. "Good question. I think Lieutenant Copeland can help us with that. I have a sneaky suspicion she's pretty important here."

"So do I." They took a few more pictures, then took a moment to remind Jon Cutting that all reports including autopsy reports were to be sent to them for first review. They proceeded back up the path to their vehicle. The plan was to head to the police station to speak with Lieutenant Copeland, who had apparently returned there while they were looking at the body. They also wanted to begin questioning witnesses starting with Jennifer Townsend, who was the first response to the scene. As they both sat down in their vehicle, Jill's cell phone began to ring.

"Simko," she breathed into the phone. Jack started the car and began backing up from their spot. "I'm happy to hear that. Very happy. It's nice to know that some things are still normal anyhow." A long pause followed as Jill nodded, then gave Jack a quick smile. "Ah, yes, all right. All right. I will call you back as soon as I can.....of course.....ok....yes....thank you." Simko closed her phone and glanced at Jack. "My daughter. She's doing better. At least her fever has vanished."

Jack nodded. "Very good." Jill made some notes on her pad of paper as the two drove in silence to the center of town, which was nothing more than a few storefronts, a post office, a town green, and the public safety building. "Would you live here?" Jack asked her quite out of the blue.

Jill smiled, "It depends, I suppose." She looked out her passenger side window as they pulled into the police station parking lot. "It depends on a lot of things."

Jack grinned and stopped the car. "Time to go see why Carmen was here."

Jill noticed that not only did Jack refer to the victim by her first name, but he also made a quick assumption, something that was very out of character for Jack. "Are you saying you don't think she was born and raised here?"

They both stepped out of the vehicle and closed the doors. The air was still very warm, almost oppressive at this point. "Call it a hunch," Jack stated and winked at her.

Jill nodded as the two approached the small police station and went inside. The officer at the front desk was a small, blonde woman with brilliant blue eyes, and a quick, nervous smile. "Hi, I'm Special Agent Simko and this is Special Agent Pellingworth. We are here to see Lieutenant Copeland." In the background phones were ringing at a steady pace and there were at least three people answering them.

She smiled wider. "Hello. I'm Officer Payland, Denise Payland. I will let Lieutenant Copeland know you are here." She quickly left her post and hurried off to a back office.

Jack and Jill moved to the side of the front desk. "We should've called the Bureau," Jill whispered to Jack.

Jack nodded. As usual Jack had the same idea. "Yes. I had hoped we could get some information on the missing boy." Although the specific case was not theirs they both felt they had an obligation to report or at least acknowledge anything outside of basic procedure. It was obvious Lake Shore had no idea how to handle situations of this magnitude.

"Let's be sure to make a call right after we meet with Lieutenant Copeland," Jill stated glancing in the direction of where Officer Payland had disappeared. Jack nodded. They stood for a minute or two more listening to the ringing phones and rapid-fire dialogue of other Officers in the building. Other than that the place was pretty quiet. "What is taking so long?" Jill hissed.

Just then Officer Payland appeared with a smile on her face. "He'll be right out. He told me to tell you that he is speaking with Detective Winsler and will be right with you."

"Thank you," Jill stated turning to Jack, who looked equally frustrated. Time-sensitive cases were just that and both Jack and Jill hoped to begin their investigation promptly. Despite this both waited patiently for another minute until Lieutenant Copeland appeared through the doorway.

"I am so sorry," he bellowed walking over to them and shaking hands. "I just finished a conversation with Detective Winsler."

"Is it about the case he is working on? The missing boy?"

The Lieutenant nodded, "Yes, yes....come into my office. We can discuss everything in there." They followed Lieutenant Copeland through the doorway he had just appeared in, which led to a long hallway with various offices. They took a right at the end to yet another hallway with offices and what appeared to be the lavatories. "Jared's down at the end here," Lieutenant Copeland muttered. "We can discuss some things, then I'll check to see if he still feels up to speaking with you." Lieutenant Copeland took a left into a rather large office with his name on the door. Jack and Jill took seats at a round table. Lieutenant Copeland grabbed a file off of his desk and settled his girth into a chair at the table directly across from the agents. He let out a sigh. "There is coffee if you would like," he stated setting the folder down and giving them a small smile.

"No, I think we're all set," Jill stated. "Jack?"

"Yes, I'm all set. Thank you."

Jill leaned forward a bit and took out her pad of paper and pen. "We'd like to start with some questions about your conversation with Detective Winsler if you don't mind, then we'll proceed to the De Santo case."

Lieutenant Copeland nodded as if he expected as much. "The Emery's are not easy people," he began. "As soon as the boy was reported missing we tried our best to get information from them. Mrs. Emery did nothing but sit on the couch and cry and Mr. Emery sat in the kitchen with a cup of coffee and a look of despair on his face. We decided to bring Detective Winsler in and he has agreed to investigate and to find the boy." Lieutenant Copeland looked down and shifted in his seat uncomfortably. "My worry is that it may already be too late or we didn't get going on this quickly enough. We spoke with neighbors, who had not seen the boy and had not heard anything during the evening or morning hours." He paused and looked down at the table. It was clear that he was as concerned for the boy as he was for Carmen De Santo.

"We are certainly not here to blame," Jill stated. "That being said, we do have an obligation to discuss this with the Bureau and explain what has been done thus far. Detective Winsler may need to discuss the case with them, if necessary."

Lieutenant Copeland nodded, "Detective Winsler is with the Emery's right now."

"That's all we need to know," Jill said softly. Obviously, Lieutenant Copeland was uncomfortable with how things had been handled and Jill wanted him to focus on the case at hand for the time being. "Now, can we talk about Carmen De Santo?"

Lieutenant Copeland focused his attention, opened his file, and looked at Jack and Jill directly. "Yes, of course."

"We would like to get a better idea of Carmen's life. The people she knew, where she worked, activities she was involved with, her husband, and things of this nature. It may sound odd, but Agent Simko and I have found that looking into a victim's life often gives us many clues into the death."

Lieutenant Copeland nodded. "Where should I start?"

"Well, first of all, was Carmen born here?"

"Oh, I see. Start from the beginning." Lieutenant Copeland grinned for the first time since they entered the office. "To answer your question, Carmen was not born here. She moved to Lake Shore when she married her husband, Armand De Santo." Jack and Jill exchanged quick glances. Score one for Jack.

"Do you know where she moved from?" Jack asked.

"Somewhere in upstate New York. Armand could help you with the exact location. Her mother still lives there."

"Do you know her mother's name?" Jill asked.

"Cheryl. Cheryl O'Dea."

Jill wrote this down. "Is that Carmen's maiden name? O'Dea?"

"No. Cheryl took her own maiden name back after her divorce from Carmen's father. Carmen's maiden name is, I mean, was Ricci. Carmen Ricci."

Jill wrote this down with another notation to contact Carmen's mother for further information on her daughter. "When did she move here?"

She moved here approximately three years ago. Met Armand at a function in Boston a year before that, they hit it off well, got married, and she moved here."

Jack looked down at his notebook. "What did she do for work?" he asked.

"She was a homemaker. Their house is rather large and needed someone to manage the particulars. Carmen was very pleased to stay at home taking care of things for her husband." Lieutenant Copeland shifted again and grinned. "She was a wonderful woman."

Jill nodded. "I'm sure she was, Lieutenant. It's not easy on anyone when something like this happens."

He nodded. "Would anyone like a cup of coffee?"

"No thank you, " the agents said as Lieutenant Copeland excused himself to get a cup before they continued.

Jill glanced at Jack. "Ah, yes, sweet girl gets toasted. We've heard this before."

"Hey, maybe she was a sweet girl." He grinned.

"Are they ever just sweet and innocent?"

"Sweet. Who said anything about innocent?" he grinned.

Just then Lieutenant Copeland reappeared. He sat down again and placed a steaming cup of coffee on the table. The bitter scent mixed with the smell of cream wafted through the room.

"Did she have any friends here in Lake Shore?" Jill asked.

Lieutenant Copeland nodded. "Just a few. She was close with Armand's brother, Nero. She also had a friend by the name of Marisca just a few streets over. I believe she visits her quite frequently."

"Does Marisca have a last name?" Jack asked.

"Maroe. Marisca Maroe. I can give you her contact information, of course." Lieutenant Copeland took a slow sip of his coffee.

"We'll also want to speak with Armand De Santo and Nero De Santo," Jack said to which Lieutenant Copeland nodded.

"Was she involved in any church or community projects?" Jill asked.

"No church projects. Carmen has made it quite clear that she did not want to be involved in that. She volunteered at the library from time to time helping with some of the children's programs and assisted with area soup kitchens. Other than that she mostly kept to herself and her home."

"Is her husband available to speak with today?" Jack asked.

"Her husband is in New York City on business. He is away quite often. We have contacted him regarding Carmen's death and he promised to take the next flight into Boston." Lieutenant Copeland took another sip of coffee.

"We would like to speak with him and perhaps visit his home to have a look around."

"Yes, of course." Lieutenant Copeland nodded and put the cup of coffee back on the table. "I'm certain he will help you in any way he can."

"Now we have to ask a couple of questions that are normally routine, however we understand this is a small town and everyone is pretty close so it's nothing personal."

Lieutenant Copeland nodded. He knew exactly where this was going, but he waited patiently for the questions anyhow.

"Have you ever received a domestic call to the De Santo house?" Jack asked.

"No," Lieutenant Copeland said simply.

"Can you think of anyone who may have wanted to harm

Carmen?" Jill asked. These were the same questions in the same pattern they asked each police department and nearly every witness in the desperate hope that perhaps this time it wasn't Renault. In the end the answers were all the same and the serial killer still continued to roam the streets in search of a new victim.

Lieutenant Copeland sat for a moment, then took a sip of his coffee. "Carmen was a lovely girl. Some of the local ladies were jealous I suppose. Carmen was young, pretty, had married one of the most eligible bachelors in town, and was stinking rich, but not enough to kill her. She did not have any obvious enemies."

"Does her husband have any enemies? A business associate or a jealous mistress perhaps?" Jack asked.

Lieutenant Copeland shook his head firmly "no". "I'm sure there are some that are jealous of Armand's success, but not enough to kill his wife and certainly not in this way." He fidgeted in his chair. "And with a woman like Carmen I can guarantee there was no jealous mistress. He loves Carmen with all his being."

Jill could tell from the tightened tone of Lieutenant Copeland's voice that try as he might he was taking this personally. "Was Carmen involved in any occult behavior?"

Lieutenant Copeland laughed a short laugh. "Oh, Carmen loved the horoscopes. She would read them aloud to anyone who would listen. In fact, one time at the corner store she was laughing out loud and driving people crazy asking if she could read their futures." He smiled like a proud father.

Just then he could see Carmen as true as life in his mind's eye. Her smile was dazzling as she ran up to him with the daily paper in her hand. She was wearing a long skirt, a peasant shirt, and small shoes that looked like slippers. Her face was aglow with her hair long and flowing behind her. "Lieutenant Copeland, oh, Lieutenant, can I read your horoscope?" she said with that lilting, flirtatious accent she had. She looked up at him with big eyes and opened the paper. "Ready or not, here goes!" Lieutenant Copeland brushed the image away by shaking his head and sipping more coffee.

"You said Carmen's husband, Armand, is away on business frequently. I would assume that Carmen is alone quite a bit."

"Well, yes and no. She has the housekeeping staff to tend to and keep her some degree of company, and she spends time with her brother-in-law, Nero. Armand likes that he keeps an eye on her while he is away."

Jill nodded making notes. "Do you know how many are on the housekeeping staff?"

"No. Armand can give you all the names you need." Lieutenant Copeland drained his cup and got up to throw it out. He settled back down in his chair and glanced at the clock.

"Can you think of anyone else we should speak to?" Jack asked.

Lieutenant Copeland sat back. "That's all I've got to start with. If I come across anything else I'll be sure to contact you immediately."

"Of course," Jill stated smiling. "Do you think Jared Prentice will be available to speak with us?"

"We have conducted an initial evaluation and questioned him on the scene and then again back here at the station. We sent him home after the evaluation, but he returned to speak with you. He is doing well given the circumstances and is very eager to help." Lieutenant Copeland leaned forward as if about to stand.

"Agent Pellingworth and I would like to discuss a couple of things privately before meeting with Jared. Is there a room we could use? We should only be 10 minutes or so," Jill stated.

"Oh, yes, of course. There is an interrogation room right across the hall. Feel free to use it."

Jack, Jill, and Lieutenant Copeland stood up. They all shook hands. "Thank you so much for your help, Lieutenant Copeland, " Jill stated. "We will be keeping in touch."

"Of course. Of course. I will let Jared know you will be with him in a few minutes. He is down the hall to your left, last interrogation room." Lieutenant Copeland smiled and seemed much more at ease. It was obvious the questions had been difficult, but necessary.

Agents Pellingworth and Simko walked across the hall to the room, closed the door, and sat down on metal chairs at the table. Jill let out a sigh and put her notebook on the table. "I hate these small town cases."

Agent Pellingworth grinned. "Me, too."

"So, what do you think so far?" She placed her head on her hand with her elbow propped up against the table.

"I think this is going to be more difficult that we had first anticipated."

"Tell me about it. I get the feeling that everyone around here is hiding something," Jill sighed.

"There's one thing that Lieutenant Copeland said that disturbs me."

"Besides the fact that we're searching for the murderer of a sweet, little dead girl?"

Jack just looked at her.

"Sorry, I'm punchy," she said.

"There's plenty of burnt coffee around here to perk you up."

Jill wrinkled her nose. "Uh, yuck, I'm not drinking that swill."

Jack let out a quick laugh. "Seriously though, Lieutenant Copeland stated that Carmen was opposed to volunteering at the local churches."

"Yes. So?"

"Carmen had a cross cut into her forehead. The cross is a Christian symbol and very well may have some meaning in this case, more than it appears."

"Yes, but Jack that's only if Renault is not our guy here. We know what the symbol means to Renault. Anyone would have heard about and could copy it, too. It doesn't have to be just *his* signature move."

"No, you're right. For now all signs still point to Renault." Jack stated.

Jill nodded. "You know, I also don't have much faith in the law enforcement around here. Small towns are just not very good at these high-profile cases."

"And that's why they bring in the big guns," Jack grinned referring to he and Jill. "I say we question Jared Prentice and Jennifer Townsend, then make a call to the Bureau to check in."

"Sounds good to me." Jill stood and grabbed her notebook. Jack remained seated. "It's been a long day for Jared." It was obvious he was not quite ready for the next round of questioning.

"Anything on your mind, Jack?"

"Just a feeling. A hunch. Well, not exactly a hunch, but a bad feeling. Worse than usual." He sat back for a moment, then let out a sigh. "I don't like that the kid is missing, too."

Jill put her notebook down on the table and let out a sigh. "Neither do I, but we're not on that case. I think we just need to focus right now and see where this gets us."

Jack nodded. "You think this is related?"

"You mean the victim and the missing boy?" Jill picked up her notebook again and stared at the wall behind Jack. "I admit it's odd. Carmen De Santo was found this morning and the boy was discovered missing this morning. Thing is, Renault has never involved a child before.

That would be very strange for him. We'll have to keep our eye open to connections." She paused and continued staring at the wall in deep concentration. "We have to keep it all in mind because it is odd and it doesn't feel good to me either. Well, not exactly like murders and missing children give me that warm fuzzies, but you know what I mean." She looked at Jack. "Keep it in mind. We'll figure it out."

Jack stood up and smiled. "I know you're right."

"I also know how you get when you get a hunch." They both walked to the door. "Ready, Jack?

"Ready." They both smiled, both very aware that this was just the beginning. Just as Jill opened the door her cell phone rang. She took it out of her pocket and glanced at the number. "It's home. I need to take this."

"Sure. I'll wait in the hall."

"Thank you." Jack closed the door behind him and stood just outside of it. He could hear the phone ringing incessantly in the front office and the hallway walls were littered with missing person's posters and notes on message boards. An unsettled feeling had been a constant presence for him since arriving in Lake Shore. He expected there were secrets here much larger than he had anticipated. Of course, these were only his thoughts and feelings. Besides a very dead Carmen De Santo, nothing was much different than any other case he had worked. He let out a sigh just as Jill walked back into the hall.

"How's the kiddo?" he asked.

"Better. Thanks," Jill said. "Still no fever. She's resting. My mom is thrilled because that means she can rest for a bit, too." Jill's eyes flashed. She was obviously quite relieved. She checked her watch. It was nearly three o'clock. "Wow. Time flies in Lake Shore."

"Let's get this over with, then get something to eat," Jack suggested.

"Sounds good to me," said Jill.

31

In silence they walked down the hall to the room Lieutenant Copeland had referred to earlier. Jack took the lead, opened the door, and entered the room. Jill followed. The room was smaller than the interrogation room they had been in previously, but still remained stark, bright, and bare. As soon as they entered, Jared nervously looked up at them, then quickly stood. He was a very tall, lanky man dressed in jeans and a polo shirt. He had sandy blonde hair cut straight and close. His eyes were round with fear and it was obvious from the way he stood moving his weight quickly from one foot to the other that he was highly anxious.

Jack stretched out a hand, "Hello. I'm Special Agent Pellingworth and this is Special Agent Simko." Jared shook both hands quickly hands. His eyes remained round even when looking at Jill, who was known for easing men with her attractive face and slow smile. All three sat down. Jack and Jill took out notepads and Jared sat with one hand over his mouth anticipating the questions.

"We know you're nervous," Jill said with a smile. "You've had a very rough day and we appreciate anything you can tell us."

Jared nodded. Same round eyes.

Jill continued. "We need to know as much about the day as you possibly can remember. Are you ok with that?"

Jared nodded and muttered a "yes".

"Okay. Why were you in the woods, Jared?" Jill asked.

"I was taking a jog," Jared began his voice wobbling. "It was very warm so I decided to take a path through the woods that I know is cooler. I knew I wouldn't be able to run for long, but I wanted to make the most of it."

"What happened in the woods?" Jack asked.

Jared glanced at Jack, then Jill, then down at his hands. "As I ran there was a reflection that caught my eye. I felt that I needed to see what it was and discovered what I recognized as Carmen's necklace."

"Describe the necklace," Jill coached.

"Gold with an amethyst pendant. She had worn it to a town picnic earlier in the summer."

"Ok, then what happened?"

"Well, I picked up the necklace, looked at it, and put it back down. I thought it was odd, but decided to keep running. When I reached the clearing…." He paused his face turning ashen. "There was this cool breeze." His eyes were no longer round, but lost in time to that moment. "And I looked ahead and saw a white form in the grass. I walked closer to discover it was…..it was Carmen." He covered his mouth with a fisted hand and his eyes were large and round again.

"Did you touch her at all?" Jack asked.

Jared shook his head violently. "Oh no. Not at all. I took out my cell phone and called the police right away…." His eyes became distant again. "I told the police that Carmen De Santo was in the woods and seriously hurt."

"Not dead?" Jill asked.

"I thought I saw her fingers move when I first arrived. I was quite certain she was dead, but I didn't want to jump to any conclusions." He put his face in his hands then looked up quickly. "It took forever for the EMT to arrive."

"Jennifer Townsend?" Jack asked.

"Yes. Nice girl. Father owns the hardware store."

"What did she do?"

"She arrived, asked me a few questions about what I was doing, then tended to Carmen. She told me to stand in a specific spot, then started making calls, roped off the area, and started taking pictures."

"Was she able to ask you any other questions?" Jack continued.

"Just asked why I was there, if I had touched her….that kind of thing." Jared put his face in his hands again.

"Okay," Jill said softly. "How well did you know Carmen De Santo?"

Jared looked up. "Not all that well. She kept to herself mostly. She was at town picnics and activities though." His eyes looked sad. "My wife likes to talk about her."

"Why?" Jill asked with a smile.

"Talk of the town, I guess. You've seen her. Even in death such a pretty girl, married to one of the wealthiest men in town, moved here recently. Lots of people like to talk about Carmen."

The door opened and Lieutenant Copeland rushed in closing the door quickly behind him. "We have a slight situation," he stated his eyes darting nervously between Jack and Jill.

Jack stood. "I'll take this," he said. "If you'll excuse me, Jared."

Jared nodded as Jack followed Lieutenant Copeland out of the room.

"So," Jill said smiling at Jared. "Carmen was interesting."

"To some people, yes. My wife thinks everyone is interesting."

Jill gave him an easy smile. "But some are more interesting than others, don't you think? Was Carmen one of those people?"

"If by that you mean beautiful and mysterious. Hell yes."

"What is it, Lieutenant?" Jack asked. He crossed his arms.

"Armand De Santo is here. Just got off the plane from New York. He wants to talk to you about Carmen. Ask you questions." Lietutenant Copeland looked down as if he were embarrassed to ask.

"We're in the middle of an interview. Tell Mr. De Santo we'll speak with him soon about his wife."

"Someone has to ID her you know."

"I thought this was already taken care of."

"He's her family and got here as quickly as he could."

"Has she been autopsied yet?"

"I think they are ready to begin. We called in a doctor from the county."

Jack let out a deep breath. "Okay. Have Armand view and positively ID her, then have her autopsied, reports and samples sent to the Bureau. Then we'll talk to him."

Lieutenant Copeland looked down again. "Armand De Santo is a very important man. He only has a question or two."

Jack could hardly believe what he was hearing. Not only was the local police department completely ill-equipped to deal with any aspect of this investigation, but they also had the audacity to include the dead woman's husband in the investigation. "No. Absolutely not. We'll see him in the morning."

"The man has just lost his wife, Sir."

"The man may be a suspect," Jack said firmly.

Lieutenant Copeland looked up his face reddening. "Are you calling Armand De Santo a killer?"

"No. I said suspect....he may be one. We'll see him first thing tomorrow morning. His house, preferably. Call forensics over to his house as well, under his consent of course. No consent? Get a warrant."

"His house isn't the crime scene!" Sergeant Copeland was clearly outraged.

"How do you know that?!"

"She wasn't found there."

"For Christ's sake!" Jack was starting to lose his patience. "We don't know where Carmen was before we found her in the woods. She could very well have been murdered in her house and dumped in the woods. We just don't know. Calm Armand down, get the autopsy completed, get Carmen ID'd and the forensics team over to the De Santo house."

"What am I supposed to tell Armand?"

Jack looked at him in disbelief. "Tell him that we understand his concerns, but that we must proceed with the investigation. Tell him he can help by allowing a forensics team and by giving a positive ID." Jack let out a deep breath and felt his frustration starting to cool again.

"Armand De Santo is not to be kept waiting."

Jack's blood began to simmer. "Tell him two federal agents will meet with him first thing tomorrow morning. That's all we can do right now. We're trying to get as much information as possible to catch his wife's killer."

Lieutenant Copeland nodded, clearly not interested in having to relay the message. "Yes, of course."

"I know it's not easy to have us come in here barking orders, but we have a very important job to do. This is very serious."

"Yes, I know. You just don't.....well, you'll see later." With that

Lieutenant Copeland turned and walked down the hall.

Jack let out another deep breath. "What the fuck," he muttered. He turned and entered the room again.

"Well, thank you very much for everything," Jill was saying. She glanced up at Jack her eyes searching his for answers to what had been so urgent to call him out of an interview. She handed a card to Jared. Jack remained standing and he smiled as Jared stood up and shook hands with both agents.

"If you think of anything, anything at all, please contact us right away," Jill stated.

Jared looked down at the business card she had given him earlier and put it into his pocket. "Yes. Of course."

Jill walked Jared to the door, thanked him again, and sat down. "What's up, Pellingworth?"

Jack sighed and put his hands in his pockets. "Armand De Santo is pissed that's what's up. Apparently Armand had some questions for us regarding the death of his wife."

Jill rolled her eyes. "Big man on campus I gather?"

Jack rolled his eyes in return. "Very." He ran his hand through his hair. "And he's a potential problem. The police department here is practically pissing their pants because he's requested it and we won't see him immediately."

Jill sat up a little straighter. "What did he want exactly?"

"He wanted to talk to us about his wife, I believe. I'm assuming he wanted to ask us questions about what's going on. I can understand his anxiety, but seriously?"

"Well, it's typical. Of course, I suppose he doesn't realize he's a suspect just based on his proximity to the victim." She grinned. Shop talk.

37

Of course he doesn't realize that.

Jack grinned back. "So, now what? How'd things go with Jared?"

"Same old. He's pretty shaken up given the circumstances. I don't think he really knows much about her at all tell you the truth. Most of his information comes from his wife, who apparently is the town gossip. He seemed a bit intrigued by Carmen. She was the beauty of the town and since she wasn't a native she was that much more exotic. The fact that she was married to Armand furthered interest in her. Armand didn't choose a local girl to be his wife."

"Are you trying to say this may have been incentive to murder her?" Jack asked.

"I'm not saying anything....quite yet." Jill grinned. "We have a lot of ground to cover."

Jack sighed. "So, where to now, Boss?"

Just then the door opened and Lieutenant Copeland walked in. His face was red as he looked down, then up at Jack and Jill. "Jennifer Townsend, first response, can speak with you now if you would like."

Jill smiled and stood up straight. "Absolutely. She may come right in here. We are ready whenever she is."

Lieutenant Copeland nodded avoiding eye contact with Jack, and left the room.

"Oh, man, what did you do to that guy?" Jill asked grinning.

"You don't want to know," Jack answered.

"I can't wait to meet this Armand character. He must really be something." Jill's eyes lit up when she said this.

"Hold on, there, girl," Jack shook his head as he talked. "Of course I do hear he's quite the stud."

She let out a peel of laughter that was highly inappropriate given the context. In this business any reason to laugh was a good enough one. Just then there was a knock at the door.

"Come on in," Jack called.

The door opened and a young girl with blonde hair pulled back in a ponytail walked in. Her eyes were wide, but steady. She closed the door behind her, then just stood near the door her hands at her sides. She was petite and round still wearing her EMS gear her name on a badge attached to her shirt.

"Jennifer?" Jill asked.

The girl nodded remaining where she was at the door.

"I'm Special Agent Simko. This is my partner Special Agent Pellingworth." Jill approached Jennifer and shook her hand. The girl gave a weak handshake, then glanced at Jack and blushed slightly.

Jack approached her and shook her hand. "It's nice to meet you, Ms. Townsend. Have you ever met with FBI agents before?"

She shook her head no. So far, she had said nothing at all.

"Well, have a seat," Jill said motioning to the chair that Jared had so recently occupied. The girl walked directly to the seat, sat down, and folded her hands on the table. She was clearly terrified. Both Jack and Jill sat down opposite her.

"Now, we're just going to ask you some basic information. Nothing too crazy here, ok?" She smiled.

The girl relaxed a bit, her eyes still wide, and nodded. Her eyes shifted between the two agents.

Jack began. "Can you tell us your full name and occupation, please?" The warm-up technique.

Jennifer took a deep breath then stated, "Jennifer Anne Townsend, Emergency Medical Technician." Her voice was soft and small.

"How old are you, Jennifer? How long have you been working as an EMT?" Jack asked.

Her eyes widened a bit. Too many questions at once, perhaps. "I'm 23. I have been working as an EMT for 2 years." So far, so good.

"How long have you lived in Lake Shore?" Jack asked again making a notation in his notebook. He glanced sideways at Jill.

"My whole life. I was born here." Her face had relaxed a bit more and her voice was steadier.

"So, let's talk about this morning," Jill said kindly. Jennifer nodded. "When did you get the call?"

"Early morning. Seven a.m.?" She hesitated. "It's in my log; the exact time. I was dispatched to the scene; a possible fatality."

"What happened when you got there?" Jill nudged.

"I got there and met Jared at the road. He was white as a ghost so I had him sit down for a moment and I gave him a quick once-over. When I saw that he was ok I told him to keep seated and asked where I should go." She paused for a moment and let out a breath. "He told me to go through the woods to a clearing. I did. That's when I saw her." She sucked in her breath quickly and her face paled. The sound echoed in the room, a sharp hiss.

"Who did you see?" Jack said careful not to influence her at all.

"Carmen De Santo. She was lying in the grass. I went over, tried to get a pulse, nothing. She was definitely dead – I probably didn't even need to take a pulse. I ran back to Jared, asked if he had moved her at all, called for backup and started securing the area." She sat up a bit, much more comfortable now that she was on familiar territory. She knew her job and she knew she had done it well.

"Did Mr. Prentice move her or touch her at all?" Jill asked.

"No. At least he said he didn't."

"All right. What were your initial impressions of the scene?" Jack asked.

"Witness was very shaken up; typical reactions displayed when discovering a body. The scene was pretty clean. No noticeable footprints to bring to the attention of forensics. No weapons or paraphernalia left at the scene. Later forensics found the necklace. I just marked off the area and waited for backup."

"Did you know Carmen De Santo at all?" Jill asked.

Jennifer grinned a little bit, then looked sideways. "Yes, I did."

Jack grinned. Jill noticed it. Their secret language. Something was up here. Let's find out if it's important. "How well did you know Carmen?" Jack asked.

"I talked to her just a couple of times, at cookouts or something. I didn't really know her all that well." Jennifer started to look a bit uncomfortable again. She bit her bottom lip and shifted in her chair.

"What was Carmen like? Outgoing? Quiet?" Jack asked.

"She was very outgoing. She'd talk to just about anyone. Very pretty. Then again she didn't have to worry. Everyone talked to her." There was something in Jennifer's eyes that needed more explanation.

"So, she got along with others well here?" Jack asked.

Jennifer's eyes shifted. "I guess."

"Did she have any enemies?" Jill chimed in right on the tail of Jennifer's words.

Jennifer looked down. "Not exactly."

"Well, what did she have – exactly?" Jill asked leaning forward slightly in an attempt to be a bit more imposing.

"Well, some people used to talk about her. In a negative way." Jennifer looked very uncomfortable now. She put her hand to her lips as she talked, a childish gesture.

"What did they say?" Jill asked her voice softer.

Jennifer let out an embarrassed, little laugh. "Well, some people say that….." She paused. "Some people say she's a witch." She looked down, then quickly looked back up. "It's stupid, I know," she said quickly.

As she looked down, Jack and Jill made slight eye contact both just as interested as the other about where this would lead. "What do you mean by witch?" Jill said slowly.

Jennifer looked up sheepishly and grinned. "You know. Vampires, werewolves, witches kind of thing. It's stupid, really, but some people around here think she has special powers."

"What makes them think this?" Jill asked.

Jennifer blushed and shifted in her seat obviously uneasy and perhaps a little embarrassed to relay the information. "I don't know. She goes out alone in the woods a lot and so some people started joking that she is doing witch things – causing mischief." She paused. "It's really stupid. It is. She's just different than everyone here."

"How is she different?" Jack asked.

"She just moved here. That makes her different enough. Most people are born here, grow up here, live here and die here." She paused. "And she has, um she had, creepy eyes." Her age was showing and she knew it.

"Her eyes were creepy?" Jill repeated to her.

"Um…..yeah……they are kind of haunting. I mean they *were* kind

42

of haunting. I think it's just the color of them or something, this sea green color. Anyway she was pretty with creepy eyes, that's enough around here." Jennifer looked up at the agents again.

Jill glanced at Jack. Neither of them knew where to go with this. "Is there anything else you feel we should know about Carmen De Santo – her life, interests – anything would be helpful." Jill asked.

Jennifer let out a slow breath of air her eyes pensive. "No. I don't think so," she stated hesitantly.

Jill smiled. "It's ok. If you think of something, anything at all, all you need to do is give one of us a call." She handed her a business card. "How's that sound?"

The girl looked relieved. "Good."

Jack and Jill stood up and Jennifer followed suit nervously straightening her clothing as she did so and pushing her hair back. They all shook hands and Jennifer left closing the door behind her.

Jill let out a rush of air. "Oh my! First response, huh?" She half-sat on the table her arms crossed.

"Don't be too hard on her. She's just a girl after all," Jack said grinning.

Jill grinned back and let out a breath. "I'm exhausted. What's next?"

"Do you think we should be here?" It was an odd question and Jack knew it.

"If you mean do I think this is Renault, I don't know. We probably won't know until after we get the autopsy report. If you mean do I think this warrants FBI investigation, I'm not sure either. But I do have to say the whole witch talk has peaked my interest." She grinned trying to keep things light-hearted.

"I don't like the missing kid," Jack said quickly and seriously. The kid was an itch he couldn't quite scratch. But at this moment it wasn't his itch to scratch. It was more like Renault was too big for this small town. He wasn't sloppy and he wouldn't be upstaged. Yet, Jill was right, all signs pointed to the fact that Renault murdered Carmen De Santo. So, what was the boy's story?

"Well, unfortunately that's not really our problem right now."

Jack looked directly at her. He decided to change the subject. "I don't like Mr. DeSanto and I haven't even met him. The police here are brainless. I wonder if Renault sliced the girl just to fuck with Armand De Santo. Quite frankly I could hardly blame him."

"Oh, stop it, Jack. Sympathizing with a serial killer," Jill stood up fully. "I'm ready to head back to Boston, do a little more research, then head back here to question Armand De Santo in the morning. What do you say?"

"Sounds good. I'll give a call to the Bureau with an update."

Jill nodded. "Excellent."

The two headed out of the room and down the hall in silence. They said their parting good-byes to the staff.

"So, tomorrow morning then?" Lieutenant Copeland called out to them coffee cup in hand.

"Absolutely. Ten o'clock. Oh, and you can tell Mr. De Santo we are eager to speak with him." His eyes flashed.

CHAPTER FOUR

Jack let out a low whistle. The De Santo house was like nothing Jack and Jill had ever seen before. Set back from the road with a long, winding drive, the house sat on carefully sculpted and manicured sprawling grounds. A landscaper was clipping the bushes when they arrived and he looked up only to wave briefly, then returned to his work. The "house" was a Spanish stucco villa the size of a small mansion with balconies off the sides and potted plants on the front stoop and side patio. The spaciousness of the front lawn continued beyond the house, as well. The agents parked in front, got out of the car, and approached an enormous, imposing wooden door. A heavy-set woman in a blue housedress met them almost immediately. Her hair was in a bun and her golden skin was shining from the heat. She gave them a soft smile.

"May I tell Mr. De Santo who calls?" she said in a slight southern drawl.

"Special Agents Simko and Pellingworth," Jill stated stepping into the marble foyer that looked just about as big as her apartment back home.

The woman smiled shyly again. "Ah, yes, Mr. De Santo is expecting you. He's in his study now. He'll meet with you in the library."

Jill glanced at Jack, who openly smirked. For some reason great wealth made Jack grin in a slightly condescending way and Jill could never quite make it out. Maybe it was the "study" and the "library" and the fact that they were forever solving mysteries that made him think there was some joke in it. A modern day "Clue" game if you would. They followed the woman in the housedress down the hall to the right of the door. The hall was plain and adorned with the occasional portrait or work of art, which Jill was certain separately cost more than her car and her favorite pieces of jewelry put together. They entered what was quite obviously the library. The room was spacious and sunny with a slew of couches and a large wooden table in the middle. It looked solid and regal and perhaps made of mahogany or something equally expensive. There was another small table with a dictionary and globe set upon it. The most spectacular aspect of the room was that from floor to ceiling the walls had in-laid shelves that were lined with books. The room overlooked the front yard and the driveway, which gave it a sense of spaciousness that most libraries did not possess.

"I can bring you tea or coffee if you'd like," the woman in the housedress said.

"Please," Jill said politely her eyes not moving from the shelves of neatly lined books.

The woman left and Jack and Jill stood in silence for a moment. "Have you seen anything like this?" Jill breathed.

"No. Not quite. This is wealth like I haven't seen in a long time," Jack stated. "Shall we sit?"

"I'm going to peek at the books. I'm curious. They must have every book ever published. My goodness!" Jill walked to the nearest shelf and began scanning the book titles while Jack sat down on a sofa with the most comprehensive view of the room. Jill touched the spine of one of the books. "This is really quite amazing!"

"I am happy to see you enjoy the library," a voice called from the doorway from which the woman who greeted them had exited.

Startled Jill whipped around and Jack stood up both feeling like intruders. Armand DeSanto entered the room. If not already breathless from the array of books and the extent of the library, Armand took the last bit of breath away. He was an extraordinarily handsome man; tall, dark-hair with a chiseled appearance and high cheek bones, smooth skin, and haunting blue eyes. He wore a suit without a tie and shoes that had just been buffed. His voice was smooth when he spoke, "Hello. I am Armand De Santo."

He walked with great confidence over to Jack and shook his hand in a warm, firm manner. He greeted Jill with an equally formidable handshake. "Agent Simko. Agent Pellingworth. We are happy to have you here in Lake Shore. Please, do sit. We have much to discuss."

He had the air of someone who was preparing to meet with a business associate, not to answer questions relating to his wife's murder. They all sat down at sofas that faced each other so that Armand could sit across from the two agents in comfort. Armand straightened his jacket and settled into the sofa. "Beatrice will be here with coffee, tea, and refreshments shortly." He looked past the agents to the window overlooking the front lawn.

Jill looked at Armand and could not help but think of how his wife appeared laying on the grass covered in blood. She found it hard to picture this woman dressed in such a plain, white dress with this exceptionally polished, if not stuffy man. However, they must have been the talk of the town, such an amazingly beautiful couple.

Before the agents could start the questioning, Armand began, "Carmen loved this room. She would climb up on the ladder over there." He pointed to a short ladder that leaned against the shelves on the far corner of the room. "I would tease her about falling and breaking an ankle or a leg or something on that thing and she would just laugh at me and float around up there finding something good to read. Her smile was so beautiful. She would just hang there, smile down at me and tell me I was silly and nothing could ever happen to her with me around." He looked off to the front lawn again and his eyes glazed over in memory. "She could laugh anything off," he muttered.

Carmen smiled. "I'll never get down. It's like heaven up here with all these books, my dear!" She laughed as he looked up at her.

"Do I need to come up and get you, then?" he asked grinning as he said it.

Carmen rolled her eyes, "Of course, Daddy. Why else do you think I climb up here?"

47

As he approached the ladder she rushed down it and ran around him. "You'll never catch me!" she shrieked laughing as he reached out to grab her. Her hair spun around her head in a torrent of curls and her smile was bright and real and red. He took two steps, caught her in his arms smelling her perfume and her sweetness.

"Oh, drat, baby, you caught me. Now what?" she pouted.

Jack and Jill remained quiet as Armand sat staring out at the front lawn for a moment. He shook his head slightly, and then took a deep breath. "Ah, yes, but you are not here to listen to my memories. How can I help you?" He smiled civilly as one would do to a cashier or clerk.

Jill began. "We've both been told you made a positive ID and we know how difficult this must be for you, but we do have a few questions for you. Anything you can't answer is quite all right. We hope that whatever you have to offer will be helpful in some way." She tried to be soft, but every word sounded harsh and clinical to her ears.

Armand smiled sadly and his eyes were glassy. "Yes, I saw her last night. She was so beautiful, that Carmen. Always beautiful. No matter what the occasion. And last night….." His words trailed off for a moment as he stared out the window at the spacious lawn. "Well, she was beautiful, but she just wasn't…..she just wasn't Carmen." He stopped for a moment and looked at both agents. "She just wasn't Carmen." He looked down at his lap.

"Armand, do you need us to come back in a couple of hours or so?" Jill asked softly.

Armand looked up and smiled sadly. "Oh, no, this is fine. This is very fine."

Just then Beatrice walked into the room carrying a tray of cookies, tea, coffee, milk, cream, and sugars. She set the tray down to a room encased in silence and arranged things. Then she stood and asked if anyone needed anything. After a quick "we are well" from Armand she silently left the room.

"That is Beatrice, correct?" Jack asked.

Armand poured tea into a small cup and lifted it with a saucer as he settled back into his seat. "Ah, yes. Beatrice is our housekeeper and manages the rest of the household staff here. She has been with us many years. She is much adored and does her job efficiently." Too much information, but at least Armand was thorough.

"Is it possible for us to speak with her today?" Jack asked.

"Of course," Armand said softly taking another sip of tea. "After we meet she will be available if you so desire."

"If you so desire, huh, my dear? If you so desire me?" Carmen teased giggling and pulling Armand close to her.

"I desire you always, my love. I always will," he answered her.

Armand blinked back the memory and took another sip of tea. "So, what is it you need from me this morning?"

"We'll just start off with some questions regarding your marriage with Carmen. Where you met, when you got married and some basic questions like what you do for work; that kind of thing," Jill started. She kept her tone soft since at this point in the game there was no need to be too harsh and sound as if she were implying guilt.

Armand nodded. "Can I start off for you?"

"Of course," Jill stated reaching forward to pour some tea for herself.

"We met in New York. Her mother is a New York socialite and there was a benefit dinner she insisted that Carmen attend. I was attending on behalf of my company. The benefit was focused on AIDS relief in Africa. We were seated close to each other and started a rather interesting conversation."

The girl next to him sipped a martini and sat straight in her chair. He noticed that she had the nervous impatience of someone who wanted to be anywhere but where she was at that moment. Quite out of the blue she leaned over to him, touched his hand, and said, "Wanna get out of here? I have a fast car and a box of cigarettes that will take us all the way to Texas."

She was pretty and when she looked up at him all he saw were her green eyes, eyes that looked as if they were glowing, but couldn't possibly be. He must have met her statement with shock because she giggled a little bit, then sat up again and took another sip of her martini, then said, "I'm dead serious. Well, at least about the car." She grinned. "I'm Carmen. Carmen Ricci."

"And what's the car?" he asked.

"She's Annabelle. A world class bitch of an Aston Martin Vanquish."

"Not bad. Not bad."

She finished her martini quickly as the salads began to be served.

"Now what is a girl like you doing with a car like that?" He whispered as he took a forkful of salad.

Her eyes flashed when she looked at him. Beautiful indeed. She was unbelievable. "Driving it, silly!"

Armand blinked back to the present time. "She was an incredible woman. I had never met anyone quite like her." He paused for a moment his eyes glazed, then took a sip of tea. "We started dating on and off for a few months, but I had to admit I was completely smitten with her from the start. I was certainly not about to let her get away."

She was wearing a light-blue dress with matching pumps and a string of pearls around her neck. She shimmered in the moonlight as he followed her out to the back patio. Inside the house the sound of music and people echoed into the night. She looked up at the moon with a soft smile on her face and let out a sigh. "Let's get out of here. Let's leave this party."

Armand put his arms around Carmen's waist. "You always want to leave parties," he teased looking into her eyes just as glowing and captivating as ever.

"I want to go for a drive. A nice drive. It's so beautiful tonight." She looked up at the moon again then met his eyes.

He kissed her gently, "Whatever you'd like, my love."

They hopped into her Aston Marton and drove at first slowly, then whipping along the coastal rode, top down, wind in their hair. It was warm and balmy and the moon was full. Carmen drove them to the beach, jumped out and ran to the water. When she reached the water she let the waves lick her feet, then she jumped back and spread out her arms like a bird. She turned around to look at Armand, then laughed.

He walked up to her slowly, stared into those eyes, and said, "Marry me."

Jack was the first to interrupt Armand's reverie. "How long were you married?" he asked.

Armand took another sip of tea and looked at him slowly. "Three years."

"No children?" Jill asked.

"No, no children," he said softly. "We wanted to wait until the timing was right; when business slowed down for me perhaps."

"Any problems?" Jack asked.

"No. Not many anyway." Armand stared out at the lawn again. "Carmen didn't like that I was away so much on business. It made sense to me, but there was little I could do about that."

"Did Carmen work? Have a day job?" Jack asked.

"No. She stayed home. I told her to get a job, even a part time job to bide her time. She was born of socialites and would laugh and say that any job here would bore her to tears."

"How did she spend her time?" Jill asked softly.

Armand looked at the agents again. "She read a lot and she knitted a lot. She used to like to sit on the front lawn and knit and listen to the birds." His eyes misted a bit. "She spent time with friends and she worked to help feed the poor and do personal errands for the elderly."

"That's admiral," Jill commented making a note in her book. "Did she work for an organization?"

"Yes. The Lake Shore Hospice Association. She assisted them, all volunteer work."

Jack looked up from his notes. "Did she enjoy the work?"

"I believe so, but she still wanted me home." He looked off sadly again.

"You said she visited friends. Any friend in particular?" Jill asked.

"She has a friend on Cherry Lane. Marisca Maroe." Armand paused. "And she spent time with my brother, Nero. Nero is kind of an odd duck, but he and Carmen always seemed to get along."

Jill looked up again and tried to meet Armand's eyes. "Now I need to ask a couple of more difficult questions. Will this be all right?"

Armand met her gaze, then sat back and straightened his top. "Yes. Yes. I believe it is. Anything to help Carmen."

"Do you know of anyone who may have wanted to hurt Carmen?" Jill asked.

Armand shook his head ferociously. "Absolutely not. Everyone loved Carmen."

"Have you ever wanted to hurt Carmen?" she asked again, this time softer.

The pain flashed into Armand's eyes. He had not expected the question.

Carmen's face was a mixture of frustration and pain. "Why do you always want to hurt me so, Armand? You always leave me. You always leave me and it hurts like Hell."

"Oh, no. No. I never wanted to hurt her."

"Did you ever hit her? Strike her in any way? Threaten her?" Jack asked.

"No." Armand looked down at his lap. "Never."

"Is there anything else you think we'd need to know, Mr. De Santo? Anything at all that could help us," Jill asked softly.

Armand looked up. "Not now. I wish I could help more. I wish I knew more." His voice was almost a whisper. When he looked up again his eyes were stormy. "I wasn't here," he said simply. "All that time, I wasn't here. And now she's gone. It cuts deeper than you could imagine." The emotion was thick in his voice as his eyes misted over again and he clenched his jaw visibly holding back the tears.

Jill was quiet for a moment. She wasn't quite sure what to make of him. "I can't imagine the pain, Armand," she said quietly. The room was quiet as Armand composed himself, sat up straight, and looked over at the two agents once again the confident man that had first entered the room.

"How else can I help you?" he said in a steady voice.

Jill gave him a soft smile. "Just one more thing really. Did Carmen have a room that she used more than the others? Perhaps this room or an office or something?"

Armand looked at her blankly.

"The reason I ask is that it's important for us to get to know your wife as much as we possibly can. I know the forensics people have already been here. For Jack and I, sometimes things start to click when we get to see everything for ourselves."

Armand nodded. He was a man of action so a specific task was just what he needed to pull himself from an emotional wasteland and get to work. "Yes. Absolutely. She has a private study upstairs. Even I don't get to go in there." He grinned sadly. "You're more than welcome to look around."

Jack got a call on his cell phone as they were walking up the stairs to Carmen's personal study. He put up a hand and took the call in the hallway at the top of stairs with a promise from Armand that the room was easy to locate.

Jill followed Armand down the expansive hall lined with artwork and family portraits. "It smells of roses," he muttered.

"What does?"

"Her room," he stated. "That's why it's so easy to find."

Jill smiled slowly. Armand De Santo's pain was palpable. Almost as soon as they started down the hall they stopped in front of an ivory door that had a wreath of dried flowers on it.

"This is her room; her private study," Armand stated. "I would join you, but I just can't right now. Not yet."

Jill nodded. "Yes. I understand. I will be only a moment. If I find something I may need to take it back with me. If you don't feel comfortable with that I can issue a warrant."

"No. Please. Take anything you'd like. Please. I mean only to help."

With that Armand strolled down the hall leaving Jill to look at the door. She paused a moment, then put her hand on the doorknob to open it. The room was small and aside from a couple of pieces of furniture it was decorated almost entirely in white. The window directly at the back of the room was rectangular and wide allowing in a great degree of sunlight. There were flowers everywhere. Dried flowers hanging from the ceiling. Flowers in vases. Flower petals on the floor and desk. Jill closed the door behind her and walked into the middle of the room, which hosted an enormous, plush white carpet. The room consisted of a daybed, armoire, spacious desk, and a small writing table near the window. Next to the daybed sat a large, plain table with a dark, antique stain and a white, silk cloth on it. The table was the only dark object in the room and thus this gave it a stately appearance. Pictures of flowers and fairies hung on the walls and there was an overall feeling of peace and tranquility in the room. The smell of roses was thick in the air.

Jill let out a slow breath and looked around the room. Where to start. Where to start. Jill looked straight ahead at the writing table near the window. A black leather bag was perched next to the chair and for some reason Jill felt drawn to it. She could almost picture Carmen sitting there writing, looking over her shoulder at her, and smiling. Jill stopped in the middle of the room staring at the desk and chair. The image of Carmen smiling had been so vivid, so unique it had almost seemed as if Carmen had been in the room with her for that one moment. Almost.

Jill shook her head. There was a slight chill in the room although the temperature outside had been about 80 degrees, and it didn't feel as if Armand had turned on any air conditioning. She stared at the table where a small black book sat neatly a decorative pen placed at a diagonal on the cover. When she had first entered everything seemed encased in white but now all she could see was the black book and the black leather bag. Jill could feel the cold of something very, very wrong here. The feeling stopped the breath in her lungs momentarily and made her fingertips grow cold. In a word there was evil here. Evil in all this white and light and roses.

Jill crossed the room and looked down at the book on the table. It appeared to be a diary or writing implement of some sort. Jill reached into her pocket and pulled out a pair of latex gloves. She quickly pulled them on never letting her eyes off the book. She put one finger on the book the smell of roses becoming stronger in the room. She spread her hand over the book and over the pen feeling an energy pulsing there, something she had never quite known before. A warm feeling coursed into her palm and wrist and it felt pleasant yet foreboding. Something was very wrong here. Very, very wrong.

"Well, that was the medical examiner," a loud voice proclaimed.

Jill jumped, pulled her hand quickly off the book and turned around. Her breath caught in her throat. "Oh my God. Jack."

Jack looked amused. "Did I scare you?"

Jill took a quick glance at the book then let out a breath with a small smile. "Oh no. Just concentrating."

Jack looked around the room and put his hands on his hips. "Well, my, my. What do we have here?"

"Carmen's room. Her study."

"Is this ok with Armand?"

Jill nodded her mind still on the book. She was certain there was something in that book that would lead to Carmen's killer or perhaps to Carmen herself. "What did the medical examiner have to say?"

"Cause of death exsanguination. Manner of death loss of blood due to wounds to the chest, neck and throat. We can stop by after we leave here for the full report."

Jill nodded and glanced at the book again. "There's something here. I just know it."

Jack nodded, then looked back at the door. "I'll take your word for it," he said wrinkling his nose. "Too girly for me."

Jill turned around and immediately touched the book. "I'll start here." Jack nodded and moved to the other side of the room beginning his usual canvas starting at the left of the entryway. Jill watched him for a moment then sat down at the seat spreading her hands over the cover of the book. She took a deep breath feeling the familiar warmth through the gloves to her hands. She opened the book. On the first page the words "Wanton Pleasures of a Desperately Deserving Woman" were written in neat, black ink. Underneath it was a symbol of some kind, a loop with a bar at the top similar to a cross. Jill frowned and turned the page. Again the same, neat handwriting in black ink. This time there appeared to be some kind of oath or agreement written out. Jill glanced at it quickly yet felt compelled to keep flipping pages, never staying on one for very long. She flipped forward. More black ink. Crushed flowers. Drawings and diagrams. Lunar calendars. More writing. Towards the back of the book what looked like recipes for potpourri and spices was carefully handwritten out. The pages seemed to move without her direction. At the end she could only close the book tightly and stare at it. Her breath was coming in gasps and her heart was racing. What was this? This did not seem like a typical woman's journal, but then again people did all sorts of strange things in life.

"Ah, bingo," Jack called out to her making her jump for the second time in less than ten minutes.

Jill turned around sharply her breath still heavy; her face flushed.

"Her computer. I found her laptop." He had pulled out the black bag and placed it on the floor. "I think we should take this." He grinned. There was nothing Jack loved more than spying especially when computers were involved. In his mind the secret worlds of many an individual were held on their personal computers and laptops.

"I found something, too," Jill managed to say breathlessly. She picked up the book.

"A book?" Jack asked frowning and clearly disappointed that the laptop computer did not send her into a fit of giggles and praise.

"I don't think this is any other book, Jack. It's a gut feeling I have."

Jack stepped forward and took the book from Jill's hands. He looked at Jill's vacant, wondering eyes for a moment then opened the first page. Almost as quickly he began scanning pages, then looked up at her again. "Wow. Yes….." he paused. "Wow." He closed the book, then opened it again. "I'm going to have to call a friend on this one."

"What is it?" Jill asked.

"I think it's what is called a Book of Shadows or a grimoire of some kind."

"Again, what is that?" Jill stood up and rubbed her hands together. She could still feel the warmth there, but now there was something else, an unsettled feeling in the pit of her stomach.

"It's a Wiccan or pagan custom. It's really just a book of notes that documents spells, lunar calendars, rituals, and important spiritual work. I don't really know enough about this kind of thing; that's why I need to call Jim. He is an expert on comparative religions. I just don't understand why it's here." He looked down at the book again.

"Wicca? You mean it's witchcraft?" Jill asked. The feeling of dread was rising in her and she felt a bit dizzy.

"Yes. Where did you find it?"

"Here. On the desk."

"Was there anything else with it? Near it?"

"Just a pen on top of it," Jill stated looking back at the desk. Was there something she had missed?

"Witches use a lot of oils, potions, herbs and things, but I didn't find anything here. Hmmmm...." Jack said more to himself than anyone else. "I'll call Jim right away. I'd like to have him look at this. This may be it. This may be a huge clue to why she was murdered."

"Do you think she was a witch?" Jill asked. She put her hand to her chest and the room swam around her slightly. The dizziness was getting worse.

"I'm not sure. I don't see any other evidence. This could belong to someone else. We just don't know for sure." Jack looked around the room. "We need a writing sample." In seconds he placed the book near the laptop and began walking around the room. His eyes scanned quickly. "I don't see anything." He paused. "Wait a second." He glided past Jill and pulled a drawer on the desk that the book had been placed on. Nothing. Another drawer. Nothing. Another. "Bingo," he said pulling out a paper with what appeared to be a shopping list on it.

"That may not be her writing, Jack."

"Her study, her writing in my opinion. Maybe Armand can verify the writing sample."

Jill nodded and looked around. "Anything else here, Jack?" she asked.

"I think we have a lot to work on for now. Who knows where this will lead?" With that he gathered the book, shopping list, and laptop. "I really hope Armand lets us take this. I don't want to have to get a warrant."

Jill smiled weakly. The sense of foreboding had vanished, but had left her quite tired in its wake. "Let's ask him."

The two agents left the room with all its white and roses and walked out into the spacious hallway. Almost instantly Armand was standing in front of them. "Anything important?" he asked glancing at the laptop and book.

"We found her laptop, a journal, and a shopping list we'd like to take back with us for closer observation. These items could all prove helpful in our efforts to find out who did this to your wife," Jill stated.

Jack took out the shopping list. "And we need your help with something."

"Yes, anything," Armand stated.

"Could you look at this list and tell me if that is Carmen's handwriting?"

Armand looked from a distance stepping just a bit closer to Jack. "Yes, that is her handwriting, yes." He looked away quickly. "Forgive me. I just can't look for long." The pain in his eyes was unmistakable.

"Thank you, Armand. Is it ok for us to take these things with us just for a couple of days?" Jill asked.

Armand stepped back. "Yes. Yes, of course you may. Take as long as you need."

"Thank you, Mr. De Santo. We will be in touch," Jack stated.

"Oh, one more thing, Mr. De Santo," Jill said as Jack began to take one step away. "Is there any way we could speak with Beatrice today? Is she still available?"

"Oh, yes, of course. I will page her and she will meet you in the library. Can you remember your way? If you don't mind I have a terrible headache and need some rest."

"Yes, of course we can find our way. Thank you so much for your time, Mr. De Santo," Jill said kindly.

They shook hands with Armand, then turned to head down the hall.

"You do remember the way right?" Jack teased.

"I hope so. This place is magnificent."

When they had just about reached the stairs they heard a voice calling behind them. "Agents! Agents!"

Jack and Jill turned around to see Armand rushing down the hallway. He was breathless when he reached them. "I almost forgot. I had a question for you." His face was ashen and he pressed his right index finger to his temple.

"Yes, Mr. De Santo," Jill stated.

"Did you find Carmen's car?"

His words made Jill's stomach feel hollow again. "Car?" she managed.

"Yes. Carmen's Mustang." He looked at them expectantly still pressing his index finger to his temple.

Jack and Jill glanced at each other quickly. Jack's eyes flashed a bit of fire.

"I am so sorry, Mr. De Santo. We are not aware of your wife's car."

"I told Lieutenant Copeland about it briefly on the phone when he contacted me about.....about Carmen. I told him that if she left the house she would have been driving her Ford Mustang so he should check for that and sure enough it is missing. Her keys are also gone."

Jack shook his head his eyes still blazing in his anger. "Mr. De Santo, we will have a conversation with Lieutenant Copeland to see where they are in locating Carmen's vehicle. We do not have any information at this time."

Armand nodded. "Thank you. I need to treat this." He pointed at his head. "Thank you. Please do be in touch." He turned and hurried back down the hall holding his head.

Jack turned to Jill. "How could they leave out such vital information?" he hissed pulling off his latex gloves.

"We'll check on it, Jack. It's ok. Lieutenant Copeland must have forgotten to mention it." Jill said softly.

Jack rolled his eyes, then looked down.

"Listen, Jack, now is not the time to get too angry. Let's just have a moment with Beatrice, then meet with the medical examiner. Once we have a second we can check on the car, ok?"

"This could be the crime scene," Jack stated looking around the house. "This house could be where it all started and we're doing nothing about it."

"Yes, we are, but getting angry isn't going to help. Maybe Beatrice knows something. Perhaps even whether or not Carmen left and took her Mustang with her, ok?" She put her hand on his arm.

Jack looked up. "Okay. But I don't like what I'm feeling. I just want all the info."

"Yes, I know. So do I. Now Beatrice is probably waiting for us. Let's go get that info."

They proceeded downstairs and down the hall to the library. When they walked in Beatrice stood up and walked over to them. "Mr. De Santo said you wanted to speak with me."

"Yes. Only for a moment," Jill stated. "Please, let's all sit and be comfortable."

Jack's haunches were still up; she could feel them. He wouldn't relax until he had more information on the vehicle. Cars and laptops....the secrets they held were infinite and could lead to a huge break in a case in Jack's opinion.

Beatrice sat down keeping her hands folded in her lap. Jack and Jill sat opposite her.

"This is very casual," Jill stated. "We need a little information about Carmen in general and about what may have happened to her."

Beatrice nodded keeping her hands clasped in her lap, back straight and tall.

"When was the last time you saw Carmen De Santo?" Jill asked.

Beatrice looked down at her lap, then back up at the agents. Her eyes were wide and watery. "Night before last. She was heading out around seven in the evening. I saw her briefly. She was very pale and hadn't been feeling well. She told me she would be back in a couple hours, but that she wouldn't be late."

Carmen smiled and draped her handbag over her right shoulder. Her face was pale, but her smile was still sunshine.

"Oh, hello, Bea. I'm heading out for a couple hours. I shouldn't be out too long, ok?"

"Are you feeling all right, Mrs. De Santo? You look pale."

"It's ok. Just a flu or something. See you later?"

She looked over her shoulder and headed out the door to the garage. Moments later her red Ford Mustang zoomed up the drive.

"Are you positive she took her Mustang?" Jack asked.

Beatrice blinked the memory away. "Yes, she absolutely took the Mustang."

"Do you know what year it is?" Jack asked making notes.

"It's new – brand new. She loved the new look." Beatrice's lips trembled a bit.

"Did Carmen seem agitated or upset about anything?" Jill asked.

"Oh, no. She seemed tired and she was pale, but that is all. She had stayed in bed all day with a flu. It was nice to see her up and about."

"What was she wearing when she left?" Jack asked.

"All I saw was a long, tan trench coat tied at the waist and black flats.

It was far too warm to wear a trench coat, but I thought she may have had a chill since she wasn't feeling well."

"Did she have anything else with her? A bag or anything?" Jack asked.

"No. Nothing. Just her car keys." Beatrice's hands began to tremble in her lap.

Jill could see that the memory was agitating her so she decided to change the subject slightly. "Did you like Carmen?" she asked.

Beatrice's eyes lit up. "Oh, very much so. She is such a nice woman. She would talk to us about all kinds of things and would even help us out with the housework every so often. After a long winter she would often let us leave early on an especially warm spring day. She said we should go out and enjoy. She expects us all to work hard and we do because we all enjoy her so much." She looked down again blinking back tears. Her lips were trembling again.

"I know this is difficult," Jill said calmly. "Thank you so much for helping us out here."

Beatrice looked up and nodded.

"Did Carmen have many visitors to the house?" Jill asked.

"Oh, a few here and there. Her mother would visit occasionally. Mostly Carmen liked to get out and be with people and help people."

"Can you think of anyone who would want to hurt Carmen?"

A solitary tear fell down Beatrice's cheek. "No. Not at all. Carmen was such a beautiful person. It's a shame; a tragedy."

CHAPTER FIVE

Dr. McKinley leaned his bulky frame back in his chair and adjusted his glasses. "This is a terrible case. We do not have terrible cases in Lake Shore. Nothing like this," he said an obvious touch of sadness in his well-practiced, polished delivery. He shook his head. "Mrs. De Santo died of exsanguination, blood loss as a result of deep and severe lacerations to her chest and throat. The throat laceration was so severe her head had been nearly severed from her body. Lacerations in the shape of a cross on her forehead, three deep stab wounds on her chest; two near her breasts and one at her stomach. Bruises on her hands and knuckles. Scratches on her arms and legs possibly from branches or twigs. My guess is that she was running away from something prior to her death. The soles of her feet have many small lacerations and are caked with dirt. Dirt under the fingernails indicates that she may have been knocked on her stomach at some point or scratched at the dirt in her escape. Toxicology will have results on blood levels and samples taken from under the fingernails. She was not raped, nor sexually assaulted, however it does appear she had sexual intercourse within the last two to three days." He paused and looked down at his paperwork. "She was dead about three or four hours prior to discovery so I would say time of death was two or three in the morning. Little to no decomp despite the heat. I suppose that is our only saving grace." He looked up. "You must understand, Agents, this is a very unusual case. I can't remember the last time Lake Shore endured anything like this."

"We understand, Doctor," Jill stated. "It's understandable that the entire town would be in shock."

"And they're afraid," Dr. McKinley stated adjusting his weight in the chair. "Fathers are worried for their daughters. Husbands are worried for their wives. Rumor has it you are here investigating a serial killer. Lake Shore will not tolerate a serial killer."

65

"We are here following some leads, yes," Jack stated discreetly. "But we are also here to help your local enforcement. We are well-aware that this kind of situation has not happened before in Lake Shore and we want to be sure that we do all we can to solve this murder."

"Dr. McKinley," Jill nearly interrupted. "Did you find any evidence of defensive wounds?" She looked up from the report she had on her lap. "I don't see any note of that here."

"No. No defense wounds. These are typically located on the arms near the wrists up to the elbows. Nothing at all."

"Any ideas?" Jack asked.

"I'm thinking she was running, took a tumble, maybe tried to crawl away and this monster was on her. She just didn't have time to respond. This was a sudden attack brought on by rage. There are no hesitations to the lacerations. The first wound hit her breast straight on and with enough impact to bruise a significant radius. The second hit the left breast and nicked her lung; same amount of force. The third hit her stomach and upper intestine, and the final blow was to slit her throat. This was a quick, forceful rage that Carmen couldn't possibly predict."

Jill looked up from the report again. "Does it appear that she was murdered in the meadow where her body was found?"

"Yes, I would say she was. Based on the amount of blood found at the scene on the ground underneath her and on her body I would say she was murdered and left at the scene. There would have been a tremendous amount of blood spray from severing the carotid artery. It's almost impossible to clean all that up in a closed space. But outdoors? It could go anywhere and remain undetected."

Jack nodded. "Would you mind taking a look at a couple of reports from cases we are working on to see how much they resemble this specific case?"

"Absolutely. I would be happy to help."

"Great. We'll be in touch."

"So, forensics is a bust," Jack stated as they walked out of the Medical Examiner's office to the car. "I could have guessed what happened to her just by looking at her for 5 minutes."

"Ok, Always-the-Expert," Jill said grinning. "Well, at least he'll look at some of our reports. Maybe toxicology will have something. I would just like to know where Carmen was going that evening. Beatrice didn't seem to think she'd be long and her car is missing. We have some kind of bizarre journal and her laptop to go by. I don't know. Nothing is really adding up here. Maybe Renault bit off more than he could chew this time around. He wants socialites and political importance, but he doesn't want anything messy. A missing car? He wouldn't take the chance."

They reached the car and sat it in for a moment. "And Carmen wasn't raped. That's a red flag right there. Maybe he's starting to decline. Maybe he's messing up now and starting to unravel like so many killers do before they are caught," Jack offered.

"Maybe. I think this one is personal." Jill stared at the dashboard for a moment. "So, what now?"

"Well, we need to follow up on the car. We've got the laptop and the book and we should talk to Nero De Santo, her friend Marisca, and the Lake Shore Hospice Association. There's a lot going on here. By the way, how are things at home?" Jack asked.

Jill smiled and looked at him. "Oh, good. Very good. We're all healthy now."

Jack smiled. "You look exhausted."

Jill let out a long breath. "I'm confused. I feel like we're missing something big here."

"Yeah. That would be the car," Jack teased. "Seriously, though,

Renault is changing his ways. Either he's changed his M.O. or it's someone else. Whatever the case we've got to keep ourselves open to anything at this point."

"Yeah. I know," Jill said quietly biting her lip. She was not so convinced.

"There's always that case, the case that begins to stir you in all sorts of ways. This may be your case, but we still have to remain objective."

Jill smiled. "Of course. What's the game plan?"

"Let's head over to see Lieutenant Copeland, check in on the car situation, then we can split up and get the interviews and the evidence taken care of. How's that sound?"

"Sounds great." Jill smiled.

CHAPTER SIX

"We're here to see Lieutenant Copeland," Jack stated looking across the desk at the clerk.

"Is he expecting you?" the female clerk asked briskly.

The police station was a bustle of commotion. There were many people roaming about and officers heading out for response.

"No, but he should be," Jack said evasively.

"He's in with someone right now. He really can't see you."

Jack flashed his badge. "Tell him we want to talk to him about the Mustang." He smiled.

The woman nodded and hurried off into the bowels of the building. Jack and Jill turned and looked around the room. "Wow, it's a zoo in here," Jill commented.

Jack nodded. "Why do you think he never mentioned the Mustang?"

"Maybe it slipped his mind?" Jill offered weakly.

"Pretty important detail to let slip don't you think?"

"It's hard to know what he was thinking. I don't think these people have ever really had to think about so many details in such a short period of time." She looked at Jack's skeptical face. She smiled. "Ok, I'm trying to be optimistic here."

The woman returned to the desk and nodded to them. "He's in with the Emery's right now. About their son. He can be with you in a few minutes."

"Did you find their son?" Jack asked hopefully.

The woman looked down. "No. No we haven't," she said softly. She looked up again. "We've been having a lot of press coverage as you can imagine. A murdered woman. A missing child. All in a span of 24 hours. It's a lot for any town or city to take on."

"Any leads on the boy?" Jill asked.

"Nothing. It's so very sad. It's like he vanished. Just vanished." Her brow furrowed, then she made a note on a piece of paper. "I'll bring you to one of the offices out back. Press have been in and out of here all day. You don't need to deal with that."

The two agents followed her down the same hall they had been in the day before to an empty office space. Once inside Jack closed the door and turned to Jill.

"Children don't just vanished," Jill said. "They are either taken or they run away. How old is this child anyway?" She sat down resting her left hand on a nearby table.

"He must be very young. Hold on a second." Jack rushed out the doorway and returned a minute later. "He's seven." A pause. "I asked the desk clerk."

Jill nodded. "I'm pretty sure seven year olds don't run away." She let out a sigh. "Can you imagine? Losing a child?" There was an instant, deep pain in her eyes.

Jack nodded. "No. I mean I don't have any kids to lose quite yet, but I still can't imagine."

"It's odd though. A child missing and a woman murdered, all in this small town all at once. There has to be some connection, right?"

Jack leaned against the wall positioning himself to be able to look down the hall from the corner of his eye while he stood. "I'm not sure. For starters, Carmen didn't have children who may have played with the boy. She didn't volunteer for a children's organization that we know of. Unless she used him for sacrifice I don't see that she would have had much of a connection to the boy." He looked Jill square in the face and grinned. "Ah, just a little witch humor, that's all."

Jill rolled her eyes. "We still don't know if she was a witch."

Jack nodded both eyes glued to the opening of the door to the hallway. "I think the Emery's are leaving."

"Really?" Jill got up and stood near Jack. She leaned forward a bit and peered down the hall. Like watching a car accident site she couldn't help but catch a glimpse of the missing boy's parents. She could only see Lieutenant Copeland's back and his head bobbing as he spoke. Then he shifted his stance to reveal the missing boy's parents.

Mr. Emery was a slightly rotund man with a protruding abdomen. He was wearing worker's overalls stained with dirt at the knees and paint on the bib. His round head had a receding hairline and his face was etched in poverty, a sad expression and deep wrinkles. He was holding something, a piece of paper perhaps that he kept turning in his large hands over and over again. Mrs. Emery was a fair woman, fair skin, fair eyes, golden hair that hung straight to her shoulders. She had a small face, small nose, pencil-thin lips, and just a dot of blusher on each cheek. She wore a common housedress with buttons up the front and nondescript brown shoes. She kept putting a handkerchief to her face and looking down, then up vacantly at her husband and Lieutenant Copeland.

"Oh, I just can't watch this," Jill said in a whisper pulling back and returning to her seat near the table. "How horrible."

Jack continued to take in the scene, then pulled back a bit so that he wouldn't be visible as they came down the hall. He shook his head. "There's something I don't like about them."

"There's something you don't like about everyone," Jill teased.

Lieutenant Copeland's voice could now be heard. "We will certainly let you know of any new developments. I can only hope we find your son quickly." The three walked close to the agents who sat just near the door trying to look as if they had not been eavesdropping. Lieutenant Copeland followed the couple out of the first set of doors and his voice became softer. Jill glanced at Jack. "Awful" she mouthed.

As soon as Lieutenant Copeland opened the doors again Jack took one step forward. He wasn't sure if the Lieutenant had seen them when he was exiting with the Emery's and he wanted to be sure to get his attention. Jack waited one, two seconds then stepped forward directly in front of Lieutenant Copeland.

"Hello there." He smiled. "We'd like a moment with you."

Lieutenant Copeland looked tired. He rubbed his face with his hand and his shoulders sagged slightly. "Yes. I can give you a moment. Would you like to come to my office?"

"Yes, please," Jill chimed in.

The three walked past the desk clerk and down the back hall to Lieutenant Copeland's office. Once seated and this time not being offered coffee, Lieutenant Copeland began. "Any updates?"

"Well, actually, Lieutenant, we wanted to ask you the same thing?" Jack said his eyes sparkling devilishly.

Lieutenant Copeland rubbed his face again. "It's the car, isn't it?" It was not a question. He was defeated.

"Bingo," Jack stated, although the quick admission took a bit of wind out of his sails.

Lieutenant Copeland looked up at them and let out a short sigh. "We haven't a clue where it is. Pretty much disappeared into thin air. No reports of any vehicles found in the area matching the description…"

"Of a red 2005 Ford Mustang," Jack interrupted. "You know where I got that little bit of info?"

Lieutenant Copeland looked at him wearily.

"From the husband, which in case you've forgotten absolutely any and all training you may have had, makes him a key suspect just by proximity to the victim. Absolutely unacceptable."

Lieutenant Copeland's face reddened. "We were going to inform you. We thought we'd have located the vehicle by now."

Jack leaned forward. "In case you've forgotten, we're running this investigation now so I suggest…"

Jill interrupted. "Do you have a missing vehicle report we can review?" Her voice was smooth, clipped and serious.

"Yes, Special Agent, we do." Lieutenant Copeland looked directly at Jill trying to avoid Jack's angry stare.

"We'd like to see that, please, and we'd like you to make finding that vehicle your first priority. I don't recall any tracks at the scene and since this vehicle is missing I'd say it's probably got something pretty important in it," Jill stated.

Lieutenant Copeland nodded and rubbed his hands on his face again. "I'll get it straight away." He stood up and hurried out of the room.

Jill looked over at Jack. "Jack, you've got to try to keep your cool."

"I am," he said sulking like a child.

"I have a hard time believing that the car just disappeared. It has to be somewhere. Of course, who knows what kind of condition it's in at this point." Jill sat back in her seat. "Pretty damn sloppy. Renault is slipping big time."

Jack grinned. "Pretty damn sure of yourself, huh?"

"We've never known Renault to be this foolish," Jill said aloud, mostly to herself. She sat back in her chair and rubbed her face.

Jack nodded, but kept quiet his eyes on the door. "Do you think he even has a vehicle report or do you think he's just making one up now?"

Jill grinned, then let out a short laugh.

Just then Lieutenant Copeland walked in vehicle report in hand. "I made this report up personally," he said as he sat down.

Jill coughed as she choked back a chuckle.

"Are you all right, Agent?" Lieutenant Copeland asked.

"Oh, yeah, I'm fine." Jill sat up and brushed him off. "Thanks."

Lieutenant Copeland put the report on the table. "If you don't mind, Detective Winsler may have some information on the missing Emery boy. I need to speak to him while you look over the report."

"Of course," Jill stated. Lieutenant Copeland nodded at both of them and left the room.

Jack leaned forward and pushed the report closer. "Well, it's a report all right. Missing 2005 Mustang GT, red, owner one Carmen De Santo. Discovered missing on…..blah, blah, blah….it's listed as currently under investigation. No LoJack. No known enhancements. Nothing very special about it except that it's owner has been murdered and this car has gone bye-bye."

"Well, and the fact that this is a pretty sweet car for a housewife. Clearly Carmen likes her cars fast and sporty. And since this is the remake of the classic 1964 model I'd say she may have known a thing or two about cars." Jill glanced at the report.

"Maybe. But then again I have a feeling there's more to Carmen than meets the eye."

"Well, seeing that "the eye" is a dead woman with her throat slit wide open I'd hope so." Jill grinned.

Jack grinned back. "We're going to Hell you do know that, right?"

"Ah....no such thing, my dear," Jill cooed. "All right. What's next?"

"Let's get Lieutenant Copeland to dig up any and all files on Mrs. De Santo, as well as her husband and family. That should keep them busy and out of the way while we do the job that needs to be done here." Jack stood up.

"Agreed."

"While we're at it let's have them dig up a file on the Emery's, as well, doesn't hurt to look for a connection even if it's weak."

"Also agreed." Jill stood up. "I'll have a talk with Carmen's friend, Marisca and I'll take a trip to the Lake Shore Hospice Association. You?"

"I'll look over the Book of Shadows and talk to Jim about it; ultimately I'd like to meet up with him to go over all this. I think he'd like to physically see it. I also may be able to do a little work on the laptop."

"Ah, yes. Always sitting back reading books and laptops while I cart my ass all over Lake Shore. What a guy!"

"Hey, I try." He shrugged boyishly.

After asking for directions to Cherry Lane with the desk clerk and leaving a request for files for Lieutenant Copeland, Jack hopped in the car and Jill headed out on foot in search of Cherry Lane. "Meet up with you in a few! Call my cell if anything comes up!" She yelled over to Jack.

"Absolutely. Oh, and Agent Simko."

"Yeah?"

"Watch out for Renault." He grinned.

Jill laughed to herself and watched the vehicle drive off leaving short puffs of dry dirt in its wake. The air was very warm and Jill could feel the sweat on her brow almost immediately. Jill started down Main Street as she had been instructed looking around her as she went. What a very small town. How in the world could a woman be murdered here and no one see a damn thing? Then again. Maybe someone had. Jill proceeded down Main Street until she could feel the sweat on her brow. Phew, was it ever hot! The trees along the sidewalk did very little to shelter her from the heat. She came to a street perpendicular to Main Street and looked up at the sign. The desk clerk had said to take a right at Plum Lane and follow to the end, then take the left at Cherry Lane. Nope. This one was not Plum Lane. Jill frowned. Maybe one more street up.

"Can I help you find your way?" The soft, male voice made Jill jump. She put her hand to her waistband where she kept her pistol and turned around quickly. The man who had spoken was tall and lanky with a face that would make any ordinary woman drop to her knees and beg for mercy. His hair was a little longer than most men with just a bit of wave to it. He wore dark jeans and a black T-shirt and he didn't seem at all bothered by the warm weather given his attire. He grinned at her his high cheekbones moving up a bit higher still. Jill felt her heart flutter. "Hmmmm.....let me guess," he continued. His voice was soft with just the slightest hint of an accent. British maybe?

She was silent as she waited for his guess. He was so tall she had to look up at him. He looked down the street squinting his eyes as if in deep concentration. "Ah, never mind. I haven't a clue." He let off a short laugh.

Jill smiled and dropped her hand from her waistband. This man's eyes were mesmerizing and blue; they almost glowed. "Cherry Lane."

"Well, you're about on your way, then." He walked past her and headed down the street.

"Hey! Wait!" Jill called.

The man turned around but kept walking so that he now walked backward. He pointed to his ears and shrugged as if he couldn't hear her then disappeared down the street. Now that was odd. Jill continued down

Main Street. Still dazed from her experience with this tall, dark-haired man with the haunting eyes and the knowing smile, she met up with Plum Lane and took a right. She followed it down to the end, took a left, and located Cherry Lane.

Fifteen Cherry Lane was a small, blue Cape slightly set back from the road with a row of hedges and flowers directly in front of it. Jill made her way up the path to the front door and looked behind her for just a moment certain that the dark-haired man was somewhere out on the streets watching her. Yeah, right. You wish, she thought. She knocked on the door.

She waited a minute. Nothing. She looked down at the ground, then knocked again this time a bit louder. She looked behind her again certain that the man was out there somewhere. Those eyes. Who else had eyes like that? Just then the door opened and Jill turned to face a short, plump, dark-haired woman. The woman's eyes opened wide.

"Marisca?" Jill asked. The sun was hot. She pulled out her federal credentials so that Marisca would have no question who she was. "I'm Special Agent Jill Simko. Can I talk to you for a moment about Carmen De Santo?" Her tone was soft. Got more with honey, right?

The woman made a small sound and put her right hand to her lips. There were tears in her eyes. She nodded. "Yes," she said her voice barely above a whisper. "Of course." She stepped back and Jill walked into a modest entryway with a stairwell directly in front of her, a side table and mirror to the left. Marisca closed the door softly then stood staring at Jill. Her eyes were big and round.

"Is it ok if we sit?" Jill asked unsure of how to begin with this kind of response to her arrival.

The woman nodded again and put her right hand to her mouth. "Right this way." They walked through a doorway to their left and Jill found herself in a small living room with furniture neatly arranged in the room and flowers on the center table. "I can get coffee......if you would like," Marisca said again so softly Jill could barely hear her.

"No. No. This is fine."

77

"Water then?" The woman was wringing her hands now.

"No. Really. I'll only be a moment. I am hoping you can help me, help all of us find out what happened to Carmen."

The woman nodded then moved past Jill to sit on the couch. Jill sat next to her at about one person's distance and folded her hands in her lap. "How are things? Things are rough, huh?"

Marisca looked down at her lap, then quickly up at Jill her eyes full of tears again. "She was my best friend." Her lower lip trembled.

Jill leaned forward. "Yes. I know. This kind of stuff is never good." She noticed the baby monitor placed upright on the side table. "You have a little one?"

Marisca looked at her and smiled her body relaxing slightly. "Yes. She's only a year old. Fourteen months actually. She's sleeping now or you could meet her."

Jill smiled. "I have a little girl, too. She's twelve. Not a baby by any stretch of the measure, but my baby none the less."

"Do you have to leave her a lot?"

"Yeah. When I'm on the road with the job. It's really tough."

"Hey, I don't….well, I'm not used to talking to the FBI." She looked down at her lap again as if she had spoken out of turn.

Jill smiled. "We're everyday people. Just doing our jobs, you know."

Marisca smiled and glanced at the baby monitor.

"So, tell me about Carmen." Marisca stared blankly at her. "When did you last see her?"

"Oh, my she's getting so big, Missy!" Carmen waved at Baby Annie and the child

grinned up at her and bounced on her mother's knee. "How's my little one?" she said to the child. Carmen slumped down onto the couch next to Marisca. "Ugh....I'm exhausted." Then she grinned and bounced up again. "Coffee? Got any coffee?"

Marisca giggled. "Stop being so silly. Tell me! Tell me!"

But Carmen was already in the kitchen from which she yelled, "And we'll run away happily ever after!" Her clear laugh trailed from the kitchen into the living room.

"She came over to visit a few days before...." Her lip trembled. "Before she was found. She came by to visit me and the baby."

"How did she act?"

"Same as always. Chatty. Happy. She was excited to see Annie; that's the baby's name."

"What did you two do while you were here?"

"Just hung out, drank coffee, chatted, played with the baby."

"Did you go out anywhere together?"

"No." Marisca looked down at her lap again. "I can't believe she's gone," she said quietly. Her lower lip trembled.

"I'm so sorry," Jill said sincerely. "Did Carmen ever mentioned being afraid of anyone recently? Anyone who may have creeped her out in some way?"

Marisca frowned and made direct eye contact with Jill. "No. Not at all. Do you think it may be the serial killer, that Renault that's been in the news? Do you think he was watching her like he watched the others?" Her eyes were wide. Apparently the news was out. The Feds are here! The Feds are here!

Jill leaned forward casually. "Where did you hear that?"

"Lake Shore Daily News. It was the top story, front page, as you can well imagine. The article said there is reason to believe that a serial killer, possibly Lee Renault, is being investigated." She glanced at the baby monitor again. "People are scared. If Renault is here in tiny Lake Shore no one is safe." Her mouth made a little frown and she glanced at the baby monitor again in agitation.

"We are investigating all angles to the case I can assure you," Jill said softly. "We are very good at what we do and we're taking everything into consideration."

"But you still haven't caught Renault. If you had maybe Carmen would still be here," she spit out her eyes flashing suddenly and tears beginning to spill.

Jill put one hand on Marisca's knee. "We are doing all we can do. I assure you." She squeezed her knee. "I absolutely assure you."

Marisca took a deep breath and sighed. "Carmen never, ever mentioned being afraid of someone – and she would have. She told me everything."

"Did Carmen have a lot of friends in Lake Shore?"

Marisca took another deep breath. "No. Not really. She had me. She had her volunteer work at the hospice. She had Nero, Armand's brother. She had Armand when he was around. Other than that, she didn't have too many friends. She got along well with everyone, but there are a lot of cliques here and Carmen was brand new so I suppose she tried to get into some but found out that it was a lost cause. She didn't complain about it though. She never really complained about anything." Marisca smiled slightly at her memory.

"You mentioned Armand. Did she ever talk to you about their marriage?"

There was a loud noise from the monitor and Marisca jumped a bit. "Oh, sorry, I need to tend to Annie."

Jill smiled. "Go ahead. Do you mind if I wait here? I have just a couple more questions."

"No. Of course not." Marisca stood up and straightened her skirt. "I'll just be a moment." The wailing sound continued from the monitor as Marisca rushed out of the room.

Jill sat on the couch and looked around the room. She could hear soft coos from the monitor as Marisca attended to the baby. Jill stood up hands in pockets glancing at the pictures of kittens and flowers on the walls until her eyes spotted pictures on the mantel above a faux fireplace. She walked over to take a look. Marisca with the baby. Marisca smiling with a tall, man with sandy hair presumably her husband. Marisca and Carmen.

Jill shivered. Carmen's smile was intoxicating if any smile could be described as such. In the picture she was standing cheek to cheek with Marisca donning a floral sundress. Her hair was a light copper brown and framed her head in an array of curls. Her eyes were a mystical green and there was a "come hither" look under the layer of happiness in her smile. Her skin was an olive reddening into a deep tan. There was a feeling of youth, excitement, and adventure about her. Who in the world would want to take that away?

"We took that at our lake house in New Hampshire. Doesn't she look beautiful there?"

Jill whipped around to see Marisca holding an angelic infant with red, chubby cheeks and a crop of blonde hair. "Yes, she does," Jill agreed smiling at the baby. "Did she go there with you often?"

Marisca looked down and let out a short sigh. "Every so often. Not all the time. I guess whenever she just wanted to get away."

"This particular weekend," Jill said pointing at the picture. "Why did she go with you?"

Marisca shifted her weight from one foot to the other. "She had an argument with Armand. She needed to get away for a bit."

Carmen grinned and leaned forward. She was sitting on the front steps of the porch when Marisca returned home from shopping at the local market. "Had a fight with Armand. He is such a dick sometime!" She let out a laugh.

"Hey, help me with these bags, will ya?" Marisca responded struggling with a number of plastic bags.

Carmen jumped up and grabbed a couple. "Are you going up to the lake this weekend?"

"Yup." Marisca fiddled with her keys for a bit then inserted one into the front door lock. "Are you saying you're coming with us?"

Carmen grinned her eyes flashing. "Yup. Sound like fun?""

Marisca managed to open the door then pushed it with her hip. "Uh-huh." Carmen followed her into the entryway, then through the house to the kitchen. "Doug won't mind, will he?" she asked.

"Oh no. Of course not." Marisca set the bags down then looked over at Carmen. Her expression was serious. "Please tell me you'll get these arguments under control."

Carmen put her bags down and grinned. "Never. Armand will always be a prick and he'll always put the business before me so I'd get used to me tagging along to New Hampshire if I were you." She gave Marisca a big smile.

Marisca let out a short laugh. "All right, but you'll need to slum it with the chores, Little Miss Socialite. There are more bags in the car."

Carmen pouted. "But I just did my nails," she whined and held up hands that hadn't seen a manicurist in months. She skipped out of the house laughing.

"What were they fighting over?" Jill asked her.

"Oh the usual. She felt that he always put the business before her. He was always gone. I don't think Carmen minded being alone. She just wanted to feel like she was cared about. Armand is all business all the time. She knew he'd never change." Marisca moved to the couch and sat down again putting little Annie on her lap. Jill took her cue and sat beside her.

"Was he ever violent?" Jill asked.

Marisca let out a short laugh, then looked down as if she had spoken out of turn. "No. Not at all. Carmen was all piss and vinegar. Armand is much more restrained. I don't think he even raised his voice. But he's stubborn and that Carmen is, was, very convincing so I don't think she liked that he wouldn't budge for her."

"Wouldn't budge? What does that mean?" Jill asked softly.

"Uh…" Marisca looked up as if asking a superior being for the right words. "He wouldn't change for her. He loved his work. It always came first. Carmen wanted to be first or at least she wanted him to tell her she was first." Marisca looked Jill directly in the eyes her own eyes beginning to brim with tears again. "She was an amazing woman. He knew that. He's probably kicking himself right now that he can no longer make it up to her." A tear spilled down her cheek and she brushed it away quickly. "He loved her….in his own way."

Jill nodded. Didn't they all.

"So, you don't think he would have harmed her at all?" Jill asked.

Marisca's eyes opened wide as if startled. "Oh no." Her mouth curdled horrified at the thought. "Absolutely not."

After Jill said her goodbyes and thank you's and headed back into the blistering heat all she could see was the horrified expression on Marisca's face at the thought that Armand could have ever done his wife harm. But.....stranger things had happened and quite frankly Armand was still right up there on the suspect list. The fact that arguments between the two had caused Carmen to leave frequently on weekend vacations did not help move Armand's name any further down that list.

Jill pulled out her cell phone and dialed Jack as she proceeded back up the street. "Hey," she said when he answered.

"Hey. How are the interviews going?" There was a hint of excitement in his voice.

"Pretty good. Apparently Carmen and Armand were not the super happy couple we would hope for. Lots of arguments. I don't like the sound of it. We'll go over everything in a bit." Jill's eyes roamed the streets looking for the street signs that would lead her back to the main street.

"Hmm…" Jack said.

"Jack, are you listening to me?"

"Yup. Marital problems….not good for Armand…..look, I got something big, Jill."

Jill spotted Main Street and walked in that direction. "What is it?"

"You're going to love this. I'm with Jim. Carmen had some secrets." His voice was strained with excitement. "Big ones."

Jill headed down Main Street looking for the Hospice Association. "Would you call it a break in the case?"

"Maybe. Pretty damn interesting I'd say. When can you be here?"

"Where's here?" Jill spotted a small white building donning a sign out front that read "Lake Shore Hospice Association" written in red letters. She stopped just in front of the door.

"We're at the town library so we can meet there. No, no, scratch that. We should probably head back to the hotel, check in with the Bureau." He was speaking rapidly which only happened when he was excited and sensed he was on to something.

"I'm outside the hospice association now. That should only take a minute."

"Okay. Head over right after. Oh, man. This is big."

Jill let out a sigh and brushed her hair from her brow already glazed with sweat from the heat. "Did you forget I don't have a car and it's like a hundred degrees out?"

There was a pause on the other end of the line. "Oh, yeah."

"Can you pick me up in fifteen?" She looked up at the sky and reached for the door handle.

"Yes. Absolutely."

"All right. See you soon."

Jack clicked off the line without a goodbye. He was certainly distracted, which meant that whatever he had discovered had to be good. Jill walked through the doorway slipping her phone back into her pocket as she went. A wall of cool air welcomed her arrival. She entered the reception area, which was very sparse with two chairs, a small table, one large, waxy plant near the chairs and a small reception desk. Walls were painted white, the carpet a neutral tan. The woman behind the reception desk was plump with porcelain skin and dark, curly hair held back with a pink headband. She looked up from her computer screen and broke into a wide smile. Her lips were a bright red.

"Hello there," the receptionist said her voice lilting a bit with a Southern drawl.

"Hi." Jill smiled and leaned against the top of the reception desk. "I'm wondering if you could help me."

The woman nodded a pleasant expression on her face.

"I'm Special Agent Simko. I'm here investigating the death of Carmen DeSanto. Is there any way I can speak with your director?" Jill pulled out her credentials and flipped them over to show the receptionist.

The woman sat forward and peered at them and then up at Jill. She smiled again. "Well, I'll be. FBI, huh?"

"Yes," Jill said smiling patiently.

"Carmen was such a nice girl," the receptionist bubbled. "Such a nice girl." She over-emphasized the word such.

"Did you know Carmen well?" Jill asked.

"Not all that well. Just a 'hello, how ya doing' here and there. But she stopped and said hello. Not everyone does that." She smiled again.

"What is your name?" Jill asked kindly.

"Molly. I'm Molly Merris." She stood and stretched out her hand.

Jill shook it. "Nice to meet you, Molly. Now, is your director available? I'll need to speak with her about Carmen."

Molly nodded quickly. "Lemme see." She picked up the phone and dialed an extension. She smiled again at Jill. "Yes, Mary Anne. I have Special Agent Simko from the FBI here to speak with you." She paused a moment, glanced over at her computer, then said a bit softer into the phone. "About Carmen." A second later she put down the phone. "She'll be right up." Molly sat back down and looked up at Jill. "Can I get you anything, Agent Simko? Coffee? Water?"

Jill stepped back from the reception desk. "Oh, no. I'm all set. Thank you so much, Molly." Jill walked over to the waiting area and sat down. Her gut was telling her there would be no answers here, but then again who knew? Her gut had been wrong before.

A tall, slim woman entered the reception area from a narrow hallway adjacent to the reception area. She appeared to be in her mid-forties with smooth skin and a stern, yet approachable expression. Her hair was an ash blonde with some gray mixed in. She wore a gray suit with pencil skirt and sensible pumps. She smiled as she approached Jill, who stood up in response. Hand outstretched she said, "Agent Simko. I'm Mary Anne Newmarth. Welcome to Lake Shore Hospice."

"Thank you," Jill said warmly. "You have a very nice place here."

"Thank you very much. We try our best." She took a step toward the hallway from which she had come. "Please. Let's head to my office. We can speak privately there. Did you want any coffee or water or anything?"

"No, thank you. I am fine."

Jill nodded to Molly who simply smiled her big smile, then followed Mary Anne down the hallway that led to an array of cubicle spaces, then to a large office. The office was decorated with a large, mahogany desk and file cabinet, a round table for meetings, and a leather sofa. Mary Anne grabbed bottled water from her desk and sat down on a large, over-stuffed desk chair. Jill sat opposite her.

"It is so hot out there," Mary Anne mused. "It will be so nice when this heat breaks."

"Yes, it is quite warm," Jill agreed. "I hope I have not interrupted you at all. I only have a couple of questions about Carmen De Santo. It shouldn't take long."

Mary Anne sat straight and put down her bottled water. "Oh, no. No bother at all. I am happy to discuss Carmen."

"I take it Carmen helped out with the hospice association as a volunteer?"

Mary Anne nodded. "Yes. She helped out in any way she could. She visited our patients and spent time reading to them or playing cards and sometime bringing food or just talking with them. Sometimes she would help out in the office to answer phones or make copies. She was happy to help in any way she could."

"How long did she volunteer here?"

"Hmmm…" Mary Anne put a finger to her lips. "Maybe six months or so."

"Did she enjoy her work?"

Mary Anne's eyes were level showing very little emotional. All business. "She seemed to enjoy her work here. Our patients loved her. She was always full of life and I think she gave them hope."

"Did Carmen say why she volunteered here?"

Mary Anne took a sip of her water. "She said she wanted something to do and she wanted to help the community in some way. A lot of our volunteers are stay-at-home moms or housewives and we are grateful for their assistance."

"Was Carmen a professional? You know, showed up for work on time, that kind of thing?"

Mary Anne nodded. "Oh. Absolutely. She was a model employee. And she was so warm and friendly. She made everyone feel welcome. She will be missed."

Jill asked a couple more questions which only continued to prove Carmen was a model volunteer, thanked Mary Anne for her time, then after a quick goodbye to Molly headed out into the blazing furnace that was the late-afternoon. Her cell phone rang.

"Ok, I'm late. I'm just around the corner." It was Jack.

"That's all right. I just left the hospice association."

"Be right there."

Jill stuck the phone back into her pocket and looked around. It was late afternoon, yet the streets were practically deserted. Of course it wasn't quite the end of the workday yet and with the potential of a serial killer roaming the town she could understand why there weren't many people milling around. Still, Carmen had to be bored out of her mind here. She had left the socialite world of New York for this. It must have been an adjustment to say the least.

Just then Jack's Ford Taurus whipped around the corner pulling up alongside her. He reached over to open the door. "Need a lift, young lady?" He teased.

She shrugged. "Well, I'm hot and there's nothing much else to do around here. Why not?" Jill teased back hopping into the passenger seat. The car was cool from the air conditioner.

"Jill, this is Jim Reynold," Jack said motioning to the back seat. "He's helping with the materials from Carmen's room."

Jill turned halfway in her seat. "Nice to meet you, Jim." They shook hands. Jim was a slight man with a sandy mustache and small, intense blue eyes. To Jill he looked the type to surround himself with books and paperwork imbibing in very little social interaction of any kind. He wore casual shorts, a blue T-shirt and a baseball cap. "So, Jack tells me you two found something very interesting," Jill said facing forward again and snapping on her seatbelt.

Jack grinned. "All in good time, Jill." He pulled out from the curb heading back to the hotel. "Anything on your end?"

Jill shook her head. "Nothing major. The association just confirmed she was a great, helpful person. Marisca told me just about the same thing. A super person with some marital problems, but super none the less."

"Marital problems?" Jack asked his eyebrows drawing together in a frown.

"Well, nothing major. She would get annoyed that her husband was gone so often and would head up to Marisca's place in New Hampshire from time to time. Still, it's nothing serious enough to kill someone over."

"Well, maybe it's something," Jack mused.

"Now, why do I have the feeling I've gotten the short end of the stick here?" Jill asked grinning. "Both of you look like you've been caught with the canary." She let out a short laugh.

"All in good time," Jack cooed.

"Oh, come on, Jack. Someone has to tell me something before we hit Boston. I can't wait forty-five minutes."

Jack nodded a grin spreading on his face. "Ok, ok...." He glanced at Jill. "Remember what Jennifer Townsend said about Carmen De Santo?"

Jill's eyebrows furrowed in concentration. "Condition of the body I'm guessing?"

"No. Something else. Something kind of odd. Childish." He paused for a moment to get the right effect. "That's right. Our Carmen De Santo was a witch."

CHAPTER SEVEN

Jill Simko blinked a couple of times a smirk on her face waiting for the punch line. Instead Jack glanced at her quickly as he drove, his eyes intense and serious. Jill let out a chuckle. "You can't be serious." She grinned.

"I'm serious," Jack said his voice low and even. "And I'm not talking about the kind of witch that flies around town on a broomstick and has a fancy, black cat. I'm talking about something entirely different." Jill sat back further in her seat. She let out a long breath of air. "Remember? I mentioned it when we found the book. I just wasn't sure that any of it actually belonged to Carmen. But it does. It's all hers. Every bit of it. Jim has taken a look at it and it's amazing. Carmen's entire life for the past eighteen months is in that book." His eyes flashed with excitement even as he kept them on the road.

"Well, to clarify. Her Wiccan life is in that book," Jim sat forward so that he could be heard clearly. "She was meticulous in documenting her Wiccan life."

Jill frowned. "No one we've spoken to has mentioned this, except for Jennifer Townsend, but that was mostly gossip in my opinion."

"Looks like Carmen had her secrets after all." This time Jack took his eyes away from the road for a moment to glance at Jill and give her a grin.

"Do you think this is what got her killed?"

Jack nodded in the affirmative. "I'm positive."

"Then that would mean you're doubtful that Renault is her killer," Jill reminded him.

"You've got that right. Even Renault's not into anything this freaky!"

They arrived at the hotel in Boston one half hour later. The day had started to wind down and come to a close but Boston was alive and bustling as always. There was a message from the Bureau at the front desk upon their arrival. Jack suggested he return the call while Jill and Jim met in the front lobby to discuss Jim's findings in Carmen's book. On the drive into Boston, Jack had agreed with Jill that finding the book had opened this case up much wider than they expected. It certainly planted the seeds that Renault may not be her killer. That kind of doubt could only put a curve ball in what could have been a cut-and-dried case. At least knowing your suspect was a huge step in the right direction. Not knowing at all only made the case that much harder. Still each case had to be reviewed with a clean slate. All along they couldn't just assume the killer was Renault. Jill had found herself doing just that, however. It was time to open up her mind.

Jill ran up to her room for a moment, took a quick shower, then met Jim in the front lobby for a drink and to discuss his findings. She ordered a glass of Chardonnay and sipped it quietly while listening.

"As I have said before, Carmen was very devoted. It is common for witches to document their practice. The ancient Pagan religions were highly scrutinized under Christian regime and thus had to practice in secret. Therefore, the Wiccan culture, although a relatively new religion by our standards values secrecy in their work. They may only speak to other witches about the complex nature of the spells they are working on or the specifics of their practice. They are encouraged to document their work in the Book of Shadows. This is exactly what Carmen did. She was amazing in how much information she put into this book, which not only suggests a strong dedication to her craft, but also that she may not have had anyone to talk to about her spiritual goals." Jim took a sip of his wine and sat back.

Jill nodded. "I don't even know what to ask you right now. So, she documents her practice in this book. What practice? What is she doing?"

Jim took another sip of wine his eyes flashing clearly excited about his work and this discovery. "Witches devote themselves to an array of Pagan gods with an emphasis on The Goddess or a female deity. In their devotion to her they follow the seasons interpreting all seasonal changes as blessings from The Goddess. Each holy day is a time of devotion in respect to the season, which generally follows the agricultural cycle. The holy days are called Sabbats. Witches also acknowledge a series of rituals, which include ritual for the new moon and the full moon each month. When they document the Sabbats and rituals they are writing down a script of sorts that is called the Ritual. The Ritual will include a protection rite for their working circle or space they are working in, the reason for the ritual and an end blessing. The actual script for the Rituals during Sabbat and cyclical rituals don't change much, but the witch may adapt someone else's developed script to begin with before he or she has had enough practice to create his or her own rituals."

Jill nodded. "Amazing. So, there's a timeline here."

"Yes. Not only a timeline. Carmen documented every herb, potion, powder, and symbol she used in her rituals and spells. I have never seen a Book of Shadows so completely exact. She took this very seriously."

"So, she documented all of this. Where's the stuff? The herbs and potions."

Jim winked. "That's what I'd like to know. She has to have a secret place for it; somewhere special and that has been blessed to keep negative energy out. In addition, she would need a special place for conducting rituals and Sabbats. Witches generally practice in what is called the sacred circle, which is a safe place to practice ritual that has been blessed and that is without disturbance."

"Do you think it could be her room? Where we found the book?"

"Not sure. I'd have to take a look at it. I'm thinking if you didn't find any potions or herbs there then it isn't her sacred space."

"Well, could her room be her sacred space and her herbs and things be stored elsewhere?"

"The herbs and potions are like tools so Carmen would use them in most rituals therefore she would need them handy. Most likely the ritual tools are kept in or very near her sacred space."

Jill sat back a moment, took a sip of wine and thought about what Jim had just said. "So, Carmen may have written down rituals and spells in this book of hers while in her room, but…"

"My thoughts exactly," Jim interrupted an edge of excitement in his voice. "Why wasn't her book with the rest of her tools?"

Jill nodded. "Yeah. I guess that's what I'm trying to say. It sounds like the book is a tool in and of itself."

Jim nodded. "It is. It is. Writing in the book is a kind of ritual, which Carmen clearly took very seriously. Most witches will keep their books with their tools in their sacred space. They would also use the books in every ritual and spell. To be without it would be….well, would be like a preacher without a Bible." Jim took another sip of wine and looked around the hotel as if he were concerned someone may be listening to their conversation. "Carmen took great care to write in her book, but I don't think she had time to devote to writing in it wherever her sacred space was so she risked taking it out of that space to write in it. She may have been conflicted about that, but it would have been the lesser of two evils. Witches are respectful of areas they have blessed as protected areas or spaces where they feel safe to worship their Goddess."

"Do you think she may have protected the area she wrote in as well? In this case her room?" Jill asked.

"More than likely."

"How do witches protect an area?"

"They perform a protection ritual or blessing calling upon spirits to keep safe watch over the space. Generally they will also incorporate what is called a "binding" or sometimes a statue of some kind to keep watch of the area. This ensures that anyone with negative influence cannot enter the space."

Jill could not help but recall Armand's avoidance of her study when they had met with him. "Would this binding be visible?"

"The binder would most likely be hidden near the door. The statue may just seem like a harmless knick-knack. Witches are very good at hiding their craft from others they feel may disturb the delicate balance of the good energy they are working to develop and maintain. Whatever the case, an expert would be able to walk into the room and have a pretty good idea what Carmen was up to in that room."

Jill grinned. "Time to get you in that room." She chuckled. "Although I have to admit. All this positive energy, ritual, and binder talk is going right over my head."

"It's a foreign world to many of us. I just happen to think that Wicca is one of the more fascinating religions." His eyes lit up as he spoke.

Jill grinned. "It is different. You've got me there. Getting back to this sacred space....a witness stated that some of the teenage kids in the area have joked that Carmen was a witch because she went out in the woods alone a lot. Do witches practice in the woods in real life for lack of a better way of putting it?"

"Nature is the perfect medium for the witch. Unfortunately, not many witches practice outdoors anymore. Development has made that difficult and many witches prefer a space within their home. However, witches are often very attune to Nature and spend as much time as possible outdoors to be close to the Goddess."

"How's that?"

"The Goddess is a natural being and thus one can find her in nature much more readily than anywhere else."

"I wonder if she had space in the woods," Jill mused.

"It's a possibility."

Jill looked up and saw Jack approaching them a frown on his face. He sat down across from them at another empty seat with what looked like a gin and tonic in his hand. "You kids having fun?" he joked.

"Jim's keeping me up to speed on Carmen's past-time," Jill nodded at Jim and upon seeing a slight flash of irritation in his eyes made the correction. "I mean, Carmen's practice."

"Interesting stuff, huh?" Jack said. His buoyancy earlier over the news had vanished. In its place was a worry in his eyes that made them slightly darker and more distant than they had been earlier.

"Very. How'd the call to the Bureau go?"

Jack shifted in his chair and took a long, hard sip of his drink. He exhaled audibly and his eyes darkened just a little bit more. He said nothing.

"That good, huh?" Jill teased hoping to cheer him up a bit. "Should I run upstairs and start packing my bags now?"

"Quite the opposite," Jack said quickly his voice harder than normal.

"What do you mean?" Jill finished her glass of wine and sat forward. Jack shifted in his seat and avoided her eyes instead glancing at a group of women nearby who were endlessly laughing and grabbing each other's arms.

"We've been asked to stay on this case," he said quietly.

Jill just stared at him. "No matter what?"

"Yes. No matter what. No matter if this is Renault or not." His eyes were stormy when he finally looked at her. He took another sip of his drink.

"So I take it Powers has really taken a liking to this case, huh?" she said referring to their supervisor.

"No, it's worse than that." Jack's eyes sparked.

Jill bit the side of her lip and looked directly at Jack who was once again looking at the group of women now walking out the front door. "I'm really confused here, Jack."

Jack glanced at Jim. Jim looked at both Jack and Jill and stood up. "I really must be going. I wouldn't want to intrude."

Jill stood up and smiled at Jim. "Will you meet us for dinner in about an hour?"

Jim smiled. "Absolutely."

"Thank you, Jim. We'll be at The Astoria, ok?"

Jim nodded and with hands in his pockets walked to the elevators.

Jill sat down perched on the edge of her seat. "Ok, Jack. Be straight with me. What the Hell is going on here?"

Jack downed the rest of his drink and sat forward only inches from Jill's face. It was clear to her now he had had a drink in his room prior to coming down to the lobby. His eyes were slightly puffy from the alcohol. "Carmen's father is Senator Ricci."

Jill's mouth literally dropped open. She would never have put two and two together. "Oh fuck," she muttered. "I'm going to need another drink on this one."

"What that means is this is one breath away from becoming a media circus."

"We have to move fast," Jill concurred.

"Tonight we stay in Boston, then I say we move our asses down to Lake Shore until this is closed. I know you don't like the sound of it but I don't think we have all that much choice."

Jill's heart sank. This meant she had no idea when she'd get home to her daughter. Cases like this sucked for all the same reasons. "Good thing I really love my job or I'd tell Senator Ricci to go screw and I'd head home to my family permanently."

Jack nodded. "I hear ya. This sucks. This is totally blowing my mind. Senator Ricci's witch daughter gets herself fucking hacked apart, and somehow even if this isn't Renault we have to stay on it. And quite frankly, Jill, I'm not even so sure this is Renault anymore. No rape. Shallow cuts. It's such a mess! Who the fuck wanted this to look like Renault?"

Jill looked him directly in the eye her breath taken away momentarily. "Jack, I've been so focused on Renault I never thought of that. If we start considering other suspects then obviously someone went to great lengths to make this look like a Renault case. Details have been all over the news so it wouldn't be so hard to copy. You don't think this means we have two of them now?"

"I don't know. I'm really not so sure about anything right now."

"Ok, so let's break it down then. Senator Ricci's daughter is dead in a similar manner to the Renault cases. Married to an important New York businessman. Some marital problems, but nothing extreme. Lots of free time on her hands. Secretly practicing this Wicca or whatever. Missing car."

"I want that fucking car," Jack said his voice hard.

"Father is Senator Ricci," Jill repeated softly.

"Damn it," Jack cursed. "Media circus. Why do I have a feeling we're totally screwed with this one?"

"We're missing something, Jack."

"Yeah. That would be the car and the fucking fact that her Daddy is Senator Ricci." Jack was getting exasperated.

"No. Something more. I'm not sure what it is. But it's something."

"I need a drink," Jack answered and got up leaving Jill there to look after him.

CHAPTER EIGHT

Jack and Jill returned to Lake Shore early the next morning bags packed and destined for an indefinite stay at the Laurient Hotel, which was conveniently located in the next town over from Lake Shore. The distance from Lake Shore would give them the opportunity to discuss the case without the interference of media and townspeople, while allowing them close proximity to the crime scene. Jack was sullen the entire drive and having had too much to drink the night before sipped coffee and simply stared out the window as Jill drove.

When they were at the outskirts of town Jill turned to Jack. "Ok, Princess. Do you want to check in first or head right into town? Up to you."

Before he could answer Jill's phone rang. She answered it, then hung up quickly. "Change of plans. That was Lieutenant Copeland. Sandra O'Dea is in town and would like to speak with us."

"Please tell me Senator Ricci hasn't arrived yet," Jack said a weary whine in his voice.

"Oh, come on, Jack. Knock it off. We both think this sucks ok? I want to be home with my family. I have no interest in holing up here until God only knows when. But you know what? I'm sucking it up, ok?" She pulled off the highway to follow the back roads to Lake Shore.

"You don't have to be so bitchy," Jack whined turning his focus on his coffee.

Jill let out an irritated sigh. "Let's just get this over with, ok? Then we can check in, have something to eat, and work on this until we finish it. I want to be home, too."

Jack nodded. "Do we know anything about Sandra O'Dea?"

"Now that's the spirit, Jack!" Jill said in a mocking, cheerful tone.

"You hate me, don't you?" He smirked.

Sandra O'Dea met them in the library at the De Santo estate. Beatrice led them in as she had the previous day with tea, coffee, and scones waiting on one of the tables. Again Jill was impressed with how substantial the house was in comparison with the surrounding homes. No one had a home this grand in Lake Shore.

Sandra was an extremely attractive woman with a long, willowing body clad in a sharp, black suit and blonde hair cut short to just below her ears that curved around with waves that seemed permanently sculpted and affixed to her head. Her eyes almost glowed blue and despite very little makeup she appeared to have no wrinkles. She could have passed for a woman in her thirties. Her introduction had been short and sweet with a brief handshake to each agent during which she made direct eye contact. If she were disturbed by her daughter's sudden death and the intrusion of two federal agents into her son-in-law's home she didn't appear to be. Her jaw was set and her eyes fierce. She seemed ready for anything.

"We are pleased you are here to help find my daughter's killer," she said evenly. "And that you'll see this matter through. It is of utmost importance to us, as you can well imagine." Her voice was polished and clear her words pronounced with direction. Politician's wife.

Jill nodded. "We are happy to be of help, Ms. O'Dea."

"Do you have any leads yet?" She uncrossed her legs, bent forward and began to pour tea.

"We've begun our preliminary investigation. There is very little to go on at this moment," Jack stated.

Sandra picked up her cup of tea and gave each of them a slow, wicked smile. "Ok, cut the bullshit. Save that line for the press, who will be here in no time. Word just got out to the city this morning. You were lucky we could hold it back that long."

Jill was not sure what to make of her. She frowned a bit and bit her lip. Was this woman even upset that her daughter's head had been cut nearly clean off or was this all business for her? Both she and Jack said nothing.

Sandra sat back in her chair and crossed her legs again. "What do you have on my daughter?"

"Ms. O'Dea, all we *have* at this time is your daughter's body and a missing Mustang, which we are hoping to find sooner rather than later. Unfortunately investigations of this magnitude take time. We want to get out of here and back home as quickly as you want to find your daughter's killer. So we're on your side. Drop the attitude and work with us," Jill said firmly.

Sandra took a moment to look directly at Jill her tea perched in her hand. The slow smile spread across her face again. "I like you, Simko." She put the cup of tea down on the table and sat back in her seat. "Now, what do you need to know?"

"What was your relationship like with your daughter?" Jill asked.

Sandra's eyes glazed as if in memory. "We have always had a close relationship. She is my only child and I doted on her." Her eyes became instantly clear. "You may think I am cold to react this way to my child's death, but it is the only way I know to act. I do not intend to cry and grovel in front of you." Her tone was condescending her jaw set.

"We all handle grief in our own way, Ms. O'Dea. Right now I am more interested in how you can help us by answering our questions," Jill said softly.

"When did you last speak to your daughter, Ms. O'Dea?" Jack followed up right on cue.

"Nearly two weeks ago. She called me around noontime. We spoke for maybe a half an hour or so."

"What did you talk about?" Jack followed up fast now. No time for emotion or blame, or lack thereof as the case may be.

"The usual. She wanted to know how things were going in New York and I shared some gossip about a couple of friends of mine. That's about it."

"Did she mention at all that she was afraid of someone or that anything unusual was happening?" Jill followed.

"No. Absolutely not. Everything seemed fine. No reason for me to worry about her at all." Sandra pulled a cigarette from a silver pouch and put it to her lips. In seconds it was lit.

"Mom, you can't smoke in here!" Carmen said giggling. "You know you can't! Armand would kill you!!" She grabbed at her mother's arm a mocking smile on her face.

"Oh, Carmen, you worry too much," Sandra said.

Carmen sat down at the kitchen breakfast bar in a huff and put her chin in the palm of her hand pouting. "Mom, you are impossible."

Sandra grinned. "Only my daughter. Only mine," she muttered.

Carmen giggled.

Sandra blinked away the memory and took a long drag of her cigarette tilting her head back to exhale to the ceiling.

"How was Carmen's relationship with her husband, your son-in-law?" The question was returned with steady eye contact.

"They were very happy together. The love they felt for each was unparallel. Armand is deeply devoted to her. It had to have been so hard for her to move here, to move away from her friends and family to be here with him. He helped her through that. He was her rock. She loved him madly." Sandra took another drag of her cigarette.

"Were there any complaints?" Jack asked. He was met with stony silence. "You said you were close so she must have told you something about her marriage. Were there any problems between Carmen and Armand?"

Sandra looked at him steadily again biding her time by taking another drag of her cigarette once again directing the exhale to the ceiling. "No. Not that I knew of. They were so happy together. Newlyweds really. They were only married two years. I suppose the real problems come after that honeymoon phase." Sandra chuckled. "Seriously though, they respected each other. That was the most important part. Armand...." She trailed off a moment. "He, uh, he isn't taking this well, you know." Greeted with silence she took another drag of her cigarette and continued. "He wouldn't talk to me about it. Not yet anyway. But I can tell. His headaches are back. He's locking himself away. I know you have to ask these questions, but Armand was an amazing husband. He would never have hurt Carmen in any way." With that she pressed her cigarette into the saucer holding her teacup and put her cup back on the table.

"Armand is a powerful man," Jack began. "He clearly adored Carmen. Could anyone have wanted to hurt Carmen to spite Armand?"

Sandra looked blank for a minute. "Do you think that is what happened?" For a moment her expression was so blank it was hard to read. Shock setting in. Her lower lip began to tremble slightly. "I never thought someone would...." She mumbled her moment of bravery lost in a mist in her eyes.

"We are not exactly sure what happened, Ms. O'Dea," Jill said softly.

Sandra O'Dea lit another cigarette. "No. I simply don't believe it." The mist in her eyes was gone and she sat up straight in her chair. "Everyone adores Armand. Everyone loves working for him. And for that matter everyone adores Carmen. No one would ever want to hurt them." She lifted her chin a bit and took another drag from her cigarette.

"Well, someone wanted to harm them. Someone wanted to harm her and did just that," Jack said.

Sandra met his gaze, then looked down at her lap. "Yes, you are right. I just can't image who," she said softly. "The media will be all over this."

At that Jill sat up straight in her chair. "Speaking of....what is your relationship with your ex-husband, Senator Ricci?"

Sandra's gaze was instantly piercing. "We are friendly enough. We'll say 'hello' at social functions. That's about all though. Richard left us when Carmen was only a young girl. There is some friction there I must admit." She put her cigarette out on her teacup saucer.

"Was Carmen close to her father after your divorce?" Jack asked.

Sandra's eyes remained hard and steady. "No. I couldn't say that. He saw her on holidays, well, mostly just Christmas, but she had me and that was all she really needed. We were very close."

"Was she angry with her father at all?" Jill asked.

"No. I couldn't say she was. She looked up to him and would ask about him, but that was all."

"Does your ex-husband have any enemies that you know of?" Jack asked. He grinned. Of course he did. Bastard.

"Politics breeds enemies, Agent Pellingworth. You must realize that," Sandra said haughtily her gaze steady again.

"You didn't answer our question, Ms. O'Dea. This if very important in our investigation," Jill stated.

Sandra was quiet a moment. "There was one in particular. He wanted Senator Ricci's spot more than anyone. Tad Winslow."

Jack grinned. Good old Tad. But would he murder the Senator's daughter? Who could say?

Jill nodded. "Thank you, Ms. O'Dea. This helps so much. Can you think of anyone else?"

Sandra sat silent for a moment. "No. No one else."

"Can you think of anything else that may help us, Ms. O'Dea?" Jill asked gently.

Sandra shook her head back and forth slowly tears welling up in her eyes suddenly. "Fuck. Fuck. Fuck," she muttered and buried her face in her hands. When she looked up her eyes were blazing. "Someone fucking tore apart my little girl." With that she buried her hands in her face breaking out into audible sobs.

"It's ok, Mommy. What's the matter? It's ok." Carmen as a child had been nothing if not angelic. She shook her reddish blonde curls and laughed out loud. "Mommy, no sad. No Mommy."

Sandra picked up her little girl and felt the smoothness of her cheek against her own. If only every day could be like this day.

By the time Jack and Jill left the De Santo estate the gated entrance was swarmed with reporters from various news stations. So far it looked as if only Boston and New York had arrived, although more would come soon enough. The daughter of a powerful U.S. Senator murdered in cold blood – this would be big. Very big.

"Oh, this is great," Jack muttered hopping into the driver's seat and eyeing the reporters at the gate.

"Maybe you can just drive right over them," Jill teased.

"Don't temp me," Jack stated putting the car into drive and started toward the gate.

"Hey, I was thinking…did you and Jim end up getting into Carmen's laptop?"

"Nah. I was leaving that to us, baby," Jack teased approaching the gate which opened to the throng of reporters that were held back by barriers so that Jack and Jill could proceed out of the estate to the main street.

Jill giggled. "Good. I didn't want to be left out." She pouted then giggled again. "When do we get to that?"

"As soon as we find that friggin' car." Jack scowled. "I put out an APB. I really hope we find that thing. I have a feeling it is all we need."

"What do you think about Tad Winslow?" Jill asked as they proceeded down the scenic road.

Jack grinned. "I like that guy. I hate Senator Ricci. I can't say Tad Winslow would go this far, however. Hack his daughter up and pretty much decapitate her? No way. And to what end? If anything it's pretty negative publicity."

"Unless that's what you're going for," Jill suggested.

"I doubt even Tad would go that far."

"Still, we have to follow up on it, Jack. It's an angle no matter what you believe," Jill said softly.

Jack was quiet for a moment. "Yeah. I know. I know."

"I could do it you know….so that you don't have to…..to be there," Jill started to say.

"No, let's follow up on it together. I want to put this senator angle to bed soon. I just don't think this has anything to do with status. I don't think this has anything to do with Renault. This is....." His eyes darted back and forth along the road as he thought of just the right word. "This is intensely personal."

Jill nodded. "I agree. Still, I feel like we're just walking around in circles and we're missing something very, very obvious. We broke it down last night. She's a Senator's daughter, married to a prestigious New York businessman, time on her hands, practices witchcraft secretly. There's a lot going on here. We should have a lot more to go on."

"I know this isn't Renault but I can just hear his lips smacking on this one. This is his bread and butter. His bon appetite." Jack's face was set firmly. "I want that car."

"Forget the car for a second, Jack. We'll get the car. Eventually. Right now we still can't completely rule out Renault. This case is still too similar to the others to completely dismiss him. I'm not feeling him here either, but he's still a consideration. We also can't rule out the fact that there could be someone who absolutely hates her to the core and may not even know who her father is. After all, according to Sandra O'Dea he wasn't too involved in her life." Jill sat back and sighed. "This one is tough isn't it, Jack?" She breathed.

Jack returned her sigh. "What happened to the easy murders? The clear-cut-husband-kills-wife kind of thing?"

"Let's go take a nice look at the laptop."

Jill's cell phone buzzed at that moment. "Yeah. Simko." She nodded and looked at Jack her eyes a little distant. "Uh-huh. Yes, that should be fine. Thank you so much." She snapped the phone shut. "That was the ME's office. Report is waiting at the hotel. They are preparing the body for burial and wanted to be sure we were ok with that. Amazing how once the Senator and the press are involved everyone is on their best behavior, huh?" She smiled.

"You're right. You're absolutely right." Jack nodded. Suddenly his eyes grew wide. "Whoever killed her didn't know about Senator Ricci."

"What do you mean?" Jill asked glancing over at him.

"The ME didn't know until the press were called in so they've been dragging their asses. Lieutenant Copeland didn't know so he's been a total dick to deal with. They didn't know about Senator Ricci or they would have behaved better with us. They wouldn't have lost that car. They would've been more helpful. But they weren't. And if our top dogs didn't know her dad is Senator Ricci than I bet her killer didn't either. I bet he's fuckin' shaking in his boots about now."

Jill mulled this over for a moment. "You're making some assumptions here, Jack. What if it's someone outside of the town? Someone who *does* know about her father? You're assuming her killer is someone in this town. And besides just because the local officials may not have known who her father is doesn't mean some of the local townspeople lacked the same knowledge."

"Yeah. I know. I know. It's all coulda's and woulda's right now. You're right. But if I'm right and that person didn't know, someone is peeing his...or her... pants right about now, and guess what? We'll smell that a mile away." Jack grinned. "I feel like the hunt is on again and I *do* love the hunt."

Jill laughed. "Are we going to the funeral then, my dear?"

"Wake, funeral, I want in on the whole fucking enchilada."

Jack and Jill ordered room service and settled down in Jill's room to look over Carmen's laptop. The light of the laptop lit up the dim room amidst plates of food. On the screen was a yawning red flower muted in a way that was supposed to demand the attention of the viewer to the very center of it. Jill took a bite of a club sandwich. "Where do we start?" she asked her mouth full of food.

Jack grinned. "Well, we've got internet history, Facebook, Twitter feed, messages, email, docs, bank records, anything we can get to without our IT guys needing to get at it. From what I find most people just aren't smart enough to hide stuff."

"Let's start with her email. I love reading email," Jill suggested.

Jack stopped and looked at her. "You're not reading mine, are you?"

Jill swatted at him. "Just open it up!"

Jack opened her email program within minutes and with the help of automatically saved passwords he had her email program up and running. Carmen had ten messages to read. About eight of them were advertisements of one type or another. The other two consisted of one from her mother and one from someone named, "Omaha". Jack opened the one from Sandra O'Dea. The writing was short and to the point.

"Carmen, How have things been lately? I haven't heard from you in days. I thought you may like to get out to New York. The heat has been oppressive. Call me soon. Love, Mom."

"That was sent two days before Carmen was found dead," Jack said aloud.

"I wonder where Carmen's cell phone could be. Maybe Sandra tried to call her, too," Jill mused.

"That's why I want that car."

Jill giggled. "Enough about that! We never asked Armand about her cell phone. We should check to see if we can get that, too."

Jack opened the message from "Omaha". Two paragraphs stretched out on the screen. Jack leaned forward to read as if doing so would help him see between the lines.

"Carmen, It's sweltering. I can't stand this heat. Maybe one day we can run up to Antarctica and catch all the cold we can and bring it down here for days like this. Then

there's only one way to warm up and you won't be so far away.

I haven't heard much from you in days and I am desperate for you. I am calling on all the lands to bring you here to me. Why are you so quiet? Why don't you come here at all? It is fine, I suppose. If you need some time to yourself this is fine. Still your smile would be comforting. I will draw a spell for you so that you may feel better. I know you have been ill lately. My dear, I want all the best for you whatever that needs to be. All my love! Omaha"

Jill looked over at Jack and put her sandwich down. "By gosh I think we've found something. Looks like Carmen had a special friend."

Jack took a bite of sandwich and a sip of beer. "Appears so. It was sent the day before her body was found. Yeah, her cell phone would be nice right about now. Let's look at what else we have from this Omaha character."

Jack did a quick sort by sender and scrolled to the messages sent by Omaha. There were ten in total.

"My darling! How are things working out? Feel any better? My dear you were on fire last night. You are most powerful I think. You will need to be careful. Such power breeds haters. Breeds mischief. I cannot wait to see you again. You are so beautiful." (3 days before discovery)

"Honey, Come over quick. I am having trouble with a spell. My future forecast. Call me." (4 days before discovery)

"I love you. I love you. Is that all? Is that all it is? Oh, Carmen, stop everything and just run. It's that easy. Oh no, it's not you say. My love! Is there nothing else when we are together? Omaha (5 days before discovery)

"Oh, my Carmen. Are you mine, my Carmen? Are you mine? Call me! I am desperate for you!! Please call." (10 days before discovery)

They went on like this from short affections to deep poetry so imbued with love and adoration that Jill's heart shrank in envy. "Someone cared very much for Carmen. Who's Omaha?" she breathed.

"That's a good question. The emails are sent almost daily but it looks like Carmen only keeps a couple of weeks at a time. I have a feeling she didn't want anyone finding an email trail with this one. I'm most interested in the one right before her death. It looks like whoever this person was she hadn't responded to his or her emails or communications. Nothing threatening here, but it may be something."

Jill took another bite of sandwich. "I guess Carmen found a way to deal with her loneliness and from the looks of it this admirer practiced spells with her."

"A fellow Wiccan? Sounds like it. I'm going to check to see if Carmen wrote back at all."

Jack clicked onto her sent folder and sorted accordingly. "Here we are. There's about five saved here."

My love, I am ill. I feel as if a truck has hit the very core of me. I pray to the Goddess for strength from this virus that rips at my very soul. Such mischief you were right. Someone is pushing this on me I can feel it is such. I have set my candles and I am desperately trying to push this off but even as I do it gets stronger. This is something beyond my control. There is an evil wind falling. Pray Goddess that I am set right again and not in pieces. Such is mischievous listening all the while. Love always, Carmen (1 day before discovery)

I am dizzy today. I don't have much time. I miss you. Carmen. (2 days before discovery)

"It was a thing of wonder wasn't it? I wouldn't worry as much about mischief. We are good and pure and we have protection. I will lay a trap to keep mischief astray. I love you. Let's meet again soon. Kisses, Carmen." (3 days before discovery)

"I will be there momentary. I have something here. Armand is home earlier than expected. Praise be!" (4 days before discovery)

"Oh my love. My darling. I'm not sure this is the right way to be. I love my husband and

I am trying to come to terms with this every day. Why would I ever betray his love when I know he means all the best for me. He would be so angry with me and I cannot bear his eyes when they are angry. I am trying. I am trying to be good. Let's talk about this my love." (15 days before discovery)

Jill was quiet a moment after reading the sent messages. "She knew someone was angry with her? I am confused. Her last sent message to Omaha sounds so ominous. It sounds like she did something and she knows someone is going to be angry with her and will try to get revenge."

"It certainly sounds like this, but I may have Jim take a look at this. Carmen mentions the Goddess in this passage and all her emails are littered with religious statements. It could be that Carmen was only worried that her work as a witch would have negative consequences."

"Or it could just be a bunch of shit she's feeding Omaha since she knows he'll believe it. She doesn't seem to be straight-forward at all in any of her emails to him."

"Let's look at her emails to other people. If she is still evasive then we may be able to surmise that Carmen was just that way with everyone not just Omaha."

Upon further inspection, emails to her mother were warm, direct and inviting. Emails to her friends were short but direct and emails to her husband were sprinkled with "dears" and "loves" and "honeys", but other than that were as direct as any other without any reference to a Goddess or mischief or any other powers beyond the day-to-day of life.

"What a strange woman! She must have been living two lives. One with her husband and family, and one with this witchcraft and Omaha. The emails are completely different in all ways as if she were two different people entirely," Jill stated rubbing her face.

"And still the Senator's daughter and loving member of the community," Jack mentioned. "This is still not enough to lead us anywhere on her death, however. There are plenty of people living different lives that are not murdered and left out in a meadow to rot in the heat."

"But then again. There are some that are," Jill stated. She stood up and began to pace a bit. "She must have spent a lot of time trying to keep these lives separate. I wonder what she was thinking."

"I think she was trying to fill her time. The girl had to have been bored watching house all day while her husband was out in the world. That time can get awkward and she clearly found a way to occupy it with this Omaha person."

"Male or female?" Jill asked.

"Male," Jack said immediately. "The male-female system would have needed to work for spells. Jim told me that spells are blessed with male and female imagery and energy. This wouldn't be a female."

Just then Jack's cell phone rang. They both jumped. Jack reached over. "Pellingworth." He paused for a bit then nodded his eyes ablaze. "It's about fucking time!" He was on the phone for a bit longer than he slid it shut. He jumped up and clapped his hands once, then rubbed them together. "The Dover police think they found Carmen's Mustang."

CHAPTER NINE

Dover, New Hampshire was about an hour and a half northeast of Lake Shore, Massachusetts near the New Hampshire coast. Jack and Jill found their way there from Lake Shore that afternoon and met Dover police on a back road near an open field. Jack was all smiles in the car but his serious no-nonsense mask prevailed as he stepped out of the Taurus and made his way over to police.

A nervous man with brown hair and an equally brown mustache greeted them and identified himself as Officer Petty. His eyes shifted. "We think we found your car. We hope we have. Dover has never had a case like this. Is she really Senator Ricci's daughter?"

"Yes, sir," Jack said steadily. "When was the car found?" He took out a notebook. Jill recognized this as a technique used to slow down the person being interviewed and also keep the questions to the task at hand.

"Just before we called you, sir. We received a call of an abandoned car on Newing's Field so I headed out and I was completely surprised with what I found. I know you put out an APB for a red Mustang and when I saw the condition of the vehicle I was certain this was your car. One check at the registration confirmed my suspicions."

"The registration was left in the car?" Jack asked. Usually the first thing to be removed from a stolen or abandoned vehicle *was* the registration. This changed things a little. If someone put a hit on the Senator's daughter one would hope they would know enough to remove the registration prior to abandoning the vehicle. "Plates?"

"Plates were removed. Maybe the guy didn't think it mattered if he took the registration," Office Petty surmised. "You'll really need to see the car to understand what I mean."

"It always matters," Jack muttered. "Even when you think it shouldn't matter it always matters." He paused. "Let me guess. Car's burned out?"

Office Petty nodded. "Let's take a look."

Jack looked down at the ground hands in his pockets as Office Petty turned to lead them to the scene. "Why do I have a feeling Carmen would have killed someone for doing this to her car?" he muttered.

"You think this was done prior to her death?" Jill asked.

"Maybe. From her email she thought someone was targeting her in some way. She blamed "mischief", but maybe she knew more than she was letting on," he said.

"In that case maybe she torched it herself," Jill suggested.

Jack's eyes went wide. "Blasphemy! Not that gal. I take it she loved her cars." He grinned. "Some gal!"

They followed Officer Petty quite a distance out through a narrow strip of clearing in the woods. Officer Petty pointed, "Tire impressions. The Mustang's. Someone drove her way out here so no one would see. And guess what? No one did, not for a while. The car nearly burned itself out before we got the call."

"No one saw anything?" Jack asked. He shook his head. "I know this is the middle of absolute nowhere and everything but I really find it hard to believe no one would have heard or seen something suspicious." He shook his head.

"No one comes out here much anymore. It's primarily conservation land, but it isn't all that monitored. Not after the Darling's girl was found murdered out here. Everyone is just too scared to venture this far out."

"How was the girl murdered?"

"Strangled. Poor thing. She was only ten years old. Smart girl. Tons of potential. Went missing quite suddenly and was found all the way out here by some hunters. Poor, poor thing. We had to clear out part of the woods to really get at her in the clearing. I guess this is where they say bad things happen."

"Did you ever find her killer?"

Officer Petty looked down for a moment his eyes distant. "Never. Those poor parents. They have never fully recovered."

"How long ago was this?"

"Well, Nancy'd be sixteen now so I'd say about six years ago. It made national news but only briefly. The rest of the world doesn't even have a clue where Dover is never mind try to find the killer of a girl out here. It's really such a shame. I hope we get that bastard someday."

"How did the parents react?" Jack asked.

Officer Petty blinked looking slightly surprised by the question. "Devastated. Absolutely devastated. What you would expect when your child is found murdered."

"How long was she missing before her body was found?"

"About a week. The kill was fresh so he must have kept her for a little while before eventually killing her." Office Petty shivered. "Poor, poor girl."

"So no one saw the smoke?" Jill asked quickly coming back to the original line of the questioning.

Office Petty stopped in his tracks. "What smoke?"

"From Carmen De Santo's car?"

"Oh, pardon me. I thought you were still talking about little Nancy

Darling. We had one report of smoke but I just assumed that a homeless person set a fire to keep warm. The report did not mention an explosion or an excess of smoke. No need coming out all this way to harass someone."

"Did you ever consider it could have been a forest fire?" Jack asked abruptly.

"It's been wet up this way recently. Frankly, the thought never crossed my mind. If anyone ever ventures out this way it is usually just someone who is lost or a homeless person. It did not seem urgent at the time." Office Petty should his head and took a slow breath. "Knowing what I know now I feel pretty stupid for not making my way out here anyway."

It had taken nearly ten minutes to make the walk through the narrow lane in the woods until the trees cleared quite abruptly. There she was. Jack instantly put his hand to his mouth horrified by what he saw.

The Ford Mustang stood in the middle of the field as if on display but well away from any tall shrubbery or trees. The convertible top had completely peeled away melting along the edges to meet the frame below it. The red paint was now scorched black and a dull gray in the spots where the worst damage had occurred. The tires had sunk into the ground as if to match the entirely defeated stance of this once powerful car. As Jack and Jill walked closer to the vehicle stinking of burnt plastic and metal they noticed that the entire middle and rear end of the vehicle was obliterated whereas the front of the vehicle had only suffered minimal damage. What fire hadn't destroyed man had taken care of. The front of the vehicle looked as if it had been struck head on multiple times the overlapping lip of the fender curled into an ugly smile. The headlights were smashed and the signature pony insignia was missing entirely.

Officer Petty stood just behind them. "We've called forensics to make a complete inspection."

"We'll call in an arson expert from the Bureau as well," Jack stated simply. No need to have this part of the investigation handled with anything but the utmost in professionalism. Jack circled the vehicle peering inside as much as he dared. When he had finished his encircling of the vehicle he squatted down in front of the Mustang and stared at the front fender.

"Looks like someone banged this up a bit," he mused. "I'd like forensics to take extra care with this section of the vehicle. I want to know if this was deliberate."

"There have been no reported incidents of any vehicle accidents in this area involving a red 2005 Mustang. In my humble opinion this looks deliberate." Office Petty offered.

"I agree," Jack nodded standing up. "Wow. Who would do this to such a beautiful vehicle?! You don't think Carmen would have done this to her own vehicle do you?"

Jill raised her eyebrows. "You just never know. I'm sure she loved this car but maybe she got desperate. Maybe something happened. We just don't know enough yet."

Jack nodded and looked over at Officer Petty. "You call your people. We'll call our people. Let's get a report out ASAP." He turned to walk away.

"Officer Petty?" Jill asked.

"Yes?"

"Who called in this vehicle? Who found it?"

"A hiker. Goodness only knows what he was doing out here in these woods. As soon as he found the car he called us to it."

"Could we speak with him? Is he still around?"

"His name is David Gwen. I'll give you his contact information."

As they headed back to the road Jack muttered, "Pretty sweet fucking car right there."

VALERIE R. KACIAN

CHAPTER TEN

It was five o'clock in the afternoon. David Gwen had proven to be another dead end. Totally legit. Found the vehicle. Called it in. Nothing suspicious about his story. Exhausted and hungry, Jack and Jill had decided to eat an early dinner at the hotel restaurant.

"Now what?" Jill asked digging her fork into a seafood salad that had fallen out of her over-stuffed sandwich.

"How the Hell can you eat that stuff?" Jack asked. "It's so vile."

"Vile? This is heaven on a stick, sweetie!" she teased.

"Yuck!" Jack said taking a drink of his water. "Leaves a bad taste in my mouth."

Jill grinned. "So, like I was saying. Now what?"

"Well, Carmen's wake is scheduled for tomorrow evening with the funeral the following day. I say we crash that party. Have a look around." Jack cut into his steak and took a slow bite. "Mmmm....now, *this* is what I'm talking about."

Jill smiled and took a sip of wine. "I want to know who Omaha is. I also want to know all the why's, where's, how's, and what the fucks of that car."

"Me, too, my dear. Me, too. But all in good time. First things first. Let's let forensics and arson run their magic. In the meantime we have the rest of Carmen's computer to deal with." Jack stated.

"Yes, but that's all so dull! I want to get out there and talk to people. Someone has to know something."

"Who's left on our list?"

Jill flipped through her notebook. "I have Nero DeSanto here but I don't know if that's going to really be much of anything. According to Marisca, he and Carmen were friends but that's almost seems mandatory since he is Armand's brother."

"Good idea to talk to him though. You never know. He could pan out."

"Sounds good. I can talk to him tonight."

"Nah. Let's hit the computer a little tonight. I think Omaha may be where we need to spend a little bit more time. There was certainly an intense connection there. Carmen certainly found plenty to fill her time with so I really don't buy that she was all that upset that her husband was away so much," Jack mused.

"Maybe that's why she found someone to fill her time. Maybe it was just an online thing that became something more before she knew what was really happening. This happens every day. Who's to say it didn't happen to Carmen De Santo?" Jill suggested.

"I just don't get it. It doesn't make much sense. Carmen De Santo, former socialite, married to a wealthy businessman, nothing to worry about, daughter of Senator Ricci, silver spoon up her tight little ass and yet she's going online trying to find someone to fill her time. And to top it all off she's a fucking witch?" Jack stated.

"I think she was unhappy. I think she had led a fast life in New York and just happened to fall in love with Armand. When she realized that the rest of her life was doomed to a life in Lake Shore she started to get more and more unhappy. Her unhappiness skewed her thinking."

"But how did she get into witchcraft and online dating?"

"Who knows? Time alone does things to you. Maybe she saw a TV show and became enchanted or read a book and thought this sounded like the right path. There are a number of different reasons for her choices. And yes, being a selfish, spoiled brat meant she didn't have to worry about working or money or anything so she had to fill that time with something. I bet Carmen wanted to fill it with something as dangerous and exciting as her fast cars and social parties in New York."

Jack was silent for a moment. "You're smiling a little, Jill. Sounds like you can relate to Carmen?"

"Well, not in the selfish, spoiled rich girl way, but in the way that when you are unhappy your mind can change and you may consider things you never thought you'd ever consider. It seems to happen so much in life." Jill finished her last bite of seafood salad. "Not me, though. This seafood salad is too yummy to hear me complaining."

Jack grinned. "So, how did Carmen go from being an unhappy wife to a dead woman?"

"That's for us to figure out, right?" Jill grinned. "We have somewhere to go here. It could be Omaha and her affair. It could be witchcraft and running into the wrong people. It could be associated with her father. It could be her husband who finds out about her affair..."

"Suspects," Jack interrupted. "Armand De Santo. Husband finds out his wife is having an affair and murders her in a jealous rage and destroys her most beloved vehicle."

"Omaha. Someone she met online who may have led her into the Wiccan lifestyle and used it to lure her into devaluing her possessions and into the woods where he eventually led her to sacrifice," Jill followed up.

"Senator Ricci competitor. Targets his daughter after some threats and eventually offs her for some personal interest in Ricci's campaign."

"Ok, let's dissect," Jill interrupts.

"Omaha – a little out there if you ask me. I find it hard to believe

Carmen went online to find love, but she could have gone online to research Wicca and somehow hooked up with him that way. Motive for killing her?" Jack followed up.

"Armand. Very probable that he could have reacted in such a way to his wife's indiscretions. How tight is his alibi?"

"Senator Ricci competitor?" Jack asked.

"Weakest of all. Motive weak. Target would generally just shoot the girl or make it look like an accident."

"Or make it look like Renault......" Jack suggested.

Jill frowned. "Perhaps. Good catch there. So....best case looks like Armand. Otherwise, we're pretty much shit out of luck on everything else."

Jack sighed. "Phew! That was exhausting. Ready for dessert?"

Jill giggled.

After signaling the waitress and ordering dessert, Jill became serious. "Seriously, though, Jack. Armand is our best guess. Everyone keeps saying how much he adored her. If he really did adore her this much, it would make sense that he would be beyond himself to learn that she was cheating on him."

Jack sat back and took a sip of his wine. "I don't feel it with him, but we'll still need to look into his alibi. If it's not as solid as we'd like we'll have to consider him." He shook his head. "I don't want this to be the husband. For some reason my gut isn't screaming that it is him."

"My gut isn't screaming at all," Jill stated.

"It should be with all that fuckin' seafood salad in there," Jack teased.

Jill giggled. "We have to consider Omaha a suspect here."

"I agree, but we don't even know who he is. We don't even know if it's a he! Carmen sure kept a lot of secrets so we need to keep our options open here." Jack paused chewing absently at the inside of his cheek and staring at the framed painting of a ship riding on a swelled wave in a storm out at sea. "The car is a biggie. Someone didn't want us to find that car."

"I agree. Or someone knew that car was extremely important to Carmen. She has other cars, right? I think I remember Armand saying something about her cars."

Jack sat up again. "You're right. I say we take a look. It may lead to nothing, but at least we'll have more information on Carmen's habits. Did she buy her cars at the same place? Did she have only one mechanic touch her cars? Quite frankly her killer could be anyone and her car is key here. Maybe Omaha is her mechanic and they had an affair and when it went bad he killed her off and smoked her car...."

"I don't know, Jack. That sounds way too clean and you know these things are never that clean...." Jill began.

"Uh, come on! I was really hoping we could make this clean as a baby's bottom...."

Jill giggled. "I think you've had one too many glasses of wine." She took a sip of her own wine as their desserts arrived.

"You know, I think you have the absolute worst taste in the world," Jack said wrinkling his nose at her dessert.

Jill looked down at her grape nut custard pudding. "Not a custard man?" she asked a smirk on her face.

"Second to the Boston Crème Pie, snot in a cake."

Jill laughed out loud, took a bite of her custard, "Mmmmmm.....got to love this snot! Really you have to try it!" She took a spoonful of her custard and pushed it at his face.

Jack pulled back his face a mixture of horror and revulsion. "Oh, God, Simko! That's so disgusting!!"

Jill laughed and the tinny sound bounced off the walls around them. "You are such a wimp!"

"Yes, but a wimp with chocolate cake." Jack took a bite. "Yum."

Jill was silent a moment savoring the smooth taste of the grape nut custard. An image of Carmen came to her mind wearing a white dress and smiling while eating a big bowl of a pink-colored ice cream. She took a bite, swallowed slowly then smiled big and wide. Her blue-green eyes blazed. "I love this ice cream. It is my absolute favorite dessert! And pink just like my Thunderbird!" She giggled and put her hand to her mouth then her eyes went wide and she put one finger against her lips. "Shhhhh......noone has to know. Noone ever knows," she whispered.

Jill jumped and put the spoon down into her bowl so suddenly it jumped back out of the bowl, took a turn for the table, bounced again, and headed directly to the floor. Jack responded instantly after noticing Jill's face had gone completely white. "Are you ok, Jill?" He pulled his napkin off his lap and leaped to his feet.

Jill shook her head and put her hand to her forehead. "Oh, I must be tired. For some reason I got startled for a moment."

"Do you need water?" Jack asked signaling the waitress.

"Thank you. Maybe too much wine." Jill blinked trying to get the image of Carmen out of her mind. The water and another spoon came instantly. Jill took long sips of water and pushed her dessert away.

"I told you grape nut custard wasn't good for you," Jack suggested.

Jill smiled. He could always take the tension off. "No. This water is doing the trick." She took another long sip. "I don't think anyone really knew Carmen," Jill said when she put the glass down.

"Why do you say that?" Jack asked.

"I just have a feeling she didn't really want anyone to know her. I think she let people think things about her. I think she gave them what they wanted to hear. I mean think about it, she is a former New York socialite married to a New York businessman and she collected fast cars on the side. She also delved in witchcraft. She also slept around on her husband. None of that really adds up."

"Maybe that is her persona. The mesh of it all. Think about yourself. Could anyone really put you in a box? You are an FBI agent but does that make you rigid and impassionate? No, I don't think so, but the rest of the world may think so. There are so many parts of our own personas. We can't think that Carmen was just one type of person just because we are placing her into a stereotype." Jack finished his chocolate cake and sat back in his chair. "Oh, man, I wish I smoked. That cake was really that fucking good."

Jill half-smiled. The image of Carmen was still so vivid. There was just something very macabre about envisioning this dead-woman in the flesh. She had heard about this happening to investigators in the past but had always considered it a symptom of something far greater, a psychological condition brought on by the stress of the case.

Jack leaned forward. Jill seemed a million miles away. "Hey, are you sure you're ok?" he said gently.

Jill shook her head quickly. "Yes, I'm fine. Just tired, I think." She sat up and took another sip of water. "I'd really like to see Carmen's other cars."

Jack grinned. "Now we're talking, girl."

CHAPTER ELEVEN

The next morning Jack and Jill decided to pay Armand de Santo an impromptu visit. The previous night Jill had gone directly to bed complaining of a headache and Jack spent a little more time on Carmen's computer only succeeding at digging up internet history to a variety of Wiccan websites. He retired early promising himself he'd have IT take a closer look at her computer while he accompanied Jill in the field. The rest and a good, hot shower had refreshed Jill and she looked focused and serious when Jack met up with her in the morning for breakfast. She ate a bagel and fruit and suggested that they meet up with Armand first thing before proceeding to visit his brother, Nero De Santo. Before they left the hotel restaurant, Jack made a call to Jim who agreed to schedule IT for arrival later that day. Jack left a note with the front desk to expect Jim's arrival.

"I see you're feeling better," Jack commented on their way to Armand's house.

Jill smiled. "Thinking about the look on Armand's face when we arrive on the scene on the day of his wife's wake does that to me."

"You sadistic bitch," Jack teased relieved that Jill's condition had greatly improved.

They pulled up to the house and parked just in front of the front door. Jill approached the door first her back straight and her jaw set. She was clearly ready for a fight, an argument, or similar altercation. Jack had seen her in action and she could be downright mean if she wanted to be. He stood one foot behind her to allow her to proceed as she saw most fit.

The door opened and Beatrice faced them her eyes growing wide when she recognized who was there. "I'm not so sure Mr. De Santo will be...." she started.

Jill smiled and took one step forward closer to the doorway. "We are so sorry to bother you and to bother Mr. De Santo. We'll just be a moment of his time."

Beatrice looked at her, then looked back at Jack and gave a little wave. "Yes, please, come in. I will check with Mr. De Santo," She said ringing her hands nervously as she made room so that they may enter the foyer. As soon as they were inside and the door closed, she scurried away and did not lead them directly to the library as she had done during their last visit.

Jack looked around him at the marble floors and cathedral ceiling above them. "Some place, huh?"

"Do you think she was right here when she waved goodbye to Beatrice for the last time?" Jill asked. She stood so that her hand was on the doorknob and her torso twisted so that she could see Jack.

"Maybe. If she parked out front," Jack said simply.

Jill looked thoughtful. "I guess it doesn't really matter. I'm just trying to figure her out, you know?"

"Who? Carmen?"

"Yes. I think it's important we know more about her. I just have a feeling that there is way more to this story than meets the eye."

"Yeah. That would be who cut her fucking head off," Jack said grinning.

Jill grinned, then abruptly removed her hand from the doorknob, stood straight, and hardened her jaw as Beatrice approached them still ringing her hands. Jack called it her "cop stop." She could stop being your average, every day Mom, and start being a no-nonsense cop in a blink of an eye. "Mr. De Santo is making arrangements for Mrs. De Santo's wake this evening. He cannot help. I am sorry." She said this so quickly and so quietly both agents could barely make out what she had said.

"Beatrice, is this the entrance where you saw Carmen for the last time?" Jill asked her voice softening, but her face still just as stern.

Beatrice paused for a moment tears coming to her eyes. "Yes, ma'am."

"Did she park out front?" Jack followed up.

"That night she did. Mostly she would park in the garage or she would have someone bring her car around." The tears in Beatrice's eyes vanished as she tried to compose herself.

"Can we see her garage?" Jill asked. "I'm interested in the other cars Carmen drove."

Beatrice frowned. "I don't think, Mr...."

"Tell Mr. De Santo that we found Carmen's Mustang," Jill interrupted. Her eyes flashed. Knowledge was power.

Tears returned to Beatrice's eyes. "You found it?"

"Yes. Tell him now. I want to see her other cars." Her voice was unwavering, crisp and demanding.

Beatrice rushed off.

"She was right here," Jill said softly to Jack. She put her hands in her pockets and looked at the door. "Now if we could only track her steps from this point forward we'd find her killer."

Jack grinned. "You have that look about you. A dog on the scent."

Jill grinned back. "I'm pretty sure I've smelled something. Only a matter of time now."

In moments Beatrice rushed back. "Can I get you anything....anything at all? Mr. De Santo will be here momentarily. Would you like to wait for him in the library?"

Jill smiled. "Oh no, this is fine," she said pleasantly.

Beatrice turned to go. Jill turned to Jack and smiled. "And that, my friend, is how it's done."

"Oh, you're real full of yourself, huh?" Jack teased back.

"You bet!"

At that Armand De Santo entered the foyer dressed in a sharp black suit his hair slicked back from his forehead a slight frown on his perfectly chiseled features. And Carmen cheated on this man, Jill thought. Armand De Santo even in his grief was one of the most striking men she had ever had the pleasure of meeting. It seemed absolutely inconceivable that any woman would have any reason to cheat on a man of this caliber. Armand looked at both of them with tired eyes and let out a slow breath.

"Beatrice tells me you found Carmen's Mustang," he said simply his voice devoid of emotion.

"So, guess what I bought today?" Her eyes were sparkling pools of green and yellow. She had met him at the door in the foyer upon his arrival from yet another business trip.

"What?" Armand asked amused by her, the consummate child.

She giggled and led him into a kind of dance. "A Mustang! I bought the absolute prettiest Mustang you'll ever lay your eyes on!!" She giggled uncontrollably her eyes continuing to flash in her excitement.

Armand blinked away the memory. He focused on the two agents one of whom, Special Agent Pellingworth, was explaining the location of the vehicle. Dover, NH. "You found her Mustang in Dover?"

"Yes. Do you know if Carmen ever visited Dover?"

Armand looked down to the floor, the room beginning to spin around him. He took another deep breath, stood up straight and pushed the image of Carmen out of his mind. "Not that I'm aware," he stated simply.

"Can you explain how Carmen's car may have gotten to Dover?" Jack followed up.

Armand took another deep breath gazing back down at the floor. "No. I have no idea." His voice was steady and devoid of emotion, yet his words resonated throughout the large foyer. They hung in the air like missiles, but he offered them nothing more.

Jack glanced at Jill. He could see her studying him. Armand blinked, shook his head slightly as if to clear it. After a moment, he gave the agents both a slight, sad smile. "Now. Did you say you wanted to see Carmen's collection?"

The garage was empty. Armand watched Carmen run around the space scaling the perimeter. She squeezed her hands together like a delighted child on Christmas Day and ran up to him.

"Is this all mine?" she asked smiling up at him her eyes sparkling little bits of fire in the emerald.

"Yes, all of it. All of it is yours." He said steadily.

She let out a shriek of delight and began running the perimeter again. She wore a white sundress that trailed after her as she ran. Suddenly she ran to the center of the space and began twirling. She lifted her hands up to the ceiling and kept twirling, twirling, twirling....

"You'll be sick, my love. Moving around like that."

She stopped abruptly, clasped her hands while bending forward slightly and laughed like a woman gone wild.

The memory faded as Armand led the two agents down the hall to a terrace and out to the small garage where Carmen kept her most prized collection. The garage was a mini-replica of the main house with a front entrance door to allow guests to enter and a side sliding door to allow for in-and-out access of the vehicles. Above the guest door the words, "Carmen's Collection" were molded out of cast-iron in ornate script. As Jill entered she felt a chill tickle up her spine despite the intense August heat.

What they walked into took the agents' breath away. Lined up neatly were housed three modern sports cars of various magnitude, a Jeep Grand Cherokee, and a BMW sedan. One space was missing near the front. At the very back of the garage was a full-service station for the vehicles. Jill couldn't help but wonder if Carmen did her own repairs or hired out, and who in the world was lucky enough to get that job. No wonder the girl was bored. She didn't even have the excitement of a good old-fashioned "break down" to worry about with a service station like this.

Jill took a quick glance at the cars. Where would they begin? Her eyes stopped on a pink Thunderbird convertible circa 2005. "Oh my God," she breathed. Her eyes instantly misted over with tears and she could feel a tingle zip through the tips of her fingers and straight up her arms. Her legs felt weak and her face instantly flushed. Despite beginning to feel dizzy she made a beeline to the car feeling as if she were being pulled to it. As she walked she put her hand up in anticipation of touching it, but when at last she reached it she could not get herself to put even one finger on it. She was so overcome with emotion she was worried she'd break down crying right then and there in the middle of an investigation.

"That's quite something, huh?" Armand called over to her.

His voice shocked her out of her spell and she shook her head, took a deep breath, and turned around. "Yes. It's beautiful," she managed.

"They don't make them in that color, but Carmen just had to have pink. And not just any pink. She had to have a pastel pink so we had it painted for her. She was so happy driving that girl around." For a moment, Armand stared at the car and at Jill standing next to it. Then after a pause, "Is there anything in particular you are looking for?"

Jill glanced back at the car quickly then rushed over to meet up with Armand and Jack again. She felt as if the car were watching waiting for her answer to each and every question. What was going on here? She had never been a woman of intuition. She had always relied on fact and fact alone to solve her cases. Now she was envisioning pink Thunderbirds and discovering them in her victim's possession. Jill shook her dizzy head. It must be the heat. Yes, the heat and the wine last night. And the small town. And that she missed her family. Yes that had to be it.

"We just want to take a quick look around. There's something you should know about Carmen's Mustang," Jack said quickly.

Armand frowned slightly and glanced at Jill. "What is it?" He put his finger to his temple.

"Arson was involved."

"What?!" Armand's eyes were wide and he instantly became pale. "Why....why would someone *do* such a thing." His mouth curled around the words as if they also disgusted him.

"That's what we're trying to figure out. We assume that Carmen's cars meant a lot to her so we thought we would look at her vehicles to try to gain some information on why someone may have wanted to set Carmen's car on fire," Jack stated simply taking the lead on this one.

Armand pressed his finger to his temple. "By all means. Take your time. I can't believe someone would do this to one of Carmen's cars. Who does such a thing?" He paused a moment then said, "I suppose I should blame myself for this. Being gone all the time. Maybe if I were around more often whoever this bastard is wouldn't have gone to such great lengths," he muttered.

Jill glanced quickly at the pink Thunderbird, then back at Armand. "Do you think this is personal? Something involving you or your business?" Jill asked.

Armand shook his head. "I don't know. I don't know what I think. I just want her back, you know. I just want her back so she can drive all her cars again, and so we can forget any of this ever happened." His face narrowed in pain and his eyes glazed over. "I should have been home with her more often."

Jill stepped forward and put her hand on Armand's shoulder. "It's ok. There's nothing you could have done to stop this. Things just happen sometime. We just need to focus and try to find out who took your wife from you, ok?" She said softly.

Armand nodded. "Yes. You are right. And I have a wake to plan. I have a wake to plan for a thirty year-old woman in the prime of her life. A woman who loved her cars and one of them is all burned up now. And I was gone and I couldn't help her." His eyes filled with tears. He pressed his fingers to his temples. "Please, take your time here. I will be back at the house if you need anything further. Keys for all the cars are on the back panel." With that he slipped out the door leaving Jack and Jill to their own devices.

"What do you think?" Jack asked looking over the inventory.

Jill smiled. "I think this place is pretty sweet," she teased. She hoped that by using humor Jack wouldn't notice her recent lapse into reverie.

Jack rubbed his hands together. "Man, I wish we could try these babies out," he cooed.

"Do you think Armand is ok?" Jill asked suddenly serious. "He looks beside himself with grief."

"Either it's just sinking in for the guy or he's good. Very good. I still think he's the best suspect we have right now. You're not getting soft on him now are you?" Jack teased.

Jill smiled. "No. No. I know he's the best we have right now, but he also seems very genuine."

"I agree." Jack walked over to a Porsche 550 Spyder. "Man, would I love to drive this around! This is so sweet!"

"It looks like a toy," Jill commented. "A tin can."

Jack stood back and gasped. "You can't be saying that. A tin can," He mocked. "You've got to be kidding me. James Dean died in one of these."

"Exactly. Tin can," Jill teased walking to the back wall to inspect the keys Armand had referred to.

"Some fast, sweet-as-pie tin can!" Jack commented. "Carmen knew her stuff. What do you bet this is genuine?"

Jill looked back at him. "You mean they make tin-can replicas?" she joked.

Jack laughed out loud, then looked at the Spyder and whistled. "Yes, Carmen knew her stuff all right."

"Hey, Jack," Jill called. "Come back here. You'll like this."

"You mean even more than that sweet Ferrari 612 Scaglietti. Man, Carmen had good taste in cars!" He walked backward never taking his eye off the Ferrari.

"Jack. Come to earth, please. I think this may be important," Jill said her voice raising an octave. "And your Scaglietti is involved. Damn, that sounds like a pasta, doesn't it?"

Jack glared at her. "You didn't just say that."

Jill giggled. "I'm serious. This is totally, fucking serious," she said between giggles.

Jack approached her. "What is it?"

Jill smiled. "Here by her keys. Each key that's hung here has a placard below it with the car's name on it with the make, model and date below in a smaller scroll."

Jack looked closer. "Wow. You've got to be kidding me. Carmen named all of them like they were her children."

"The missing key here..." Jill pointed to an empty spot. "Candy Apple, Ford Mustang, 2005," she read. "But even better over here....." She pulled her finger back and pointed to one placard.

"Omaha, Ford Thunderbird, 2004," Jack read. "The pink T-bird is Omaha?" he asked incredulously.

"I say we search the Thunderbird. Why do I have the feeling this Omaha in her emails has a connection to that car?" Jill grabbed the key from the key ring and walked directly to the T-bird. This time no images, or sense of foreboding crowded Jill's mind. She stopped as she approach the car then bent forward and peered into the window. The inside of the car was pristine, black leather. There was something on the passenger's seat she couldn't quite make out. "There's something on the passenger seat," Jill breathed. She used the automatic unlock on the key to open the doors and reached forward to open the passenger-side door. By this time, Jack had circled to the driver's side and began opening the door.

A black, leather handbag sat neatly on the passenger seat as if awaiting its owner on a drive out to the country. Jill reached into her pocket for latex gloves, pulled them on, then picked up the handbag. She unsnapped the clutch and peered inside. Inside was lipstick, a mirror, a small wallet with a few credit cards, and a lighter. No random papers. No litter. No license. Just the very basics. "Nothing unusual here."

"You know I just thought of something," Jack stated. "We still haven't located her cell phone." He slid into the front seat of the T-bird and rubbed his hand lovingly on the steering wheel.

Jill put the handbag back on the passenger seat. "Let's ask Armand about it. I'm thinking that it was in her Mustang. Maybe Armand can give us her service provider and phone number so we can pull her records."

"Remember, this man is still a prime suspect and we still need to verify his alibi," Jack said gently.

"Ok, IT is supposed to be working to locate the phone and they'll run a record for us when they find it. I'll make some calls today to verify Armand's whereabouts the night of her death. I'm assuming at that time of night he was sleeping in his apartment but we can at least try."

Jack reluctantly got out of the T-bird and closed the door. He let out a low whistle appraising the vehicle. "Then again some businesses work unusual hours." When Jill looked at him skeptically he added. "And some men have extracurricular activities."

"You think Armand was cheating on Carmen?"

"He better hope so or otherwise he may have absolutely no alibi."

Jill looked down at the T-bird again while Jack began looking over the other vehicles. Why in the world would she name this car Omaha? A dull headache was returning to her temples. "So, are we done here"?

Jack looked up and pouted. "Yeah. We're done."

"You're such a child," Jill teased.

Just then Jack's cell phone chimed. Jill followed Jack out of the garage as he answered, "Pellingworth." He nodded and looked over at Jill. "Yup. Yup. Great." A pause. "Any idea if there was a cell phone or handbag in the vehicle?" Pause. "Yup. Yup. Ok, cool. Thank you." Jack closed his phone and the two agents started up the path back to the house and thus to their car. "The report on the Mustang should be at the hotel when we get back."

"Anything? Cell phone? Anything?"

"Nothing."

"So, the car was cleaned out of everything but the registration?"

"Seems that way." Jack shrugged hopping into the driver's seat.

"Do you think Carmen could have torched the car herself before she died?" Jill asked skeptically.

"No. Doesn't sound likely. I think Carmen left to go meet someone and something went terribly wrong."

Jill nodded. "She only told Beatrice she was going out. Not where she was going exactly. I would think if she were meeting Armand or even a friend she would have mentioned where she was going."

Jack shook his head. At the gate their car met up with a growing crowd of paparazzi. The crowd parted just enough for them to pass through to head back to the hotel. "One would think, but Carmen seems to be full of secrets. Lots of secrets. Maybe she didn't tell anyone anything about her life. If that's the case she certainly wouldn't have told Beatrice."

"You're right." Jill shook her head. "Ok. This case is already giving me a headache."

"Let's just hope Jim has more for us when we get back to the hotel."

"One can only hope."

CHAPTER TWELVE

They had hit a wall. Jim had nothing more to tell them than that Carmen had visited a number of Wiccan sites to order some supplies, but did not seem to have any communications in Wiccan chat rooms or sites. Her Facebook account did not reflect any of her pagan interests and she did not use Twitter. Her communications were primarily in email to the alias, "Omaha". The computer was on its way to IT for deeper analysis. The report on the vehicle was as expected. The fire had damaged most of the car beyond recognition. It was speculated that the car was driven into something repeatedly to damage the front fender, but for what reason no one knew. Carmen's belongings must have been discarded from the car prior to its gas bath in Dover. Armand De Santo's alibi cleared. He had worked that evening until 8:00pm then headed to his apartment. The apartment's alarm system was activated at 8:45pm and shut off at 6:00am presumably for when Armand left to return to work. Jill and Jack decided to run all of Armand's records including bank, phones and credit cards to determine whether or not he hired someone out to murder Carmen while he enjoyed a safe evening in the city. Now they waited. They both decided to attend the wake and funeral to determine whether or not there were any other leads they needed to follow up on. Jill desperately wanted to interview Nero De Santo, but they both decided that after the wake and funeral they would get a better response from him. And they would need to speak with Senator Ricci, as much as Jim squirmed at the thought.

The evening arrived quickly. The wake was being held from 6:00pm until 8:00pm and given the horrendous condition of Carmen's body there was a closed casket planned. Jill met Jack in the lobby of their hotel dressed in a somber black pantsuit.

"Well, you look the role," Jack said dryly. He looked off in the distance a slight grimace on his face.

"Jack, are you doing to be a total baby about this?" Jill asked hand on her hip.

"You know how much I hate wakes and funerals," Jack whined. He looked at her his eyes pleading as if he thought she would give the go-ahead to spend his evening in front of the television in his room.

"You think they give me the warm fuzzies? Come on! It's just part of our job. And tonight we need to do our job."

Jack rolled his eyes and stomped his foot like a child. Then he looked at her and smiled. "Gotcha," he exclaimed triumphantly. "Ok, I get it. Time to get to work."

Jill grinned as they headed out into the balmy evening. "Do you think this is going to be a circus?" she asked.

Jack looked up at the sky. The stars were large, swelling bulbs above. Every so often one of them winked at him if Carmen herself was in on a cosmic joke. A couple of stray clouds gracefully opened up to reveal a full and pregnant moon. Jake shuddered despite the warmth in the air. He plunged his hands into his pockets certain someone somewhere would try to grasp his hands. It was an odd thought, but one none the less. The night was creeping him out. Big time. "Absolutely. Tomorrow will be worse."

"Only the vampires will be out tonight," Jill mused glancing up at the moon.

"Fucking bloodsuckers," Jack said lightly trying to joke. He looked up at the moon again. Then he let out a little chuckle thinking about his apt description of the paparazzi. "Did you ever think we would be on a case where the paparazzi were this involved?"

Jill got into the passenger seat of their sedan. "No. Absolutely not. In fact, I've tried to avoid this like the plague."

They drove out in silence the moon in all its glory enough of a presence to keep the conversation at bay. Jill was mystified by this large shining mass in the air. There was a certain draw to it that she couldn't quite explain, almost a magnetic impulse that compelled her to gaze at its infinite beauty.

As they rounded the corner to Fleming's Funeral Home, Jill began to feel the first touch of sadness as the severity of the situation set in. She had a feeling they were about to experience something for which they weren't prepared. Melancholy had reached its arms out the front door of Flemings and into their car slipping ice-cold fingers around her throat. She shivered. She glanced over at Jack's somber face. He refused to look at her his jaw tightly clenched. She put her hand on his knee. "This is going to suck," she whispered. He nodded.

They had to park nearly a block away from the Funeral Home. Cars littered the street and parking was impossible any closer. It appeared the paparazzi were keeping their distance. Massachusetts State Police were manning the front door and were providing a strong deterrent against fearless reporters. As Jill and Jack approached the state police they flashed their badges. A stoic man nodded once and opened the door for them.

Flemings was like every other funeral home they had visited. It had the appearance of all the comforts of home without providing true comfort at all. For starters the reception area was too quiet. A tall man, the undertaker, dressed up in a stark, black suit pallid in complexion stood near a reception table made of marble. He nodded to them with a sympathetic expression that must take years to perfect, then handed them a small paper memento made of gloss stock with a Christian prayer on the back and Carmen's picture and name on the front. In the picture, Carmen looked like a young girl smiling and vibrant before them her green eyes sparkling. It only made the tragedy and the evening all the more macabre. The undertaker nodded to them again and gestured for them to proceed to the viewing room. Jack and Jill paused for a moment then entered the room. The room was packed with people dressed in somber gray and black attire. Some sat on steel chairs. Some sat on comfy, plush sofas. Most stood with their heads down shaking them in disbelief. At the front of the room an amazing coffin made of the finest mahogany and meticulous etching was displayed on a frame similar to an altar. A cross hung on the wall just behind the coffin and a stool stood before it for those who wished to pray for Carmen's soul. A woman with dark brown hair knelt before the coffin her hands clenched so tightly in prayer that they were white, her eyelids closed just as tightly. She wore a plain, gray two-piece dress suit that was worn from age and use. Jill recognized her as Mrs. Emery. To the left of the coffin stood an imposing bouquet of flowers and a large picture of Carmen De Santo's face smiling so widely and her eyes dazzling so intensely it was as if she had shared a private joke with the photographer. The picture alone made her seem as if she were still alive and in the flesh before everyone. Jill shuttered. The smell of the flowers became sickening and sweet as Jill looked to the right of the coffin. Armand De Santo stood stiff and uncomfortable in a crisp, black Armani suit. His eyes were glazed over in grief and he looked down more than he looked up. At that particular moment he glanced up and his eyes fell upon Jack and Jill. He stared at them blankly for a moment, then looked down again. Jill looked over at Jack, who kept his eyes on the remaining members of the wake party. Following Armand was Shelly O'Dea with another older gentleman and further down the line stood Senator Ricci himself. Jack's eyes sparked as he looked at the man he despised. Senator Ricci's face was a perfect mask of sadness. He looked down and periodically put his hand to his forehead.

"He's faking," Jack whispered softly.

Jill looked over at Senator Ricci. He glanced at them briefly his eyes paramount in sadness tears beginning to well around the corners, his corneas swimming. "No, he's pretty moved," she whispered back.

Jack and Jill found their way to the back of the room without paying their respects. Jill watched Mrs. Emery place her hand on Carmen De Santo's coffin her eyes welling with tears. She looked up at Armand De Santo and at that moment she looked incredibly helpless and alone. Armand walked over to her silently and embraced her. He whispered something in her ear, then motioned her to a chair that another gentleman had cleared for her. She nodded numbly and continued to stare at the coffin. Her eyes were wide and dull in grief.

Jill felt tears coming to her eyes overcome by the feeling of complete and utter loss that enveloped the room. Countering that loss she felt a presence that was similar to the draw of the moon. Jill looked at Carmen's picture displayed in all its glory and she couldn't help but feel that Carmen's presence was here. There was a slip in the gravitational pattern surrounding Armand that could only be explained by the presence of his wife. Jill glanced at Armand who looked around stunned and dull in his anguish. She looked at Mrs. Emery who stared at the picture of Carmen and the coffin with shock. Her eyes were wide as saucers and pooling with tears. Poor thing. To have a child that is out there somewhere, missing, and now to attend a funeral. Jill could only imagine what she feared the most. Could this be her son in a week, a month, a year? Jill glanced at Jack who was staring intently at the entranceway to the room.

In walked a gentleman that Jill would never forget. He was tall. He was dressed in jeans and a black shirt open save for a few buttons at the bottom. His hair was a chocolate brown and slightly long pulled back into a ponytail. He had a patrician nose and intense, brown eyes. He rippled into the room as if his body were made of rivers slipping past the picture of Carmen and the coffin to approach Armand. Armand looked up at him briefly and nodded. The man nodded back and took a place next to him in the reception line. Shelly moved over to let him in her face pinching in distaste. The man smiled at her and moved in to whisper something in her ear. Shelly smiled despite herself and put her hand on his shoulder in response.

Jill looked at the man in horror her eyes opening wide her breath caught in her throat. She turned to Jack and pulled at his hand. "I know this man," she managed although her voice sounded too loud in her ears.

Jack leaned in close. "How?"

"I know him. I met him on the street when I was looking for Marisca's house." She sucked in air, then breathed out slowly. She watched as the man scanned the crowd, then looked over at the coffin. His eyes glazed over black and his jaw clenched when he looked up at the cross. Jill noticed he ripped the remembrance card they had been given upon arrival.

"What did he say?" Jack asked.

"Nothing really. I asked him if he knew Marisca's street and he avoided the question. He's very strange." Her whispers sounded like shouting to her ears and she half expected the strange man to look up and recognize her.

"He must be someone we need to talk to. He's right next to Armand," Jack breathed into her ear.

Jill looked at the man again. He was leaning into Armand whispering something in his ear, then he turned and looked directly at Jill and Jack. Jill could feel the wind knocked out of her chest and the room swam around her for a moment. She looked down at her lap to concentrate.

"I bet that's Nero," Jack breathed.

The room swam again. Jill breathed in and out deeply and grabbed the side of her chair. "Nero?" Her eyes were wild when she looked at Jack.

"Are you ok?" Jack asked instantly concerned. "Are you feeling ok?" He grabbed her arm. "You look as white as a ghost."

Jill sucked in air. "Yes. I'm fine." She looked up at Nero again. He was staring at the coffin a look of disgust on his face. He whispered something to Armand again.

"So, you're saying I already met Nero De Santo?" She breathed. The air felt heavy and the scent of flowers made her want to vomit.

Jack leaned over and placed his hand on the shoulder of the man next to him. He whispered something to him. Then he turned back to Jill whose eyes were still glued to Armand and this man next to him. "Confirmed. Nero De Santo," he said.

The room swam again. Jill looked down at her feet hoping her breath would recover. The smell of lilies in the room made her stomach turn and she broke out into a sweat. She glanced quickly at Nero and his brother Armand. Armand leaned over to his brother and whispered something in his ear. Sandra glanced over at them a disapproving glare in her eyes.

Jill sucked in air hoping the spinning would stop. Why was Nero bringing on this response? Yet the room kept moving and moving until Jill couldn't take it anymore. "Jack, I need some fresh air."

Jack nodded. Jill got up and moved past the group feeling as if she were a million miles away. All numb. She pressed against the wall at times and didn't even feel it. The room tilted again as she headed out. She snuck one last look at Nero De Santo who at that exact moment met her gaze and winked at her. It was so fast Jill wasn't sure she even saw what she saw. She glanced at Carmen's picture all smiling and beautiful and she instantly needed the moon like water in a desert. Jill smiled weakly at the undertaker, then she rushed out of the funeral home into the thick, hot night. At the top of the stairs Jill gasped and looked up at the sky. Just trees. No moon. She needed the moon. Jill gasped for air as the state police officer stationed just outside the door looked at her with concern. She rushed past him, past all the cars parked and into the field called a "green" at the center of town. There she sat on the grass and looked up into the sky. The moon moved from behind the clouds and shined down on her with all its glory. Jill smiled. She kept her eyes glued to the moon certain her fate was this very moment in time. She watched the clouds move by and by until she felt a hand on her shoulder.

"Hey." It was Jack. Jill looked up at him the reverie broken. "It's time to go."

Jill stood up. "Did Nero leave?" she said calmly.

"No. He's still with Armand. What happened to you?"

Jill remained seated her eyes wide. "I don't know. I honestly don't know." She glanced at the moon. "I think I'm totally fucking stressed out about this case."

"Get your rest." Jack pulled at her arm. Jill stood up and followed him blindly to the car. "Funeral's tomorrow."

CHAPTER THIRTEEN

The next morning Jill woke up with a pounding headache. She felt as if the previous night had been a dream bordering on a nightmare. She needed to prepare herself for seeing Nero again at the funeral. He would most definitely be there and she would need to keep her composure if she wanted to do her job properly. Jill had no idea why she had such a strong reaction to this man. It wasn't just attraction, although he was wildly handsome. It wasn't fear. It was more like she was drawn to him and was at the same time horrified that she was drawn to him. It had to be because she was functioning on too little sleep. There was no other logical explanation.

She met Jack downstairs in the restaurant for breakfast. Jack looked at her with concern. "How are you feeling this morning?" he asked.

"Like shit," she answered nodding at the waiter for coffee. "I have to admit, Jack. I'm really weirded out by this case."

"It's a weird case," Jack said biting into a piece of toast.

"But we've handled weird cases before, Jack and I've been just fine." She took a sip of her steaming coffee and winced when she burnt the tip of her tongue. "I don't know why this one if freaking me out so much."

"Look, we've got a girl who got herself killed and just for starters she was a witch. That's totally freaky. There's freaky like Renault who is psychotic who strangely enough is somehow easier for people like us to understand. And then there's freaky like ordinary people getting into some pretty strange shit. That's almost scarier because those people are considered normal and well-adjusted." He put his hand on her arm. "I wouldn't worry about it too much. I think you're doing just fine."

Jill gave him a weak smile. "I hope so. Maybe the funeral will be better."

The funeral was a media circus. It was all Jack and Jill could do to fight their way through the crowds of paparazzi and those who wanted a glimpse of Senator Ricci in his moment of despair. Badges flashing, Jack and Jill were finally escorted through the front door of St. Mary's Church. Jill slumped against the wall of the intricate foyer and breathed in deeply. She still wasn't feeling well and the breakfast from that morning sat like a lump in her stomach. She and Jack found a seat in the back set of pews and sat quietly awaiting the funeral to begin.

The funeral procession was like a wedding procession except that everything was black and somber. Pallbearers walked he casket containing Carmen de Santo down the aisle with Armand De Santo leading the procession, Sandra O'Dea at his side. Armand's head hung low and his eyes were puffy with despair. Jill scanned the funeral procession and noticed that Nero De Santo was nowhere in sight. The funeral mass began, and yet still no Nero. Jill kept finding herself looking for him barely able to keep her focus on the actual mass. She looked over at Jack at one point and saw that he was sternly looking at the funeral party his eyes piercing as he analyzed everyone's movements.

Jill moved close to Jack and whispered in his ear, "No Nero."

Jack nodded. He had noticed, too. As the funeral ended and Armand sat down overcome in his grief, Jack and Jill stayed seated. Jill noticed Senator Ricci walked over to Armand to console him. Sandra O'Dea kept her distance and kept staring at where the casket had stood throughout the funeral mass. Slowly Armand stood up and the group proceeded out the front doors. Jill continued to scan the crowd intently looking for Nero. He must be here. She must have missed him. The party moved out the front doors into the balmy late-morning and the other attendees started to file out. Jill saw Marisca and her family. Marisca dabbed her swollen eyes and whispered something to her husband, who quickly glanced at Jack and Jill. At nearly the end of the line Jill noticed Mr. and Mrs. Emery. Mrs. Emery clutched her black purse to her chest with wide-open eyes – deer caught in headlights – following behind her husband. Mr. Emery glanced over at Jack and Jill briefly his eyes unfocused. Jill felt a cold chill run up and down her spine. The room spun for a moment and she had to close her eyes tightly to right herself.

"Ready?" Jack whispered to her.

Jill opened her eyes to see a nearly empty church. She nodded. "Why wasn't Nero here?"

Jack shook his head. "Don't know. Let's get to the cemetery."

Jack and Jill pushed through the ever-growing paparazzi to get to their car. They joined the funeral procession to the cemetery, which was only a few minutes up the street. Jack and Jill parked their car behind the procession and climbed out.

No matter what the circumstances and even on a day as warm and sunny as this one, cemeteries always gave Jill "the creeps". The overwhelming sense of loss everywhere and the distinct scent of roses contributed to this reaction. The funeral party including Armand De Santo, Sandra O'Dea, and Senator Ricci stood in front of the casket and newly unearthed ground. Each held flowers in hand. Armand hung his head low his body shaking time and time again. Senator Ricci continued to stare at the casket his eyes wide and vacant in his loss. The priest began the first of the series of prayers blessing Carmen De Santo in her quest for eternal life in Heaven.

Jill caught a hint of movement to her left. The shape in black seemed to glide over to the mourners. She blinked off the sun in her eyes to see Nero De Santo making his way up to the group huddled around the casket and open earth. Jill swore she could hear him humming to himself. Was this for real? As he got closer the humming got louder. The priest paused. Armand looked up. Sandra's eyes narrowed. The Senator looked blindly in Nero's direction. Nero continued to walk past the group still humming his eyes flashing. He approached the priest and stood at his side.

He stood tall. "She would not have wished this!" His voice was strong, commanding, yet soft and giving. There was a lilt that Jill did not recognize. As he spoke a slight breeze began to stir the air. It was much cooler than any current weather conditions. Jill shivered. "She would have wished for more than this!" Nero continued.

Nero held up his hand, which contained some kind of object, and muttered something as he turned to the casket. He placed the item on top of the casket, then bent low to kiss the top of it. His kiss lingered on the fine mahogany, then he knelt and bent low. The priest looked over questioningly to Armand who nodded as if to tell the priest to hold off for a moment. Nero stood up and made a sweeping motion over the casket. He reached into his pocket and poured a substance into the open earth. He looked up to the sky spreading his arms wide. He muttered something unintelligible.

Jill smiled. A warmth filled her body as she watched him. She couldn't help but feel a sense of hope and fulfillment as she watched him sway and continue to speak softly to himself. The sun felt refreshing on her skin and made her feel alive. The open earth felt more inviting. She could not look away from Nero. She was captivated in the moment.

Nero looked at the casket again and smiled for a moment. He placed his hand on the casket and began to chant softly. He bowed low, then stood to join the rest of his family his head hung low. The priest looked over at Armand who nodded for him to continue.

Nero looked up. "No," he said simply and softly. He stepped forward and put one hand on the priest's shoulder. "She would not have wanted this."

The priest nodded, then looked over at Armand. Armand looked down in his grief then stepped forward to put his flowers on Carmen's casket. His face contorted as he looked down at the casket realization donning that this was his last moment with his wife. The family quietly followed behind him each placing flowers on Carmen's casket. Each took another moment to quietly say goodbye to a wife, a daughter, a friend.

Jill couldn't help but stare at Nero who was walking back the way he had come. He walked past all the vehicles and continued on his way down the street. Jill continued to feel a great sense of hope and relief. She looked up at Jack who was staring at Senator Ricci his eyes sharp, his jaw clenched. Jill looked up at the sky, then to where she had last seen Nero De Santo.

She leaned toward Jack. "We need to speak to Nero."

"I agree. Something's up with Nero," Jack whispered back. "He knows she's not Christian."

Jill glanced in the direction Nero had vanished down the street. "I need to talk to him now."

Jack shook his head. "Probably not a good idea. We could talk to him tomorrow or maybe even later today."

"No. Now's the best time." Her voice was soft. "I'll be back soon." Before Jack could respond Jill found herself tracing Nero's steps. The sense of freedom, release, and renewal became all the more prevalent.

"Jill!! Jill!!" Jack hissed behind her.

Jill ignored him and continued on her way. The grass moved easily under her feet and she traced Nero's path. Her breathing slowed and the world around her suddenly seemed very unreal. The only reality in front of her was Nero rounding a corner and walking further away from her. She had no idea if she were walking slowly or running to catch up with him. Speed, space, time did not matter. Suddenly a rush of cool air behind her stopped her in her path.

Jill turned and stared dully at Jack, who held her arm. "I think maybe tomorrow," Jack said. Jill blinked a couple more times before the world became clear again.

"What is going on with me, Jack?" Jill breathed.

"The heat?" Jack suggested concern etched in his eyes. He glanced up a second to where Nero had exited. On foot. No car. "And the fact that this case is so friggin' strange?" Jack did not let go of her arm as Jill continued to blink as if she had been in a deep trance. She rubbed her forehead with her free hand.

"I think it's the heat," she said softly.

Jack smiled at her. "Doesn't help that Nero is quite a catch either, does it?"

Jill looked at him seriously for a moment then started laughing uncontrollably. She doubled over as Jack let his hand fall from her arm. Muffling her face in her arm she looked up at him tears in her eyes. "Oh, God, Jack. This is so inappropriate," she gasped.

Jack grinned. "Let's get you something cool to drink," he said. Jill nodded and stood up to her full height. They headed back to Carmen De Santo's burial spot, which was further away than Jill had realized. She had definitely covered some ground while transfixed on Nero De Santo. As they rounded a small bend Jack muttered, "Shit."

"What is it?" Jill looked up toward the burial site and saw two figures standing near the casket; one a woman wringing her hands; one a man in what appeared to be overall jeans.

"The Emery's," Jack breathed.

"What are they doing here?" Jill asked, her eyes wide.

"Time to find out."

As they got closer Mr. Emery looked up at them briefly his eyes looking glazed.

"Mr. Emery!" Jack called. "I didn't see you here earlier." His tone was friendly and warm. Mr. Emery said nothing. Mrs. Emery looked up at that moment her eyes filled with tears. "Oh, I'm so sorry. We have not been properly introduced," Jack continued. He extended his hand. "I'm Special

Agent Jack Pellingworth from the FBI. This is Special Agent Jill Simko."

Mr. Emery looked down at Jack's hand for a moment, wiped his own hand on his overalls, then shook it briefly. Mrs. Emery continued to wring her hands and did not offer her own hand to the two agents. She took one small step back behind her husband.

"I want to offer my deepest sympathy to both of you. This must be an incredibly difficult time for you," Jack continued. "Please know that local authorities are doing all that they can to find your son and we are here if you need us, as well."

Mr. Emery nodded. Mrs. Emery's eyes widened as she looked past Jack to a cluster of shrubs at the side of the graveyard.

Jack glanced up just as the machine gun sound of shooting cameras approached at such a rapid speed they nearly took his breath away. Four paparazzi cameras glued to their faces hovered just outside the gravesite taking pictures of anything and everything.

After the initial shock of what could only be termed an assault Jack took a few steps forward and yelled in an abrupt, deep voice, "Stop! Stop right now. Stop those fucking cameras!!" The paparazzi ignored him and continued snapping pictures.

Jill pulled out her badge out and pushed it in front of the cameras. "FBI. You will stop now or you will be arrested!"

Jack took two more steps forward pushing his badge up to the lens of their cameras. "FBI. Get the fuck out of here. Now!!"

A man in the front pulled his face back from his camera, quickly nodded and then the entire group ran right back from whence they had come. Jill kept her badge out until they were out of sight. "What was THAT all about?" She asked rhetorically.

"Who the fuck were they?" Jack asked.

"Paparazzi, dude," Jill stated. "They are anybody and everybody who wants to make a quick buck by being at the right place at the right time."

"We're getting those pictures." He put a hand through his hair. "How creepy is that?!"

"Speaking of….the Emery's are gone."

Both Jack and Jill looked around them. In the chaos the Emery's had disappeared into a puff of smoke. "Why were they here, Jack?" Jill asked. Her voice sounded tired. It had been a trying morning.

"I don't have a clue. Let's go make sure we get those pictures and we can put our heads together and figure out what is going on around here."

CHAPTER FOURTEEN

Obtaining the pictures was easy. The court order was a no-brainer and Jack and Jill would have them in their possession in no time. Whether or not some or all of them would have already hit the "market" would be another question entirely. Some things were beyond everyone's control. Answering the question of why Mr. and Mrs. Emery were at the gravesite was another matter entirely. It would certainly make sense that they would attend the funeral since nearly everyone in town was there. Only close family had been invited to the burial so for Mr. and Mrs. Emery to arrive there after the service was highly unusual. When they got back to the hotel Jill went straight to her room to rest. She was feeling a little feverish and had come to realize that her strange episodes must have just been the result of an impending illness. Jack went down to the bar for a drink and to contemplate the Emery's. He sipped his beer as he gazed up at the TV screen playing a football game and tried to bridge the gap that was the Emery's and Carmen De Santo. Why were they there? Were they just fascinated with the case like everyone else or was there a real connection here? From what little Jack could gather Mr. and Mrs. Emery were of an entirely different social class than Carmen De Santo. Despite the fact that Lake Shore was a small town their paths would not have crossed easily. Carmen was known to do charitable work, however, so perhaps she had worked with them at some point. Then again even though the Emery's were certainly not wealthy, they may not have been poor enough to require assistance either. It was hard to tell. Jack looked down at his beer and watched the condensation run down his glass. There was definitely something there and there was really only one way to answer the question. It was time to talk to Mr. and Mrs. Emery. Jack paid for his beer, then sent Jill a quick text. In only a few seconds he was on the road heading back to Lake Shore.

The Emery's house was down a dirt road at the outskirts of town. Since Lake Shore was small this still meant they were in walking distance to downtown, just not as close as they could be. The home itself was a nondescript two-story brown building with a small porch in front and a large detached barn to the left side of it. A beat up, dark-blue pick-up truck with a couple of rust spots on the back door was parked just outside the barn doors. Jack stepped out of his car and shut the door with a loud thump. He looked around. There was not another house in sight and he wondered how close the next house actually was. Whatever the case it was incredibly quiet. Jack looked up to the sky. The sunny skies from earlier that day had faded making way for dense clouds and the distinct feeling that rain was on its way. Jack took a deep breath, dug his hands into his pockets and approached the front porch. The concrete on the porch stairs was chipping in places and the railing looked flimsy. Surprisingly, the floorboards on the porch were steady as Jack walked across and knocked on the front door. He waited his breath audible in the silence. Jack shifted his stance to the right trying to get a view of the inside of the house, but all seemed quiet and dark. He knocked again, then turned his back on the door to get a look of the front yard from the porch. His tan Ford sat alone on the side of the road. Darker clouds were moving in now. A storm was eminent. Still nothing at the door. Maybe they were out back.

Jack descended the stairs carefully then walked around the house so that he approached the truck and the barn. The wind picked up slightly as he rounded the corner the sharp smell of ozone heavy in the air. Jack walked around the truck and proceeded toward the barn doors. There was a small footpath that led to the back yard of the property. The barn loomed in front of him the front doors closed. Another slight breeze picked up carrying with it a sweet, maple smell of what could only be a dead animal in the nearby woods. Jack wrinkled his nose a bit. He felt a couple of raindrops fat and heavy on the top of his head.

"Hey!" a voice boomed from behind him. "Are you lookin' for somethin'?"

Jack turned around to see Mr. Emery again in overalls holding an oily wrench in one hand wiping it off with a rag in his other hand. Jack smiled widely. "Ah…Mr. Emery. Indeed. Just the man I was looking for!"

"It's Tom," Mr. Emery said shortly.

Jack walked up to him and could smell engine oil. Tom Emery's eyes were dark and piercing. Behind him the pregnant clouds continued to loom. It would be any moment now before the rains would come down hard and heavy.

"Can I talk to you for a moment, Tom?" Jack asked. "I'm so sorry about the cameras at the cemetery this morning. We have confiscated the photos so you needn't worry about your family being exposed. I know this is a very difficult time for you."

Mr. Emery nodded his eyes shifting to the barn, then quickly back to Jack. "Could we talk on the porch? I think the rain's comin'."

"Yes, of course." In silence he followed Mr. Emery as he lumbered to the porch and up the steps. From the shelter of the porch Jack could see large, fat drops of water on the front walk. There was a low rumble of thunder in the distance. Mr. Emery put down the wrench he was cleaning and turned to face Jack.

"So you came here to apologize?" He blinked slowly.

Jack smiled. "Sort of. I realized after seeing you this morning that we haven't had time to chat with you yet. We've been meeting with many of the people who live in Lake Shore to talk to them about Carmen De Santo."

Tom Emery just stared at him for a moment. "I don't know Carmen De Santo."

"Did you have any interactions with her, Tom?"

Mr. Emery looked at him for another moment. The fat drops of rain began to come down quicker the air rich with the smell of earth and water.

"Annie may have. But I never talked to her."

Jack glanced at the front door a smile on his face. "Is Annie around? I'd like to have just a second of her time if she is."

Tom glanced at the door as well, then directed his gaze to the front yard. Just then the skies opened and the fat drops of rain became a torrent of beating rain. "She's not feeling well. She gets migraines in this kind of weather." His tone was flat and even.

"Sure. Wow, it's really coming down!" Jack commented jovially. A few drops of rain blew in under the porch roof with the wind. "Well, I hope Annie feels better. I'd like to stop by again so we can talk to her. It's really important that we find out all we can about Mrs. De Santo. We want to be sure this is an isolated case and that more harm doesn't come to Lake Shore."

"Annie is sick a lot. Her migraines," Tom said simply.

Jack could tell when he was being stonewalled. What is it that these people knew? What was going on here? "I'll tell you what, how 'bout you have Annie call me when she is feeling better and I'll be right over. I promise it's just a couple of questions. She can even just talk to me on the phone if she feels more comfortable." Jack reached into his pocket and pulled out a business card. He handed it to Tom, who paused a moment, then took the card. He looked down at it, then looked back at Jack.

"Ok. That sounds good."

Jack smiled. "All right then. Wish me luck in this storm!!" He ducked out into the rain and dashed to his car. Inside the car the rain sounded heavier and more menacing than ever. He exhaled and looked through his windshield at Tom Emery who put Jack's business card into his pocket, then turned to enter the house. Jack started the car. He was pretty sure that Annie was not going to call him, but for some reason he got the distinct feeling that he'd be back here real soon.

After two full hours of solid sleep Jill woke up in her hotel room feeling much more refreshed. She took a quick shower then went to retrieve the messages on her cell phone and hotel phone. From Jack's text he had headed off to the Emery's house. Interesting. The message on her hotel phone indicated she had received a package downstairs. She ordered herself some food from room service, then took a walk down to the lobby to retrieve her package. While in the lobby she noticed it was raining buckets outside. She hoped Jack was all right and that he was getting the information he needed. The package was a large envelope. Jill thanked the attendant and opened the top of the envelope as she walked back to the elevator. She peaked inside to see a sheet of paper and slew of photographs.

Back in her room Jill hopped on the bed and pulled out the sheet of paper. The photographs were exactly what she expected; the pictures from the paparazzi at Carmen's burial site earlier that day. The letter stated that the cameras was easily confiscated but that there was no guarantee that they had not already been released. Modern technology made release almost instantaneous. The photographs in her possession had been printed and delivered by a bureau courier as quickly as possible. Jill spread the pictures out and sighed. Just then there was a knock at her door, "Room Service!"

Jill jumped up, retrieved her food, then hopped back on the bed and began sipping on her ginger ale. She leaned forward and started flipping through the photographs. Senator Ricci staring dully at the coffin. Mrs. O'Dea with her gloved hand to her mouth. Armand De Santo staring at a point just beyond his wife's coffin. Nero dropping something onto the top of Carmen's coffin. A wide shot of the entire group mourning their loss. Jill following Nero beyond the gravesite. Then there it was. Just what she had been looking for. Tom and Annie Emery walking up the street that bordered the cemetery. Tom and Annie Emery walking toward the gravesite. Tom and Annie Emery staring dully down at the coffin. Annie putting her hand to her mouth her eyes filled with tears. Tom staring just beyond the coffin his face stern. Annie leaning forward to look directly at the top of the coffin. Annie her eyes round as saucers looking up at her husband. Jack and Jill approaching. Jack with his badge out his face red with anger.

Jill looked up from the photographs strewn about the bed and looked across the room at the cabinet hosting the television. She took a sip of her ginger ale, then hopped off the bed to grab a roll that had come with her soup. Her stomach turned. What was she missing? What was she missing? Something extremely important. What was it?

She chewed on the bread and sifted through the photographs again. Her fingers stopped at the one where Nero was placing something on the top of Carmen's coffin. She picked up the photograph and looked closer. Something was dangling from his hand. A necklace? She looked closer still. What was that?

Just then her cell phone rang. She jumped, then took a deep breath. She noticed her hands were trembling as she put the phone to her ear. "Simko."

"Hey. It's me." Jack. "How are you feeling?"

"A little better. I'm trying some soup." Jill glanced over at her untouched soup.

"Any good?"

Jill ignored his question her hands continuing to tremble. Jack will know what she is missing. She felt a little dizzy. Perhaps she did need more rest. "The photographs came. I think there's something you'll want to see."

Jack knocked on her door a moment later and moved the photographs from the bed to a nearby desk. He spread then out, placed them in chronological order, and stood back to look at them. Jill sipped her soup and watched him.

"You look terrible by the way," Jack said smiling smugly at her.

"Oh. Thanks!" Jill said chuckling. It felt good to laugh.

Jack was quiet for a moment staring intently at the pictures. "This picture is so odd." He picked up the picture of Nero with a necklace dangling from his fingers. Jill leaned over to look.

"How so?" Jill asked.

"I don't even know if it matters. Why would Nero be giving Carmen a necklace?" He pressed his lips together in concentration. Then he squinted to look closer at the picture. "I wish I could see it better. Nero doesn't quite seem the type to throw a tantrum, and he made quite a spectacle at the burial."

"Then again, Armand seemed very tolerant of this," Jill noted. "Maybe Nero is prone to strange episodes. He is awfully eccentric." Jill put the bowl of soup aside. She was feeling very tired again. Jack continued to scrutinize the picture. "Wait a minute. Wait a minute," he said quickly. He began picking up photographs and staring intently at each one until he found exactly the two he was looking for. "Look at these. What's different here?"

Jill sat up straight tucking her legs under her to sit cross-legged. The two photographs were of Nero DeSanto. One was as he approached the group at the burial site. The other was of him walking away. Jill looked closely but the more her eyes probed each picture the more lost she felt. Finally she shrugged. "I don't see it, Jack."

He pointed to the first photograph. "Look around his neck."

Jill looked closely. At the folds of his black shirt was a shiny, silver necklace with a pendant of a pentagram hanging from it. It looked so natural on him that she never even noticed it. "A pentagram," she whispered. A shiver went down her spine and she could not stop staring at the photograph and the pentagram. The image suddenly looked like a painting to her.

From what seemed like far off in the distance Jack said, "And look at this one. Look at his neck."

It was a photograph of Nero walking away from the burial site his hair slightly hiding his bronzed face. Jill focused on his neck. No pentagram. Another chill zipped down her spine and she felt her hands tremble again. This is what she had been missing. Of course Jack would notice something like this. She forced herself to pull her eyes away from both pictures. She had a feeling this was a critical moment and that she should sit real still so that she could soak up every minute of it. Any movement may shatter everything. "No pentagram," she managed in a whisper.

Jack nodded and sat down next to her. "What do you think that means?"

"Nero knew. Nero knew about her," Jill breathed. The photographs dropped from her hands and she looked over at Jack. Critical moment. Something here was opening up and she felt it like she did in all cases when there was an unraveling.

"Absolutely. That's why she 'wouldn't' have wanted it this way'. She wouldn't have wanted a Christian burial," Jack said. "Nero wanted to be sure there was some semblance of her real life that would go with her in death. Thus, dropping off the pentagram. I cannot wait to talk to Nero DeSanto. I bet he's something else."

"But it's not that he just knows about her, Jack. He understands her. Armand may have known about her, too, but he's giving her a Christian burial so there's no way he took her seriously. Nero took her seriously and I think to some degree he must identify with her. Or at the very least he respects her decision to do something different from others." Jill looked down at the photographs again.

"He's wearing the pentagram in the first photograph. I'm thinking he may also practice. He may not only understand her; he may be just like her. Who's to say she didn't learn about Wicca from him?" Jack's face was slightly flushed with excitement. "This could all get very, very interesting."

"We can't rush to judgment. We just know that he dropped off the pentagram to her or at least that's what it appears to be what happened. That's all. We just have to go on that for now. We'll meet with him tomorrow and perhaps he will give us some more information. Answer our questions."

"He could even be the killer," Jack said in a rush.

"Jack, at this moment anyone could be the killer. You know that," Jill said patiently. "I think talking to him is our best bet. What I really want to know is what the Emery's were doing there. Let's look at those pictures."

"Oh shit!" Jack exclaimed rushing to the table and pulling two more photographs off of it. He sat next to Jill his excitement palpable. Jill looked at the photographs. One was of the Emery's looking at Carmen's burial site. The other was Annie Emery looking at her husband her eyes wide. "They saw it. They saw it!!"

"What? The pentagram?" Jill asked looking closely at the photos again.

"Yes. Do you see Annie's face there?" Jack pointed to the look in her eyes.

There was a distinct horror in her eyes as she looked at husband. "What would the pentagram mean to her?"

"What it means to anyone who doesn't understand. Satan. The devil. Jim told me that although the pentagram is a common symbol in Wicca to symbolize the four elements and the fifth being the self, most people associate them with Satanic ritual. If Annie is a God-fearing woman she may have seen this and would have been absolutely horrified."

It was true. A burial site with a crucifix replaced by a pentagram would be quite shocking to someone who spent most of his or her life taught that these symbols were a direct call to Lucifer himself. Jill studied the photo. "By the way, how did your visit to the Emery's go?" she asked off-handedly.

"A big, fat zero," Jack said. "Tom keeps pretty quiet. He said he didn't know Carmen and that Annie might but she was sick with a migraine or something. I got the feeling he didn't want to talk to me at all and that he couldn't wait for me to leave. I'm thinking I may stop back there tomorrow."

"Maybe he feels uncomfortable talking to anyone but Detective Winslow and the locals here. A lot of people are suspicious of the Feds. I think stopping back is a good idea, though. At least to talk to Annie. I'd like to come along if you don't mind." Jill stretched.

"You sure you'll feel up to it?"

"I've got to. I'm sure after a full night's sleep I'll be perfect again." Jill looked down at the picture again. "Jack, Annie's face in this picture is just so horrified; as if she had been tricked or betrayed."

"That makes sense if she knew Carmen in some way and would never have seen her as an "evil" influence. It may have her questioning everything. Her. Senator Ricci. Armand De Santo. Everything and everyone."

Jill looked up from the picture and placed it back down on the bed. "Should we talk to Detective Winslow yet? Out of courtesy at least."

"I say we talk to the Emery's again tomorrow and if we get nowhere or maybe even if we get somewhere we take a moment to discuss with Detective Winslow."

"Sounds like a plan." Jill smiled, then nodded. "Jack, I feel like we are just spinning our wheels here. Do we even have any real suspects yet?"

Jack walked over to the desk and grabbed the complimentary notepad and pen. "Let's see. One, Armand De Santo. I'm relatively convinced he is free and clear, but as far as we can tell his wife was cheating on him and that is never pretty. Two, anyone associated with Senator Ricci. The Senator has some pretty controversial policy. It's hard to believe anyone would murder his daughter over it, but we can't rule it out right now. Three, Renault. The manner in which she was killed was brutal and her social status would have excited Renault. We can't rule him out just yet. Four?" Jack looked up from his notebook.

"Four. Anyone she may have been associated with Wicca or who opposed Wiccan practices. The only problem with this one is that we don't know for sure of anyone else who may have been involved in Wicca with her." Jill rubbed her forehead. She needed to rest. Tomorrow was going to be a long day.

"Five. Omaha. Her lover and confidante. Maybe she tried to break it off and he went crazy."

"Yes, I always love a good love triangle," Jill grinned. Most things came down to love and greed for them. The same old, same old; different people, different time and place.

"You look absolutely beat, my dear," Jack cooed putting down the notebook. "And I need to clear my head. It looks like we have a very busy day tomorrow."

Jill sighed. "Good night, Jack."

CHAPTER FIFTEEN

Jack and Jill met for a quick breakfast the next morning. The sun was high and bright in the sky streaming its glorious rays into the hotel restaurant. Jill had woken up feeling more like herself again attributing it to a solid night's rest. Jack had woken refreshed and optimistic about their work that day. It was almost 10:00 a.m. when they left the hotel to head back to Lake Shore. The storm had successfully drawn the heat out of the air leaving room for a cool, refreshing feel. Jill breathed in deeply.

"Ahhh. Now that's the stuff. No humidity. Just clean, fresh air," she said opening the door to let herself into the car.

"I hear ya! This is fantastic!!" Jack said slipping into the driver's seat.

As they headed down the hotel driveway to the road leading to Lake Shore Jill leaned an elbow against the side of the door and looked outside. "While in the shower this morning I was thinking about connections," she said softly. "Mostly how the Emery's could possibly be connected to Carmen De Santo."

Jack nodded, but kept silent. He knew Jill enough to know she had more to say.

"You wouldn't think they'd be connected at all. She's super rich. They live in near poverty. But maybe that's the connection. Carmen was known for helping out her community, especially with Lake Shore Hospice. I can't say I agree that the Emery's were people who needed Hospice help but perhaps she helped them in another way."

"Could be," Jack nodded. "And that would explain Annie's face in the picture. If Carmen were helping them out of the goodness of her heart it would have been shocking for Annie to learn that Carmen harbored a secret like this. She may even be too sick to talk to someone like me coming 'round shortly thereafter." Jack grinned.

They kept quiet the rest of the way to Lake Shore each in their own minds thinking over the case. It was a big day and they would both need to concentrate on everything. The further they got into the case and the longer the case dragged on the more they had to concentrate since it was all the more likely that either lies would be uncovered or lies would be buried for good. It wasn't long before Jack pulled up to the Emery's' house. The house did not look all that much more cheerful than it had yesterday with the oncoming storm.

"Wow. It's amazing that one little town can have a place as beautiful as the De Santo house and then this. This place is falling apart," Jill commented.

They both got out of their car and stepped over puddles leftover from the storm on their way to the Emery's front porch. Jack knocked on the door and waited. Nothing. Another couple of seconds passed in silence. Jack knocked again, this time louder.

"Too early?" Jill asked. She checked her watch. It was nearly 10:30. Still nothing. Jack knocked again this time calling out, "Tom? Annie?" Nothing.

"Well, maybe they're working," Jill offered.

"Let's check." Jack led Jill off the porch and they walked across the damp lawn to the side of the house in front of the barn where the pickup truck had been parked the previous day. The truck was gone. "Maybe they both went out. It looks like they have only one car. I assume Tom must work. And Annie? I don't know."

"Maybe Annie's inside? I hope she's all right." Jill looked back up to the house. "Do you think we should try the back door? Maybe she can't hear us."

Jack looked up at the house. It stood very still before her. "Maybe."

They began to approach the barn, which had a small footpath next to it leading to the back yard. As they did they heard the crunch of gravel indicating a car approaching. Jack and Jill turned around to look. Perhaps the Emery's were back. A black Honda sedan parked behind them along the road and sat idle for a moment. Just as Jack began to approach the car the door opened and Detective Winslow stepped out. His lips were set evenly and his eyes squinted with suspicion.

The agents both smiled and walked over to him in greeting. "Detective Winslow," Jack said kindly. "We are so pleased to see you!" Jack offered his hand.

Detective Winslow hesitated for a moment, then smiled widely and shook Jack's hand with gusto. He shook Jill's hand giving her the same smile. Although appearing to be warm the smile cracked at the edges making Jill a little uncomfortable.

"Ah, Special Agent Pellingworth. Special Agent Simko. What brings you here?" He looked past them at the house as if distracted by it.

Jack kept a steady gaze on him. "We came to speak with the Tom and Annie about Carmen De Santo. As you know, we are making the rounds. Talking to everyone."

"Ah, yes, Tom told me you were here yesterday. Did you think of something else you needed to ask him?"

Jeez. News traveled fast. "Well, I spoke with Tom, but Tom didn't know Carmen very well. I wanted to speak with Annie but she was not feeling well yesterday so I thought we'd stop by this morning to speak with her."

"Ahhh," Detective Winslow breathed looking past them to the house again. "I don't know what's the best way to say this, Agents, but I don't really know if this is the best, er, time to be asking them questions."

"Did you find their little boy?" Jill asked quickly.

"No. We have not." Detective Winslow looked at both of them sadly. "And that's why I'm thinking it's not the best time. I know you are talking to everyone and that you're trying to make everything right for Mrs. De Santo, but there are just some people who are grieving and worried sick and could probably care less about Mrs. De Santo. Your questions while important to you may not be as important to them."

Jack's eyes glazed over in anger, but he kept his cool. "The Emery's were at Carmen's funeral yesterday. They clearly feel for her family and wanted to pay their respects. I would hope that they would want to help us since we would do anything in our power to help them find their little boy. All of this is tragic, but unfortunately it all happened at the same time and lives intersect. We need to make sure we try every path. We have no idea which one will lead to Carmen's killer."

"And you think the Emery's are your path to finding her killer? Are you kidding me?!" Detective Winslow scoffed.

"You know best that they could know something that would put us on the right path; the one that leads to the killer. They may not even realize they know something important," Jack responded.

Detective Winslow drew in a deep breath and looked past them again. "You are certainly barking up the wrong tree, my friends. I can assure you the Emery's do not know Carmen De Santo."

Jack's jaw twitched in anger. Jill stepped forward. "Thank you, Detective Winslow. We mean no harm by coming here. We really just want to find as many answers as possible. And we are being gentle here. We understand the situation. Jack and I have worked on missing children's cases and they are terrifying. We get it." She smiled kindly. "But it doesn't look like they are home anyway. Could you please let them know we were here? That is, if they think they may have something that could help us."

"Of course," Detective Winslow said. He seemed braced for a verbal attack and when he didn't receive one he almost looked as if he would lose his balance.

"Let us know if we can help you with anything while we're here, ok?"

"Yes, of course," Detective Winslow said unsteadily.

Jill nudged Jack. "Well, we've got more paths to follow," To Detective Winsler she said. "Have a wonderful day. It was a pleasure seeing you again."

Jack remained silent all the way back until they reached the car with the doors shut tight. "What the FUCK is going on here?!!" He exploded.

Jill grinned. "I'm so proud of you," she gushed. "You really held it all together."

"I hate that guy."

"I'm with you there," Jill agreed. "What a slime!" She shivered. "I can't believe he's working a missing child case. What a creep!"

"I just don't understand what's going on here. I'm feeling like we're being stonewalled. Two days in a row and we can't get through to the Emery's?"

"I'm sure they are being protected to some degree. We're the Feds. No one likes the Feds. The local guys don't want us snooping around. The Emery's have probably been told not to talk to us. You know how it is. How it works." Jill breathed out.

"Yeah. I know," Jack said. "But I don't have to like it."

Their next stop was back to the Lake Shore Hospice Association. Jill asked to stop there again so that they could check to see if Carmen had ever been assigned work for the Emery's. This time they both walked into the spacious waiting room, which was vacant. Jill walked over to the reception desk and cleared her throat. The same receptionist, Molly, popped her head around the corner from a back room.

"Ahh…Agent Simko. How are you?" She said it with such warmth and hospitality Jill almost felt as if she had been invited here.

Molly walked around the corner a cup of coffee in her hand. She set the coffee down and shook Jill's hand. "And who do we have here?" She asked looking Jack up and down with a smirk on her face and a slight blush on her cheeks. She clearly liked what she saw.

"Agent Jack Pellingworth," Jack stated stepping forward to shake her hand. Molly's shake was warm and she held Jack's hand for a bit longer than he thought was necessary.

"Well, welcome, Agent Jack Pellingworth." She smiled. "Can I help you both with anything?"

Jill smiled. "I just have a quick question for Ms. Newmarth. Is she available?"

Molly smiled back. Playing the game of being polite. "Mary Anne is away for a couple of days. Occasionally we do work outside of Lake Shore. I'm sorry. Is this something I could help you with?"

"Well, this probably breaks all privacy compliance but we were interested in knowing if Carmen De Santo ever did any work with the Emery's or visited them on your behalf?" Jill said hesitantly.

"Tom and Annie?" Molly looked incredulous, then she shrugged. "You're right, I'm not supposed to tell you about that." Jack and Jill glanced at each other. "But I'm going to tell you something anyway, and when push comes to shove you didn't hear it from me." She had lowered her voice as she spoke the second part of her sentence.

"Of course," Jill said.

Molly ushered them to the seats in the waiting area and sat down on one herself. Molly leaned forward balancing her weight on the edge of the seat. "Carmen didn't do any work through us for Tom and Annie. But," she paused her eyes shifting to the door. She let out a short breath. "She did tutor Mark Emery. Not for long. Maybe for like a couple of months. He was slipping behind in school and she offered to help him out. She was just the sweetest. She couldn't stand watching anyone slip through the cracks." Her eyes beamed for a moment, then she looked down sadness deep-set in her eyes when she looked back at the two Agents. "What a waste," she whispered her lower lip trembling.

"Did she ever talk to you about the tutoring? How things were going maybe?" Jill asked.

Molly let out another deep breath. "No. I had heard she was going to tutor them. That's all. Carmen was very sweet and all, but she was also a professional and she didn't gossip about clients. She knew this is a small town and word travels fast." She paused for a moment. "People here are saying there is a connection. It's just too strange that Carmen was found murdered and Mark Emery is missing all at the same time. Personally, I don't know that there is one. I just think that God works in mysterious ways sometimes. It's probably about time Lake Shore had its come-uppance."

CHAPTER SIXTEEN

The morning was heating up. The sun was high and the morning cool was fading to make way for tolerable warmth. Jack was grinning from ear to ear as they headed to the car. As soon as they sat down he said, "I knew it. I knew it. I knew Carmen was somehow connected to the Emery's."

"I wouldn't get too excited about it," Jill said softly. "This is a small town. A lot of people are connected to the Emery's. The good news is that it gives us all the more reason to meet with the Emery's again whether or not Detective Winslow likes it."

"I agree. But why do you think Tom lied about not knowing Carmen."

"Maybe he didn't lie. Maybe he didn't know her. Maybe Annie knew her and only she was there when Carmen met with Mark. Or maybe Carmen met with Mark at the school. You just don't know."

Jack frowned. "Yeah. I guess so." He started the car. "But you know how much I love catching someone in a lie."

Jill smiled, "Yeah. I know. So, where to now, hot shot?"

"Back to the Emery's to have a little talk with Detective Winslow."

"No. No. I don't think that's a good idea." She pressed her palm to her forehead where a slight headache was beginning to develop. "Let's let that rest for a little bit. Let it sit. We can talk to Detective Winslow later."

"You're no fun," Jack pouted.

Jill smiled. "Awww, poor Jack." She ruffled his hair. "Ok, so I say we have a little talk with Nero De Santo." She grinned.

"Sounds good to me," Jack agreed. "This is a big ticket item. I'm excited to see just how much of Carmen's extracurricular activities he knew about."

"Well, let's do it, then."

They took the short drive in silence. Jill watched the road as the small downtown green made way for lush vegetation and dirt roads. They passed a couple of magnificent fields that looked perfect for a quiet picnic. As they approached the border of Lake Shore the dirt roads became narrow. Jack decreased his speed and turned off onto Nero De Santo's street, Lilly Bell Lane. The street was nearly unpassable. It was extremely narrow with a slight overgrowth of brush. Lilly Bell Lane hosted one home, that of none other than Nero De Santo. The pain in Jill's head had increased to a full-blown headache by the time they parked their car just outside a path that led to the Nero De Santo's house. She tried to ignore it figuring it was just the remnants of her flu or perhaps even hay fever. Jack killed the motor and they sat for a moment listening to the sound of birds chirping.

"This is amazing," Jill whispered. "You can actually hear the bees."

Jack and Jill climbed out of the car and shut their doors as carefully as possible. Jill couldn't explain it. The sound of the bees, the birds, and the light wind rustling through the trees and bushes was not only peaceful, but demanded a complete and utter respect in nature. This was the world as it should be without the smog and cars and tall skyscrapers. Jill leaned against the car for a moment and tilted her face to the sun. She closed her eyes and listened to Nature as a symphony.

"Feeling ok?" Jack asked. In the time she had taken to take in and feel the surroundings Jack had rounded the car and taken a moment to look at her. She looked pale and distant.

Jill opened her eyes. "Oh, sorry, Jack. I have the worst headache and the sun felt so good. This is a beautiful spot."

"Shall we?" Jack gestured toward the narrow path leading to Nero De Santo's house, which was currently hidden behind the brush and vegetation that surrounded the entrance gate.

Jill nodded. A sense of peace continued to pervade. They pushed past flowering bushes to open a small, unlocked gate. Once through it, the brush opened up to a footpath that led through a series of intricate gardens ultimately ending at a charming cottage. The cottage was straight out of Hansel and Gretel except instead of candy intricate stonework made up the beautiful façade. Ivy crept up one side of the cottage. There was a small porch in front with large potted plants decorating it. They walked up the footpath. Jill felt as if every plant were looking at them and assessing them. Were they all calling out to Nero collectively? "You have a visitor!" Despite the fact that the entire experience could be unsettling, the assessment wasn't one of distaste and ignorance. It was one of interest and acceptance. Jill felt at home here. She could even picture herself among the plants choosing just the right bouquet of flowers to go with dinner. Carmen must have loved this place. Just as she thought this Jill felt something cold on the right side of her face. The cool sensation had been so unusual it stopped her right in her tracks.

Jack paused, too. "Jill? Is everything all right?"

Jill looked at him quizzically for a moment. "Sure. Sure. I'm fine."

"Are you sure? You look like you've just seen a ghost."

Jill took a deep breath to steady herself. "I'm fine." She continued to follow Jack but could not stop thinking of the cool sensation. She put her hand on her cheek, but it felt warm. She looked up to the sky, then she peaked behind her to look at the path. Still feeling a little wobbly she followed Jack up the steps of the front porch. The front door was an intricate door with an arch at the top that resembled something straight out of a fairy tale. On the front of the door was a placard that read, "Blessed Be" in simple script. "Blessed be," Jill muttered.

Jack turned around. "Did you say something?"

Jill looked at him. "No." Then after a second. "No."

"Are you sure you are feeling all right? I need you here for this. I mean really here. All senses alive now. I can't have one thing slip by us." He said this gently, but sternly.

Jill shook her head as if to clear her mind and took another deep breath. "I'm here. Let's do this."

Just as Jack was about to knock on it, the front door opened as if by magic. Jack lowered his fist and took one step backward. As he did Nero De Santo stepped into the threshold. "Welcome. Both of you! I have been waiting for this moment."

Jill blinked and looked up at him. Nero De Santo was one of the most exquisite men she had ever seen. His dark, wavy hair was tied back exposing high cheekbones, brown eyes with a hint of mischief in them and a strong, even jaw line. His skin was the color of honey kissed by the summer's sun. He was about six feet tall with a long, lanky build. Jack noticed he wore a necklace with a pentagram on it and his fingers were adorned with rings.

"We have a few questions for you regarding Carmen De Santo," Jack said as Jill gazed in awe at this man. This response could most definitely prove problematic to the investigation if she couldn't keep her senses.

Nero grinned. "Well, then by all means, come in." He stepped back from the threshold and motioned for them to enter his bejeweled fingers glistening like the wings of dragonflies in the sun.

Jack entered first his back straight and jaw set, all business. Jill entered a little more cautiously. The entryway was small and decorated with a number of plants in a way that mimicked the gardens one traversed before entering the house. A silver watering can was perched just by the door.

Nero led them down a short hall to what appeared to be a living room. The room was small crammed with a large leather couch, a smaller, leather sofa, more plants, a bookcase stuffed with books, and piles of books here and there on the floor. A cabinet with a glass door slightly ajar to reveal amber bottles held its place at the back of the room.

Jill expected more from the brother of a business tycoon. The room was small, cozy and actually very comfortable, but didn't have any of the vastness and intricacies of his brother's house. And yet there was something so much more personal and down-to-earth in this little house. She couldn't help but find herself very soothed and almost smiling as they entered the living room.

"Please, take a seat," Nero said in his lilting accent motioning to the couch and sofa. "Can I get either of you ice tea or coffee?"

"No, thank you," Jack said making his way over to the couch. In comparison to Nero, Jack's voice sounded strangely crisp and hard. Jill knew this was his "business" voice, however she still cringed inwardly when she heard it. That kind of voice did not have any place in this house.

"No thank you," Jill managed softly. She sat next to Jack on the couch and smiled kindly up at Nero. Nero settled down into a chair that was covered with a number of blankets. He crossed his legs, then his long fingers and looked at them expectantly a calm expression on his face. This man was ready for anything, but not in a combative way.

"As you may have guessed we are speaking with anyone who knew Carmen De Santo. Carmen was your sister-in-law so you may or may not have information that can help us. Our job is to ask a few questions and go from there," Jack said.

Nero nodded, "Proceed."

"When did you first meet Carmen?"

Nero smiled softly. "Armand invited me to dinner. He had met a young woman who he was mad for and they were planning to be married."

"What did you think of Carmen when you first met her?"

"I was pleasantly surprised. She was much more grounded than I had expected for the daughter of Senator Ricci." He chuckled, and managed to get a slight smile out of Jack. "Mostly I was happy for Armand. He had had a long string of desperate women mostly interested in his money. I thought it would be good for him to marry a woman who was not only educated and charming, but also had money of her own."

Jack paused cuing Jill that he was ready for her to pose a question of her own instead of gazing over at Nero in rapt fascination. "Did you spend any time with Carmen without Armand present?" she asked. She had no idea why she had decided to cut to the chase so quickly, but she had.

Nero smiled kindly at her. "In fact I did. Carmen and I became close friends. Armand traveled so much and he worried that Carmen would become lonely. She had moved out here - in the middle of nowhere - for him. That was sacrifice enough. He asked that I visit her, which I did."

"What did you two do together?" Jill asked.

Nero's eyes glazed over for a moment and Jill sensed a moment of discomfort. He clasped his fingers. "We went for walks in the woods. We spent time in the garden here. We ate meals together. Simple things." Nero let out a short laugh. "I'm not one for shopping and getting my nails done."

Jack let out a forced, jovial laugh. "Was Carmen?"

"No. She was fascinated by...." He paused searching for the best word. "By Nature. She loved being outdoors. Long walks with a friend would be more satisfying to her than any spa treatment."

"Did Carmen have any other friends here in Lake Shore?" Jill asked.

"Yes. There was Marisca mainly. She did spent time with a couple of the older ladies in town, but those weren't real friendships. Most of the women around here were a little jealous of Carmen. Some had hoped to marry Armand themselves so I'm not so sure they were happy with a New York socialite moving in. Carmen was nice to everyone and tried to change people's minds with a kind smile, but not everyone was so open to her."

"Anyone in particular?" Jill asked.

"There was Marjorie Gray. Marjorie wanted to keep the town quiet. When Carmen came to town she was the first to really gossip about her and question whether or not Carmen would bring the New York scene to Lake

Shore. She never liked Carmen no matter how nice Carmen was and no matter how much time went by. It was just too bad." His eyes were distant and soft.

"Did this bother Carmen? Did she know Marjorie didn't like her?" Jill asked.

"Yes. At first it bothered Carmen, but she was resilient and she eventually shrugged Ms. Gray off and wished only good things for her, that she'd find peace with Carmen at some point."

Jack and Jill glanced at each other. Although Marjorie Gray may not be a murderer she had to be checked out. Stranger things had happened. It depended on how far Ms. Gray was willing to go to keep things the way they had always been.

"Anyone else?" Jack asked.

"Not specifically. Many people were very curious about Carmen. She was a very different person. A lot of people in this small town had never met anyone like her." He smiled slightly. "For starters she had more race cars than anyone in this county." His eyes sparkled.

Jack let out a sharp laugh. Jill thought it sounded forced. "You got that right. She has some collection."

Nero looked pensive for a moment, then nodded. He recrossed his legs and tapped his glittering fingers on his knee. "She loved those cars," he breathed. "They were her children. They were her everything." His eyes glazed over at that moment a profound sadness settling in.

"Look, Nero, I'm going to set this straight because I don't know any other way of doing it." Jill's voice surprised even herself. It was direct and bold and had come from someplace she didn't even know existed. No games. Nero wasn't one to play them and he would smell them a mile away. "We saw you put the pentagram on Carmen's grave. We saw how upset you were. What's going on? If you don't tell us, we're never going to find out who murdered her. Or better yet. We're going to start thinking you murdered her."

Her words hung like bullets in the air. Jill pictured them hovering around Nero, who then had to decide whether or not to receive them and be shredded or to shrug them off. Nero surprised her then. He smiled and leaned forward his elbows on his knees. Jill envisioned him eating the bullets joyfully. Yum, candy. "Clever, clever girl," he cooed. Jill could feel Jack's protest before he began and she gave him a quick, warning glance. If there was anything that Jill had learned through years of service to the FBI, it was to play the interviewees game. This usually yielded great results. This time around Jill called it instinct. Her mind had been yelling at her to just "cut the bull shit already".

Nero looked at Jill with great interest. His eyes glittered. For a moment Jill wondered how Carmen could have resisted this charm. "Carmen was a Wiccan, love," he said softly. "She was Pagan. She believed in so much joy and love and beauty in this world." He paused and looked at some point beyond Jack and Jill, a memory perhaps. "She believed further than even herself."

Ok, he was cryptic. Jill would give him that. And cryptic no matter how charming wouldn't help solve Carmen's murder. "Nero, Carmen is dead. Her throat was slashed and she was stabbed multiple times. No amount of magic and love saved her. What happened that night?"

Jack looked over at Jill this time his eyes warning her. Jill ignored him. Her instincts were screaming that he needed the dream world to become as realistic as possible. Cut to the quick.

Nero continued to smile at her, as if her bullet-words had no effect. "I know how Carmen died. It's everywhere and it's disgusting what her beautiful life has become. As for the pentagram, Ms. Simko, Carmen was Pagan and thus the pentagram was most fitting. She would have wanted to be buried with it. Armand would never have understood. She never talked to him about her beliefs and her practices. He would have freaked out and would have worried about her even more than he already did. She wanted to save him from herself, you see."

"Do you practice Wicca, Nero?" Jack asked softly in an attempt to balance out Jill's approach.

"I understand it. I use elements of magick to some degree. Carmen believed in its force and its power like no one I've ever met. She held the Goddess at her right side. With every decision she made she consulted the Goddess. She was dutiful to her core." His eyes glazed over again. "She did not deserve what happened to her, but no one deserves that. I imagine Carmen as a Goddess herself. She was meant for a more ethereal life and I truly believe she now has it." He smiled sadly and sat back in his chair.

"When did you last see Carmen?" Jack asked.

Nero eyes become cold crystal at that moment and he shivered as if instantly chilled. "Did anyone else feel that?" he asked.

Jack and Jill stared at him soundlessly.

"That cold. It may sound absolutely crazy, but sometimes I feel like she is reaching out to me. I feel a cold that cannot be explained."

Jill shivered thinking about the cold she had felt in the garden.

Nero looked at her. "You know what I mean." His voice fell like lead in the room, a bowling ball that fell flat and rolled across the room to her in his words. Jack looked at Jill for a moment and noticed that she looked a mix of awe and fear. When had they lost all control of this conversation?

"When did you last see Carmen?" Jack asked echoing Jill's question.

Jack glanced at him for only a moment, then directed his attention to Jill. "The night she died. I saw her that night." There was no pretense. It was bluntly stated.

Jack felt his own chill rise up his spine. Was Nero a suspect then?

"She was sick. She had a flu. I persuaded her to come to me for a poultice." Nero paused. "In case you don't already know, I'm an herbalist. People locally come to me for remedies when prescriptions aren't working or are making them feel less than adequate." Nero smiled. "As you can well imagine, Carmen did not care much for allopathic medicine." He chuckled to himself. "Carmen was always a big baby when she was sick. She agreed to come for a poultice. I gave her one. She visited for a bit and relaxed on the couch you're sitting on, and then she left. She said she was tired and really needed to get to bed. I agreed. Rest was the best option for her."

Jack couldn't help but look down at the couch they were sitting on. "Does a poultice have any controlled drug in it?"

Nero let out a hearty laugh. He leaned forward again and grinned at Jack. "No illegals, I'm afraid. That would make it too easy on you now, wouldn't it?"

Jack clenched his jaw. Nero's cockiness was far surpassing what he permitted, but he needed answers and he had a feeling if he pressed, Jill would weigh towards the side of Nero, and that was all he needed. Keep the peace.

"Nope. Carmen took her poultice and left. That's the last I saw of her." His eyes misted over for just a moment. "I wish I had seen her…." He paused and pressed his hand to his mouth. "In better spirits."

Carmen was at the door her hand on the door handle and her eyes glazed over with her flu. Her lips were nearly blue and her skin pale. She smiled weakly at Nero. "I'll call you tomorrow, love. I just need to rest. You understand, right?"

Nero had nodded sadly and kissed her cheek. "Call me in the morning."

She had grinned and for a glimpse of a moment looked well. "How could I forget?"

At that moment a sharp knock on the door made Jill jump and gasp slightly. She blinked and looked at Nero.

Nero stood up. "I must apologize. I have a patient scheduled that I need to attend to. I'll only be just a moment." With that he silently left the room.

Jack looked over at Jill. "What do you think?" he whispered. They could both hear murmured voices at the front door, Nero and his patient.

"I'm stunned. I have to admit this is all very, very strange. I feel like I can't quite keep up," Jill answered quietly.

"I think we're getting closer," Jack responded. He got up and began walking around the room glancing at artwork on the walls and books in the bookshelves. On one table was a picture of Carmen and Armand arm-in-arm. Carmen's smile was wide and bright and her eyes danced. Her hair was shorter and very curly all around her head. She wore a yellow sundress and her skin was sun-kissed. Armand was looking down at her pride evident in his beaming expression. Jack felt his heart fall to his knees and a rush of sadness pour in. He wasn't sure how old this picture was, but it was so clear that Armand and Carmen were deeply in love and had enjoyed each other. What happened? What in the world happened to this poor girl? This girl who kept secrets from her husband about her religion. This girl who confided in her brother-in-law. This girl who volunteered in her community and tutored a poor family in town. This girl who was alive and happy and beautiful. What in the world happened? Wasn't it easier when the victim was a prostitute or drug user and you could pretend for a moment that they had deserved their fate?

"I must postpone our talk," Nero's voice bellowed into the room. Jack was yanked from his reverie and whipped around to see Nero hovering at the doorway. Jill was already standing up and approaching him with a smile on her face. "I greatly apologize. My patient needs a bit more time and I really feel I should attend to him. Please feel free to return so we can continue. I am available tomorrow all day," he said kindly.

"We'll plan on doing that, Nero. You have been most kind," Jill's voice continued but faded into the background for Jack.

"Just one more thing," Jack stated interrupting Jill who stopped mid-sentence and slowly looked at him. "Did Carmen ever mention Mark Emery to you?"

Nero eyes flashed anger. "She tutored Mark. I can say this to you simply. Tomorrow I will tell you more about her work with Mark. I wish I could now. Please, come back in the morning. I insist. You will be interested in hearing about the Emery's." He clenched his jaw, then released it as he breathed in and out deeply.

Bingo. Jack could feel the connections coming together. Even though Nero was at the very top of their suspect list at this point, Jack had to admit that he could not wait to return in the morning for more puzzle pieces. Jill continued to thank Nero for his time as they headed for the door. Nero bowed graciously to them as they walked out the door, then quietly closed the door behind them. Jack and Jill walked through the gardens to the car in silence. They both got into the car and Jill slumped in her seat.

"I am exhausted," she said softly. "He is an exhausting man."

Jack looked over at her. He had to agree. "You've got that right. But he knows something. He has to know something. For all intents and purposes it sounds like Carmen confided in him most of all."

"I think he understood her. I think he just does that. He understands people," Jill said. "I feel like he had sized us up as soon as he met us. It was almost like he already knew our questions before we even asked them."

"That is, until my question about Mark Emery. I'm curious. I don't even want to wait until tomorrow morning to get the answer. I'm not sure we even have that time," Jack said sternly. He hated to wait on anything that may hold up this investigation.

"I think whatever Nero has to tell us is something that we'd find interesting, but may not be pivotal to this case. Whatever it is, it's more information on Carmen and that's what we need right now."

Jack started the car. "I call him as Primary. Right now he's the person we know saw Carmen last, maybe even hours before she died. Maybe as she died. He's Primary."

Jill nodded. "Yeah. You're right. He doesn't seem like a killer at all and I have no idea what his motive would have been, but you're right. He's Primary. There's no one else closer right now." She didn't look happy about it.

"Ok. I'm starving. Let's get seafood."

Jill felt rumblings in her own stomach. "Sounds perfect."

They pulled away from Nero's house and started up the narrow drive. "As for motive, I'd say love or unrequited love at the very least. Jealousy maybe," Jack muttered. He sensed this was walking on dangerous territory with Jill, who appeared smitten with him.

Jill stared at the road ahead watching as the ground moved under them quiet for a moment. She shivered. "I feel like we're missing something big time here." Her voice was soft.

Jack nodded. "I agree. So, let's review. We've got a victim who is a young socialite married to a prominent businessman and whose father is a controversial Senator. She is a volunteer in the community and keeps a relatively low profile, except that she has some of the most coveted vehicles in America. She was a tutor to a young boy who was discovered missing the same morning she was found dead. As if that's not enough she's a Wiccan or a Witch by most people's definition and has kept this a secret from her husband. Actually the only person who even knows about this is her brother-in-law. Her relationship to her brother-in-law is yet unknown, however it is known that she was romantically involved with someone other than her husband. Maybe someone knows this. It looks like Carmen likes to keep secrets, at least from her husband, that is."

"Oh, God, you can't make this stuff up, can you?" Jill breathed. "Now that you've put it out there, Carmen seems so disillusioned."

Jack nodded. "I think Carmen needed to figure a lot of things out. Either she had a lot of time on her hands or she just liked a lot of mess."

"So, who the fuck was she messing around with? Nero?" Jill looked at him her brow furrowed with frustration. "Because quite frankly he's the only one who makes any sense. Who else would it have been?" She looked exacerbated and her face was slightly red from the persistent heat. She took a deep breath in and out. "Ok, yeah, I need seafood, and I'm totally frustrated." She sunk into her seat.

Just then Jill's phone buzzed. She answered it, "Simko." She nodded her jaw tight and her eyes narrowed. "Yes, of course, sir. Of course we will. We are doing all we can, sir." She nodded as she glared at the road buzzing by underneath, looked at Jack, and rolled her eyes. The Bureau. "We'll move faster. Yes. I totally agree. Yes." A pause. "Thank you, sir."

Jill closed her phone and glared at Jack. "Guess who?" Jack nodded. "As if this case isn't fucking bad enough, our lovely boss wants us to close it up soon. Renault may have struck again and he doesn't want to waste our time on this if he doesn't need to. He's doing a favor for Senator Ricci. The faster we can get this buttoned up the faster we can get back to the Renault case." Her tone was flat. She could only guess Jack's response.

Jack's eyes blazed fire. "Are you fucking kidding me? Renault *is* our case! We've worked on him for, like, forever. And this is how we're paid? Working Senator Ricci's daughter's crazy, fucked murder!! Who's running Renault?"

Jill was quiet and her face flushed. She swallowed, then looked over at Jack and said, "Bailey."

"Fuck!" Jack screamed into the car's interior. The sound was everywhere for a moment. "Fuckin', Bailey."

Special Agent Sean Bailey had been Jack's competitor from day one. They had survived Academy together but were neck-in-neck even to the end. Jack's ability to procure the Renault gig had been the final nail in Bailey's coffin. And now this.

"Have I told you how much I hate Senator Ricci?" Jack said.

"Maybe you nearly beheaded Carmen De Santo then," Jill said snidely. After all, there was still a victim. It didn't matter about politics. Carmen De Santo was dead and no matter what their personal affiliation, the girl's killer was just as important as anyone else's.

For a moment, Jack eyes glared searing into the pavement in front of them. The seconds of silence ticked by until Jack finally said, "You're right. I get it. I just hate Bailey." Then he let out a laugh decompressing the tension.

Jill grinned. "Jack, you always close to give me a heart attack. Let's just get some seafood and get back to Nero De Santo. Right?"

VALERIE R. KACIAN

CHAPTER SEVENTEEN

The moon was high. Light wisps of clouds caressed its face. Jill breathed in deeply looking up at the beauty that was the moon's face. She let out a breath feeling a deep peace seep into her bloodstream. She breathed in deeply again. Breathed out. The moon seemed to twinkle at her and the clouds continued to adorn Her face.

"Jill." The voice was a high, tinkle of a bell. "Jill."

Jill looked away from the moon. She was in a meadow in the middle of a forest somewhere. She had no idea how she had gotten here. She looked around for the voice. Out of the mist a woman appeared wearing a long, white dress. She was barefoot and her red hair sparked fire in the night. She glided closer to Jill as if she walked on air. She smiled her lips a deep red spreading showing perfectly white teeth. Her eyes, a steel-gray snakeskin sparkled in the moonlight. "Jill," Carmen said her voice a sharp bell in the air.

Jill breathed deeply but no words would come. The moon hovered over her like an omen. Somehow despite the moon she couldn't look away from Carmen De Santo.

Carmen stepped forward and took Jill's hand in her own. Carmen's hand felt like air, but somehow had the ability to grip and hold. Carmen continued to smile the mist seeping all around her.

"Jill, I'm ok. I'm really ok," her voice was soft and loving. "This is the place I need to be right now." She looked up at the moon her white skin smooth, her face peaceful. "Ah, She is beautiful isn't she? I love the moon."

Jill looked up at the moon, then back at Carmen. She still had nothing to say. Carmen giggled. "My car's a wreck. I loved that car." Her eyes looked sad for a moment, then she laughed again, and her laugh echoed into the night. "Look around you, Jill. I loved my car and yet you miss so much."

Jill looked back up at the moon. She couldn't help it. There was such a draw to the white fullness and the warm, white light.

Carmen let go of her hand and smiled wide again. Suddenly she clutched her stomach. Her eyes rolled in pain and she buckled forward. She wheezed loudly her red hair falling forward in torrents. Jill glanced at the moon again. Carmen stood up again, but this time her hand was still on her stomach and her eyes were more desperate. Jill looked down at Carmen's stomach and could see red seeping through her white dress and through her hands. "Oh God," Carmen breathed and cursed at once. She wheezed and hissed in pain. Carmen's green eyes went wide and filled with pain. Carmen stumbled back a few steps. The red continued to seep through her hands and soak into her dress.

"Jill, look for Omaha," she breathed. "You missed Omaha. On the mantle. On the mantle." She hissed again and bent over. A slow wail rose out of her. When she stood up again more of the deep, red blood was seeping through the fabric that covered her chest near her left breast. With one hand on her stomach and one hand on her breast Carmen let out an unholy scream brimming with anguish and pain. Her eyes blazed fire and her red mouth curled. "You don't want to see this. You don't want to see this. What comes next. Oh, what comes next," she hissed through her pain. "Find Omaha. He's innocent. Send my love to Omaha." She continued to step back into the fog. She faded becoming part of the night again. As Jill looked back up to the moon to find some peace and solitude, Carmen let out a blood-curdling scream that echoed through the forest.

Jill sat up her chest heaving, her skin soaked in sweat. She looked around the room wildly seeing only blackness for a moment. The silver light fading into the blackness slowly revealed the desk, armoire and walls of the hotel room. Jill bowed her head and waited until her breathing slowed down. Then she got up and walked to the bathroom. The light was bright and hurt her eyes when she turned it on. She splashed water on her face and then dried it. Even the cold water couldn't make her forget Carmen's screams. She looked at her pale face in the mirror her dark hair pulled into a ponytail. There were dark circles under eyes and her skin looked blotchy. With that Jill left the bathroom, shut the light off and rushed to the bed. She pulled the blankets up to her chin. Carmen De Santo in all her beauty, grace and pain was trying to tell her something. But what exactly?

Jack met her for breakfast the next morning. Jill sat with coffee, a bowl of fruit and nothing else. She was just staring at the table bags under her eyes, her skin pale when Jack finally put down his coffee and sighed. "Are you ok, Jill?"

Jill smiled softly and took a sip of her coffee. "I had the strangest dream last night. It was just so real." Jill told him about her dream and Jack shrugged.

"Dreams are like that sometime." Jack said and scooped up a forkful of scrambled eggs. "They resonate."

"No, you don't understand." Jill put her hand out to him on the table her eyes desperately searching his. "Carmen visited me last night."

Jack put his fork down and looked at her one eyebrow raised.

"It was just so real." She pulled her arm back defensively. She could feel Jack judging her. She took a deep breath, sat back and closed her eyes for a second. "It was horrific. She told me to look for Omaha. To send her love to Omaha and that he's innocent." She paused for a moment. "I know this sounds crazy, but for some reason I feel like we should pursue this more. I want to know who Omaha is."

Jack sighed and continued to eat his eggs. His silence began to unnerve Jill who sat up, then settled back in her chair, then sat up again. She took a sip of her coffee. "Ok. You think I'm crazy."

Jack looked up at her. "No, I don't. I think this case is affecting you for some reason and I'm a little worried, but not enough. I think your passion for this case will help us solve this. I'm thinking about next steps right now." He ate a bit of toast followed by a long swig of coffee. "I'll call IT. Have them try to piece together this Omaha. You're right. Carmen was having an affair on her husband and we haven't nearly been putting enough effort to gather information about this. We need to speak to this Omaha. For all we know he could be a suspect. Whatever the case, he certainly knows things about her her own husband doesn't even know."

Jill sipped her coffee and gave Jack an exhausted smile. "Thanks, Jack. Mostly, thanks for not calling me crazy, because I'm feeling more than a little crazy right now."

Their first stop that morning was to visit Marjorie Gray. During the ride over to her house Jack had called IT and instructed them on what to look for on Carmen's computer. They had been pulling all references to her Wiccan practices, which was, of course, valid, however Omaha would become the central focus from that point forward. Jill was relieved. It seemed crazy to think that Carmen may actually be making requests from beyond the grave, but Jill also knew it was insane to ignore a cop's instinct. Jack had explained that he felt that Carmen's voice in Jill's dream had been more of Jill telling herself what to focus on in the investigation.

Marjorie Gray lived in a white house with red shutters and a white picket fence. She was a short woman in her seventies with her white hair pulled up in a bun and abundant wrinkles on her face. A light layer of pink lip-gloss dusted her lips and a dot of blush accented each cheek. She kindly welcomed them in and served tea and "biscuits". Once both Jack and Jill were poured a cup of tea she settled onto a Victorian-inspired armchair and looked at them expectantly.

"Thank you so much for all of this, Ms. Gray. This is quite lovely," Jill said kindly. "We're here to discuss Carmen De Santo with you. We've been talking to a lot of people in town to get an idea about what may have happened to her. Did you know her?"

"Not personally, I'm afraid. She did not attend church and that is where I meet most folk." Marjorie took a sip of tea.

"There's a rumor here that you were opposed to her coming into town once she married Armand De Santo. Is that at all true?" Jack placed his cup of tea on the table and looked over at Ms. Gray.

Marjorie looked at him a moment her lips pursed. "When I heard that Armand had married a socialite from New York, I must admit I was concerned. I was worried she may bring her New York crowd here."

"Did she?" Jack asked.

"No. Carmen kept to herself mostly. She was gentle. It's just too bad she didn't partake in the church here. She would have been a wonderful asset, that I am sure." She smiled weakly.

"I'm sure she would have, Ms. Gray," Jill said kindly. "Can you think of anything else that may help us find who hurt Carmen?"

"She spent too much time in the woods," Marjorie said simply. "I'm not surprised she was found in those woods. People shouldn't spend so much time alone in the woods. It's dangerous." Marjorie shook her head and took a sip of tea.

"How do you know she spent time in the woods?" Jack asked.

"I saw her one day." Marjorie's lips were pursed as she said this. "I was out for a stroll and I saw her entering the woods with a bag over her shoulder."

Marjorie had been curious. She had followed Carmen at a safe distance. Carmen had seemed in a world of her own staring up at the sky from time to time and adjusting her bag. In minutes she had reached a clearing in the woods. Marjorie watched as she opened up her bag and pulled out candles, bags of dried herbs, water in a small container and a container of what could have been sugar or salt. Carmen sat for a while after setting out her items and rolled her head back and forth her eyes closed. When she opened her eyes she began to chant and light the candles. Marjorie had been so afraid she had fled the woods and headed straight home.

"What do you think Carmen was doing out there?" Jill asked.

Marjorie's eyes were wide, then she scowled. "I have no idea, but it was most certainly not God's work, I can tell you that," she said firmly.

A few minutes later Jack and Jill thanked Ms. Gray for her time and headed back to their sedan. "Waste of time," Jack grumbled.

"I agree, but at least now we know it's a waste of time. Seriously, can this town have any more busybodies?"

They proceeded back to Nero De Santo's house in silence. It was another bright, hot day in what should have been the waning of the summer season. For all intents and purposes it felt more like mid-July with an extra dose of humidity sprinkled in. Just as they rounded the curve to Nero's house Jill muttered, "Carmen told me I missed something on the mantel."

Jack glanced at her with a bit of concern. "Carmen did?"

"In my dream." Jack parked the car and pulled the key from the ignition. "She said something about the mantel when she was talking about looking for Omaha. Do you think she means Nero's mantel? After all, we were just there…"

Jack looked at her his eyes soft. "I say we go in there and ask Nero about Mark Emery and Carmen's relationship to him. If you feel better taking a look at the mantle while you're at it, go for it."

Jill slumped in her seat. "You think I'm crazy."

"No." He paused and looked out the window. "Well, maybe a little." He gave her a grin. "But that's what it takes some time, right?"

Jill grinned back. "I hope so. I don't want to just be totally off my rocker for no reason."

The sun beat down on them as they approached Nero's porch once again. This time although enchanting the hot weather overshadowed any reason to linger in the gardens.

"Somehow I feel like I've been here before," Jack whispered when they got to the door, as Jill giggled.

Nero opened the door with his usual flourish. He nodded to each of them. "Welcome. Welcome," he said in his lilting voice. "I must apologize for yesterday. I have some patients who need special treatment and this was one of them," Nero stated simply as he led them to the living room once more.

"That's certainly all right," Jack stated. "We understand your position here and do not mean to intrude. It just seems that you were very close to Carmen and being so you may actually know more about what could have led to her death than you may realize."

Nero nodded for a moment and looked pensive. Jack was not sure but in that moment he thought he might have seen a tear in his eye. "Would anyone care for coffee or tea?" Nero asked breaking his own trance.

"Coffee would be great," Jill responded.

"Then I will return." Bowing slightly Nero left the room to retrieve their coffee.

"I needed him gone. I need to look at the mantle over there." Jill got up and walked over to the fireplace mantle. There were a number of pictures on the mantle and she wanted just a moment to inspect each one. Quite a few of them were pictures of Carmen with her husband, with friends, with her mother, etc. There did not seem to be anything unusual since the pictures were of family. Then Jill's eyes narrowed in on one item that didn't quite match the others. It was a picture of just Carmen and Nero leaning against a car smiling. Carmen's hair was long and wavy and she wore sunglasses on her head. The item was a brilliantly colored postcard in bright orange and red with a scene behind Carmen and Nero. Above their heads was written "Nebraska" as if it were a postcard that someone would send someone else that had gone to Nebraska. It was just a campy, cheesy memento from a past vacation, however there was something in the picture that did not sit well with Jill.

Just then Nero reentered the room carrying a tray with a coffee pot, cups, spoons, cream, and sugar. Jill whipped around quickly as if she had been caught stealing or staring at someone changing near an open window. Nero gave her no notice as he set down the tray and began pouring coffee.

"So, you were telling us about the Emery's. You didn't seem very happy yesterday when we brought them up in conversation," Jack said accepting a cup of coffee.

Jill crept back to her seat and tried not to stare at the mantle. What had Carmen been trying to tell her? Jill accepted coffee and tried to concentrate on what Nero was saying.

"Annie and Tom Emery are not very nice people," Nero started. He sat back in his chair cradling his cup of coffee. "I don't even like saying that about them, but it's true. I like to think there is something redeeming about everyone, but it's hard to find that in these people." He took a sip of coffee trying to collect his thoughts. "Carmen began tutoring Mark Emery last year. His grades had slipped severely and when she heard about this and knew they were receiving aid from the town she knew they would not be able to afford a tutor. She volunteered to help and wanted to try to convince Annie Emery that tutoring would help her son tremendously. Although Annie did not seem too worried about her son's education, Carmen explained to her that the tutoring sessions could always be stopped if there didn't seem to be much progress. Carmen went over there once a week and sat with Mark Emery and helped him with all of his assignments. Tom was never around when she was there and Annie kept an eye on her at first, but then resigned herself to drinking wine and watching TV. The house was filthy. Mark's clothing was always dirty. Yet Carmen persisted. His grades got better and with each session Mark talked to Carmen more and more. One would think this was progress even if his parents didn't seem to care one way or the other.

"Well, one day Carmen noticed a large burn on Mark's arm. She sought out Annie in the living room and asked her about it. Annie said Mark had burned himself on the stove by accident. Carmen accepted this as a plausible explanation. Then things got strange. Carmen began to notice bruises and what looked like cigarette burns on Mark. She was beside herself upset and did not know what to do. When she visited the following week she noticed that not only did Mark have a black eye, but Annie's face was bloated and red and she, too, had a black eye. Carmen confronted Annie right then and there and told her she would be happy to get them help. That they could leave immediately to go to a shelter. Somewhere Tom would never find them. Annie cried and tried to lie and say that they had both fallen down the stairs, but Carmen did not believe them. It turned into a huge argument and Carmen became even more worried about Mark and Annie Emery. After she left that day she returned two days later and Annie met her on the porch. Annie explained to Carmen that Mark would no longer need tutoring from her and that she needed to leave immediately. She was angry with Carmen and insulted her good standing in the community, her money, and even her cars. Carmen had left feeling dejected and upset that she could not help the family. She had nightmares. She was physically sick when she thought about it. She did not want to report them to the police for fear that Mark would be removed from the home and further damage would be done. She tried to visit Annie again on more than one occasion but no one answered the door. She began a series of ritual and protection spells for the family since she had no idea what else to do. She also called on the Goddess to give her better insight on how to help this family. She was completely torn. Finally she simply resolved to find peace in what she could and could not do and she continued her spell work for the benefit of the family. It was all she could do, but she never forgot them." Nero shook his head.

"Maybe a month or two ago Carmen was at the local hospital picking up some supplies for the Hospice Association. While she was there she walked by a room and happened to glance in. What she saw nearly made her sick on the spot. Mark Emery was having a cast fitted on his right arm and Annie Emery was standing right next to him tears in her eyes. Carmen was glued to the spot and couldn't help but stare. Annie looked up at her at that moment and Carmen said the look in her eyes could have killed. Carmen had rushed off to finish her errand. The next morning she reported Tom and Annie Emery to the local police."

Jill was glued to the story the postcard nearly forgotten. There she was chasing postcards and here was an incident right in front of her that was far more significant. Mark Emery was missing. Carmen was dead. What had happened? There was most certainly a link. Or was there?

"Well, what happened?" Jack asked. "Did the police do anything?"

Nero looked over at them, rolled his eyes and pursed his lips. "She was told to stop being such a busybody, of all things. Lieutenant Copeland was less than sympathetic to her condition. He said that both Tom and Annie Emery had never caused any trouble in town and although they were poor that did not automatically mean that abuse was involved. He promised her he would visit the Emery's for an inspection, but Carmen did not feel too comforted by this. A couple weeks after making her initial report she tried to speak with Lieutenant Copeland again to ask him what had resulted from his visit, but he simply told her it was police business at this point and confidential. Carmen was never able to resolve the issue before her death." Nero sat back his eyes glazed with tears. "She wanted that boy to have a normal life."

Jack leaned forward. "What do you think happened to Mark Emery?"

Nero sat looking out across his living room in thought for a moment, then his eyes shifted back to Jack and Jill. "Honestly, Special Agent, I hope to God he ran away. It was his only chance."

"Did Carmen ever contact Mark directly after speaking to police or perhaps even before?" Jill asked.

Nero shook his head. "She did not want to scare the boy. She didn't think it was her place to approach him directly. She wanted to work with his parents and the authorities on this. These were the proper channels."

"So, there's no way Carmen could have told Mark to run away or attempted to help him get away?" Jill asked directly.

Nero looked at her for a moment. His manner was much subdued from their conversation yesterday and although he may have taken offense at her question he merely shook his head. "Not a chance."

Jill glanced back up at the mantle. The mantle itself and her dream suddenly seemed grossly insignificant compared to what Nero had just told them. This was concrete. This was real. They needed to run everything down and verify Nero's story. And she had a funny feeling they were running out of time.

After verifying that that was all Nero knew about Carmen's involvement with Mark Emery, Jack and Jill gave Nero their business cards and told him to call them if he could remember anything further that may help. When Nero took the card, Jill noticed that on his left hand near his thumb were tattooed the letters NB. Jill assumed the letters were the initials of an old or current girlfriend and couldn't help but grin when she saw them. It was one of the strangest places to have a sweetheart tattoo she had ever seen.

They walked back to the car in silence. The sun had disappeared behind mammoth, gray clouds and Jill was convinced it would rain again. She hoped that this time the rain would cool everything off for a couple days. The oppressive heat was becoming overbearing.

Once back in the car she said, "Is this how it always is in New England?"

"What?" Jack asked turning over the engine.

"Hot, then gloomy?" Jack only looked at her. "Sorry, this heat is really getting to me."

"Speaking of heat, I have a feeling things are really heating up with this case." Jack grinned as he put the engine in drive and pulled away from the curb.

"Ha. Ha. Very funny," Jill said letting out a bit of a chuckle. She couldn't help herself. Jack's occasional cheesy jokes always made her smile. Even on her worst days. "Seriously, though, Jack, this is all so crazy. I don't even know which way to turn at this point. Carmen was a Wiccan in a very Christian town. Carmen was cheating on her husband. Carmen's father is one of the more hated men in America. And now this. Any one of these could have gotten her killed." Jill leaned back in her seat and let out a deep breath.

"True. But remember Nero was the last person that we know of to see her alive. She left his house and never made it back home. He has no alibi. We need to verify his story. Quite frankly, this could all be just made up junk to lead us off the path that would lead us directly to him."

"But what's his motive? Seriously, what is it?" Jill asked wearily.

"Jealousy. Maybe Nero was romantically interested in her and all the poultices in the world wouldn't make her change her mind about Armand. He finds out she's cheating on Armand and when he realizes it's not with him he goes a little crazy and kills her." Jack looked at her expectantly.

"Maybe. Anything's possible. But that just sounds so complicated."

"Look, Nero is a super strange guy! He spent a significant time with Carmen. She was a beautiful, vibrant woman. He would be crazy not to fall for her. If he found out she was with someone else, it would break his heart. Especially if she didn't even confide in him as a friend."

"Or maybe he did know. It sounds like he may have been Carmen's best friend around here. Maybe she did tell him and he tried over and over to convince her to stop seeing this person and maybe even threatened to tell Armand. It's quite possible that evening she came over they were arguing and one thing led to another," Jill said. "You're right. He's still our major suspect. He's everywhere in this." She paused for a moment in thought. "We need to talk to Lieutenant Copeland. And we need to talk to the Emery's. Now we may know why Tom lied to you about knowing Carmen. He certainly doesn't want us around asking questions. And if

Nero's story is true, we need to know what happened to Mark Emery. We don't know if Carmen approached him and told him to run away. The more I think about this, none of this is making sense."

"Well, sounds to me like we have ourselves a real mystery here," Jack said grinning.

Jill grinned back. She couldn't help herself.

CHAPTER EIGHTEEN

That afternoon Jack and Jill again found themselves in Lieutenant Copeland's office. Lieutenant Copeland looked over at them a sea of papers on his desk, then sat back in his chair. "Any news for me?" He looked tired. Dark circles hung below his eyes and he kept blinking like he was trying to ward off sleep. He took a sip of coffee.

"Well, actually, more like a question for you," Jill started. "This may seem kind of unusual, but did Carmen ever report an incident or incidents of child abuse or domestic violence concerning the Emery's?"

Lieutenant Copeland looked at them for a moment. "Well, you have been busy," he said softly. He was quiet for a moment. "Yes, yes, she did. About two months ago."

"Do you have a copy of the report?" Jack asked.

"Yes, of course." He sat up in his seat. "Look, Carmen always meant well. She just had a lot of time on her hands and she was extra-sensitive about everything. If she saw a paper cut on your arm she'd think you were being abused or mistreated in some way. She came in here very emotional and said she had seen Mark at the hospital getting a cast on his arm. She was worried there had been some kind of child abuse since she said she had also seen a couple of bruises on his arm at one point. I tried to calm her down as best as I could and I told her to please allow us to do our jobs to investigate her claim. I told her I'd visit the Emery's."

"Did you visit the Emery's?"

"Yes, it's all in the report. I visited them. Nothing seemed out of the ordinary. Mark was quiet while I was there, but this was not unusual for him. His arm was in a cast and when I asked him about it, he explained he had fractured it playing football with his dad in the backyard. Tom verified the story. They immediately brought him to the hospital. I even went so far as to check the hospital reports and speak to a couple of people there and by all accounts no one at the hospital suspected a child abuse case."

Jill nodded. It sounded as if Lieutenant Copeland had done his job the best he knew how. "Did Carmen ever follow up with you again after initially speaking with you?" she asked.

"Yes, she asked what we were doing about this and seemed even more upset about it. I simply told her that this was a police matter at this point and therefore it was confidential. I explained to her that I was doing all I could to investigate and monitor the situation. I did not tell Carmen this, but I had asked Annie why Carmen wasn't tutoring for her anymore. Annie was very upset and said she had had an argument with Carmen and discontinued her services. When I asked what the argument was about she was embarrassed to tell me that Carmen had accused them of abusing their son. I had not realized Carmen had spoken to her directly about the issue and was rather shocked by this. I offered my sympathy and gave her the name and number of someone who would be willing to continue tutoring services. This person was also an undercover investigator with the police and would be able to continue monitoring the household covertly. The investigator tutored Mark once a week in a similar manner to Carmen and reported no evidence of child or spousal abuse. We tried everything we could to thoroughly investigate, but there was nothing there."

"We'll need to speak with the investigator if possible. And we'll need to speak directly to Annie and Tom Emery. We've been having trouble getting in touch with them, although we've made several attempts." Jack said simply.

"Special Agent Pellingworth, with all due respect Tom and Annie are scared to death for their son. They are trying to grieve. The possibility of this child being alive at this point is slim to none. Let's just be honest here. The last thing they probably want to do is talk about Carmen's death when all they can think about is their own son."

"Then why would Tom tell me he didn't know Carmen?"

"He didn't. Annie knew her. Tom was working in the day. I don't think he ever even met Carmen." Lieutenant Copeland let out an exasperated sigh. "Look, I'll talk to Detective Winsler and get you some time with the Emery's. I'll get you time with my investigator. And I'll get you those reports. We have a lot going on here in Lake Shore. More than ever. We want to find this boy and we want to find out who killed Carmen. Putting this all to bed will do wonders for the community. Everyone is flat out scared to death. Mothers won't leave their children's sides. Young women won't walk alone anywhere. We get more calls about potential break-ins and people of suspect than you can imagine. We want our town back." He let out another tired sigh. "We deserve to have our town back."

"I couldn't agree with you more," Jack stated. "That's why it's so important that we get that time we need with the Emery's. They may know more than they realize about what happened to Carmen. We're getting there, and we hope that we can get this wrapped up soon so everyone can feel safe again. Absolutely."

"You'll have your report in a matter of hours. I'll see what I can do about the other stuff."

Jill picked up the report and looked it over while Jack ordered a tuna melt and French fries. They were at the local diner catching a quick lunch before they met with Detective Reynolds, the investigator from across state who Lieutenant Copeland had asked to work with the Emery's. As luck would have it he would be in the area early that afternoon and had agreed to meet Jack and Jill at the police station to discuss his findings.

"Well, it's all here. No question. Lieutenant Copeland wasn't lying. He was trying to help as best as he knew how," Jill said. She put the report back on the table and looked up at Jack. "I just...I know there's something more here. We're missing something."

"It's become complicated," Jack said. "Like it wasn't complicated enough."

"Anything from IT from her computer?" Jill asked.

"Nothing yet. If they had something really juicy they would call, but it's certainly worth checking in with them."

"Well, I'm looking forward to getting some face time with the Emery's. They are totally creepy and I think in some ways they are being protected. Detective Winsler especially seems to be protecting them."

The lunches arrived and Jack picked up a French fry and dunked it in ketchup. "This is Detective Winsler's case and quite frankly a lot of time has gone by and he hasn't done a damn thing. At least our case is dead. He has a live case. He should be all over the place on this." Jack used the French fry to accentuate his point.

Jill giggled. "Never underestimate a man with a French fry."

Jack grinned.

Jill speared her salad with her fork. "I'd say Detective Winsler has reason to be worried. No one likes the FBI snooping around criticizing everything. You know?"

"Then he should do his damn job. And stop getting in our way," Jack said the French fry still in hand.

"Would you just eat the damn French fry?" Jill giggled.

On the way back to the police station, Jill got behind the wheel and Jack made the call to IT to discuss their findings. Although they were working hard, Carmen had made very little effort to hide anything. Email exchanges with her lover were rather banal with little to none of the overt sexual content that was usually discovered. It did not appear she spent much time on the web and when she did she was researching spells and Pagan ritual. Nothing new there. He thanked them for their time and continued efforts and told them to report anything unusual ASAP.

"Well?" Jill asked.

"Nothing unusual. Even the email exchanges with her lover were pretty clean. They are still looking and trying to make connections. They are working on trying to determine the location of the boyfriend she was emailing. This would help tremendously in our efforts."

"Because quite frankly, we need to speak to this person. This person could know something or may be our killer." Jill parked the car and turned off the engine. "Ready, Captain?" She asked grinning.

Jack grinned back. "Ay. Ay."

They met Detective Reynolds in one of the private interrogation rooms. This would allow them the privacy they needed so that Detective Reynolds' previous cover would not be blown. Detective Reynolds was a tall, attractive man in his early thirties. With light-brown hair and an engaging smile, Jill could see why he was chosen for this type of undercover mission. He had more of an air of a social worker than of a police detective. He crossed his legs, tented his long fingers and gave each of them a kind smile.

"Thank you so much for agreeing to meet with us, Detective Reynolds," Jack said kindly.

"It is no trouble at all. I will do what I can to help. This is such a tragic set of events." His voice was calm and unassuming. Jack imagined that many a person in the past had told this man things they probably wouldn't have admitted to anyone else.

"We understand that you worked with the Emery family undercover after there was a report of domestic violence in the household," Jill started.

"Yes, I did. Lieutenant Copeland told me there was a report, which I now understand was from Carmen De Santo. He asked if I could work with the boy, Mark, posing as a tutor to monitor the household situation. He told me that a previous tutor had felt there was some abuse present. I was happy to help. After clearing with my own station, I started working with them right away."

"What was your impression of Tom and Annie?" Jill asked.

"Initially, I was shocked at the state of their home. It was quite grimy and not necessarily the most hygienic place for a young child to be growing up. I tried to keep my focus on the task at hand, however, which would be actual physical abuse and not the living conditions. I only met Annie at first. She was very quiet and preferred to stay in the living room during our tutoring. She seemed almost fearful of me. I did not meet Tom right away, although I did meet him shortly before Mark went missing." He uncrossed, then recrossed his legs. "Tom was an interesting man. He had a lot of questions about what I was helping Mark with in school. His eyes were piercing and he almost looked angry that I was there. I got the distinct impression that he was a rather intense man. But "intense" doesn't mean that he was an abuser so I tried to keep an open mind."

"What about Mark?" Jack asked.

Detective Reynolds smiled slightly to himself. "Mark is actually a brilliant boy. I don't think either of his parents realized how smart he really is. Maybe they don't even care. He was quiet at first, but after a while he started warming up a little. He is certainly not a gregarious child by any means, but it was nice that he became comfortable with me after a couple of weeks."

"Did he talk to you about his parents? If there was any abuse? Any issues?" Jill asked.

Detective Reynolds chuckled softly to himself. "When I said he opened up a little it was to talk about sports and movies. He most certainly never said anything about his parents and I didn't pry. I was there to observe."

"Did you observe any signs of abuse?" Jack asked.

"Abuse of alcohol, absolutely. Annie was never without a wine glass when I did see her. I got the impression that this was her usual behavior. There was nothing else. Annie, although half in the bag most of the time, did not have any bruises on her face or body. Mark was also clean. No bruises. No marks."

"What do you think may have happened to Mark Emery?" Jack asked the difficult question.

Detective Reynolds was quiet for a moment. He stared off across the room then turned his attention back to Jack and Jill. "I wish I knew. Maybe he ran away. Kids do that sometime. But we all know the time-frame here and most likely if he ran away he'd have had second thoughts by now and would have returned home. If someone did take him, I can only hope he is safe and well. Or at the very least not in any pain." Detective Reynolds looked pained himself at the very thought.

"Did you ever at any point get the impression that Carmen De Santo may have told him to run away? Did Mark ever say anything like this?" Jack asked.

"No. Like I said, Mark may have opened up to a point, but we didn't talk about everything. He never even mentioned Carmen to me. I didn't even know she was the one who reported the Emery's until just now."

After verifying that there was nothing further Detective Reynolds could provide, they both thanked him for him time and left the station. As they headed out, Lieutenant Copeland called out to them that if they had time they could meet with Detective Winsler in another hour or so. They both agreed to come back. After jumping in the car, Jill leaned the back of her head against her seat and sighed.

"I feel like we're running around and around in circles here. Do you think maybe Carmen was just insane?" Jill said. "I mean, it doesn't look like anything was actually happening with Mark Emery."

"But he's missing. And she's dead," Jack pointed out. "So, something was going on."

"Look. We just need a few minutes with them, ok? I don't really care if Annie and Tom would rather not talk to us. Carmen had a direct relationship with the family. And we're talking to everyone. So, I don't care. They have to comply," Jack said. As he talked he placed his hand firmly on the table and looked over at Detective Winsler with an expression of both anger and determination.

Trying to diffuse what could be an ugly confrontation, Jill interjected before Detective Winsler could speak. "We all want good results here, Detective. We're trying to find our killer and the clock is ticking. Same for you trying to find Mark Emery. We all need answers. And we need them fast. Lieutenant Copeland has expressed to us that this town is terrified and I can understand that. We need to work together. Annie and Tom need to work with us. They may not be comfortable speaking to FBI agents. That can be scary to some people, but if you encourage them to speak to us, we may get more answers together then we ever could separately. They could know something they don't even realize they know."

Detective Winsler looked at both of them for a moment as if sizing them up. Then he leaned back, tented his fingers, and smirked. "Honestly, I was worried about having the FBI in here. I thought you'd try to get involved in Mark Emery's case even though that's not what you are here for…"

Jack began to protest his back straight as a board as he puffed out his chest in agitation.

"Hear me out, Agent," Detective Winsler warned raising one finger. Jill looked over at Jack her eyes wide with protest. "But you've stayed on your side of the fence and so have we. I agree we need to join forces. It's evident that Carmen and Mark had a relationship and therefore here we are with our paths crossing." He paused for a moment looking at them. "I will convince the Emery's to talk to you. I only ask one thing."

"What is it, Detective?" Jill asked gently.

"I would like to sit in on the interview. And the Emery's can meet with you at the place of their choosing."

"Sounds like you're telling us more than asking, Detective?" Jack seethed.

Jill glanced at him worriedly. "This is fine by us. This isn't an interrogation, Detective. We aren't accusing them of anything. We aren't involved in the allegations of abuse. We just need to know about their previous relationship with Carmen. That's all. It's pretty simple actually. Nothing out of the ordinary. We've talked to a lot of people here. And we'll be understanding with them. We know this is difficult."

"Ok. Tomorrow. I'll call you." With that Detective Winsler stood up and exited the room without even a handshake with either of the agents.

"What a fucking prick," Jack muttered.

Jill couldn't agree more.

VALERIE R. KACIAN

CHAPTER NINETEEN

It was midnight. The moon was high and there was hardly a cloud in the sky. Jill was walking through the woods enjoying the warmth of the night on her skin. It would not be long before Fall and Winter would be here and the evenings would bring a bone-numbing chill. Jill walked along looking out over the forest until she reached a clearing.

A young woman sat in the clearing her back to Jill. Jill thought she saw a flash of red in the woman's hair as she moved. The woman was kneeling on the grass busy with something in front of her. Jill saw a warm, yellow glow in front of the woman and as Jill walked closer she could smell incense in lavender and cherry in the air. The woman was softly chanting to herself. As Jill got even closer, the woman swept her arms up above her head and arched her back to the sky. In the moonlight it was obvious who she was. Carmen De Santo. Carmen called to the sky, "Bless these gifts we have before us! Bless this child!!" Her voice carried itself as if autonomously into the night. At that moment Carmen returned to a supine position, then turned around slowly to face Jill. Her green eyes sparkled and she grinned. "Welcome. Our first guest has arrived." Her voice was soft, but with an eerie, ethereal tone.

Jill could not help but be mesmerized by her. In the glow of the candlelight Carmen's head looked like it was on fire and her eyes cast an almost unearthly glow. She looked more a spirit than a living, breathing creature.

"Come. Into the circle," Carmen breathed. Her mouth curved into an inviting grin. Jill walked closer to the candles and sat an arm's length away from Carmen. Carmen faced the candles again and began a chant. As she did her hands waved about as if she were shaping patterns from the air. She closed her eyes and said simply, "There are mysteries to solve." Jill remained silent. "Close your eyes, Jill. When you open them a puzzle piece to your mystery will be revealed to you."

Jill did as she was told not only because she wanted to, but also because she felt compelled to do so. Carmen's voice was soft, yet had a tone that could not be ignored. Jill began to breathe in the incense deeply in and out. In and out. In. And out.

"Open your eyes, Jill."

Jill opened her eyes to see Carmen running across the field as if she were a child. Her feet were bare and her sheer, white dress billowed around her. She giggled as she ran. Just beyond her Jill noticed that a pink Thunderbird had been parked. Carmen ran over to it and squealed with joy. Leaning against the Thunderbird was none other than Nero De Santo. Carmen leaped into his arms giving him a huge hug. She turned around and smiled as if awaiting her picture to be taken.

It was then a series of pictures flashed before Jill's eyes. Nero De Santo's mantle from a distance. Carmen as she turned to welcome Jill to her circle. A close up of the postcard of Nero and Carmen in Nebraska. Zeroing in on what was behind them. A Thunderbird. A pink Thunderbird. The NB tattoo on Nero's hand. Carmen's wide smile. Jill felt dizzy as if the entire world was spinning, but she couldn't add it all together.

Carmen giggled loudly. The sound shook Jill as if cold water had been poured on her face. She looked over at Carmen and Nero who remained frozen posing for the picture in front of the Thunderbird. Then she had it. She knew. She knew. Jill felt as if her head would explode and that she couldn't breathe. The air kept pulling itself from her lungs. She gasped and sunk to her knees. She looked wildly at Carmen, who was becoming more and more blurry. Oh no. Oh no. What was happening to her? Now that she knew! Jill tried desperately to draw a complete breath. The forest around her was spinning, spinning, spinning.....

Jill sat up and drew a deep, loud breath. Jill looked wildly around the dark room unable to orient herself. After a few breaths she recognized the room as her hotel room. She looked down to see her tank top was nearly soaked with sweat. She continued to look around wildly. What was it? She felt as if an answer had come to her. She searched her brain to remember what had gripped her before she started to have trouble breathing.

And then it hit her. "Oh my God. Oh my God. Oh my God." She began chanting this as she rushed out of her bed and threw on her complimentary robe. She rushed out of her room the door slamming against the wall upon her exit. She ran across the hall to Jack's room and began knocking on his door. She knocked until her fist began to ache.

Suddenly the door flung open. Jack glared at her his eyes blinking away the lights from the hallway. "What?" he said to her rudely.

"Jack. I know. I know who Omaha is," Jill breathed.

Jack took her arm and pulled her into his room. He closed the door and looked at her. "Jill, you look insane. It's 3:00 in the morning. Are you sleep-walking?"

Jill grabbed both of his arms. "Jack, it's Nero. Omaha is Nero."

It was 4:00 in the morning. Jack had brewed two cups of coffee from the mini-coffee machine in his hotel room. Jill sat in her bathrobe stirring a mini-moo creamer into her coffee and staring at the floor. Jack sat next to her.

"So, you got this from a dream," Jack started.

Jill looked at him. "No. It was more like my dream drew together all the images from the past couple of days and gave me the answer. It's the postcard on the mantle. The tattoo on Nero's hand. That postcard was of Carmen and Nero on some vacation with her Thunderbird in the background. Her Thunderbird is named Omaha according to its placard and Nero has a tattoo with the letter NB on it. Nebraska. I don't know what happened between Nero and Carmen on this trip to Omaha, Nebraska, but it was clearly important to them. Enough to be just about everywhere." Jill took a sip of coffee.

"Jill, this is huge. This is paramount. It makes Nero De Santo our number one suspect. As far as we know he was the last to see her alive. That is besides the killer. And now this. Do you have any idea how insane this is?"

"But remember everything he told us checks out. We know about the Wiccan stuff. And she definitely talked to the police about the Emery's. I can't see any lies here." Jill looked at him puzzled.

"Nero could be the perfect liar. He's good. But we never talked to him about a romantic relationship with Carmen. That could change everything." Jack paused and took a sip of coffee. "We need more proof."

Jill looked at him her eyes wide. "What do you mean? More proof? I think I brought a lot to the table." She was annoyed.

"You did. But it's nothing that absolutely points to him. I'm not saying it's not enough to talk about it, but I wish we had something more. Something absolutely concrete."

Jill put her coffee cup down suddenly and her eyes were wide. "You're right. What if it's not Nero? I can one hundred percent believe that Nero and Carmen had a romantic relationship, but we can't prove he killed her. Someone else would have had to have had a way bigger motive." She sat up straight looking Jack directly in the eyes.

"Armand," Jack said softly. He looked away. "He was away. He had an alibi. There are witnesses to prove his alibi."

"Do you really think Armand De Santo would get his hands dirty for this?" Jill asked incredulously. "He could have hired out."

Jack was silent for a moment. "This is what we do. We talk to Nero again and we squeeze him this time. No Mr. & Mrs. Nice Guy. It's all business. He's a suspect and a primary one and maybe he was using the Emery's to throw us off and buy himself some time. We push. Hard."

"And we pray like Hell we have something concrete on his romantic connection to Carmen," Jill concurred.

Just then Jack's phone buzzed. Text message. He glanced at it. As he did so a smiled started to warm his face. "Look at this."

Jill got up and looked at the phone in his outstretched hand. It was IT informing them that the computer connection to Omaha was from a person who resided in Lake Shore, specifically in Nero De Santo's neighborhood. Party of one. Jill looked up at Jack. This couldn't have come at a better time and she couldn't help but wonder if they were getting some otherworldly assistance on this one. "Puzzle piece received. Thank you, Carmen."

VALERIE R. KACIAN

PART TWO: A SET OF CIRCUMSTANCES

CHAPTER TWENTY

Jack didn't like it one bit. Not one bit. After showering, changing for the day and getting breakfast, Jack and Jill had received a call from Detective Winsler. The Emery's were willing to speak with them at the police station at 10:00 that morning. This was about the same time that Jack and Jill had planned to arrive unexpectedly at Nero De Santo's door. Jill had suggested that they split up to take care of both meetings and to avoid wasting any more time. She had explained with some earnestness that she felt they were losing time on this case and they needed to finish it up. Although Jack had to agree he also desperately wanted to interrogate Nero, as well as meet with the Emery's. Since they both couldn't agree who should go where, they drew straws. Jill had drawn Nero. He had drawn the Emery's. In his opinion this was an abomination, but Jill had gotten what she wanted. He couldn't imagine that Jill would be able to effectively interrogate Nero alone. Just the sight of the man made her weak at the knees. And, on the other hand, he wasn't so sure he could keep his cool with the Emery's. The amount of protection they were receiving was unsettling to him. They had decided that Jill would take the car so that if she ran into any trouble with Nero she could get out of there fast. She could also always call Jack, who would be at the station with several police officers ready to assist if necessary. Jill didn't know it but upon arrival to the station Jack had asked if one of the police officers could run surveillance in the area, then tuck away out of sight to watch out for Jill should she need any additional help. When cornered potential killers could strike out like cats and that could be very dangerous for an agent out alone.

Jack sauntered into the conference room ten minutes early, and since no one else had yet arrived, helped himself to a cup of coffee. He looked out the window that overlooked the back campus of the police station. Autumn had arrived overnight to Lake Shore. That morning had been quite chilly despite the sun. Weather reports promised highs in the upper seventies, however it was evident that Summer was making Her final exit.

Jack took out his cell phone. He drafted a text to Jill. "Where are you?" He couldn't help but worry about her. They had been on separate interrogations during past investigations, but for some reason Jack worried more about Jill losing her rationale than her personal safety when she spoke with Nero. He knew this sounded strange given Jill's mission, but he couldn't help it. Jill seemed unusually susceptible lately. Although Jill had also come to some striking conclusions in her sleep, Jack was worried about her mental health. They needed to get this case solved. And fast.

The door opened. Jack turned around to see Detective Winsler entering the room. Behind him Annie and Tom Emery hovered. Detective Winsler smile. "Ah, you are here already," he stated. "Great to see you, Agent Pellingworth."

Jack smiled and shook Detective Winsler's outstretched hand. He looked past the detective to where the Emery's stood. This was going to be interesting.

Jill parked outside of Nero's house as her cell phone beeped a text message communication. She shut off the ignition and searched for her phone in her purse. Her hand gripped it and she pulled it out to view. It was Jack. Jill rolled her eyes. The moment they had pulled their locations she knew that Jack would have a problem with it. It wasn't that he was worried about her safety. She knew that. For some reason Jack thought her judgment had been skewed when it came to this case. Especially when Nero De Santo was involved. She had to admit. Nero was an incredibly attractive man, but she was a professional. And as such she was ready to drill into Nero this morning with the force of a great white shark. She would be relentless until she had her answers. Jill shook her head and texted that she was at her location. She hoped Jack would leave it at that.

Jill took a deep breath and couldn't help but silently call out to Carmen to give her strength. She opened the door and entered the chilly air. She made up her way up to the front door, took a deep breath and knocked loudly.

She waited a moment. When she was just about to knock again, the door opened. Nero De Santo stepped into view shirtless with only his pajama bottoms on. He looked at her quizzically. Jill took another deep breath. This would be interesting.

Tom Emery entered the room first. He was wearing a pair of dirty blue jeans and a red and black-checkered shirt. For all intents and purposes he looked like a lumberjack. His face had the reddish tinge of a chronic drinker and his eyes were a piercing blue. As he entered the room Jack felt a chill. He felt his jaw flex as he took a step forward and shook Tom Emery's hand. His hand was warm and rough with callous.

Following Tom was Annie Emery. Jack was curious about her. Besides a quick view of her at the police station and the graveyard he had not seen her up-close and personal. Annie walked tentatively behind her husband. Her eyes looked down at the ground. Jack noticed she was a very plain woman with mousy, dark-brown hair pulled back in a ponytail affixed to the nape of her neck. Her skin was quite pale and she wore a plain, brown dress that only made her appear all the more pale. Jack approached her to shake hands. She quickly gave her hand, which was cold and small like a bird's. It was gone as quickly as it had come. She never made eye contact with Jack, despite his attempt to connect. Detective Winsler pulled back seats for the two, then sat next to them.

Jack proceeded to sit across from all three of them and took a deep breath. "There is coffee," he said by way of a beginning of conversation.

He was met with silence.

Jill swallowed. Nero De Santo's chest seemed to be made of marble. He was carefully sculpted his skin the color of honey. "Agent Simko," he said simply. "What a pleasure." Her presence did not seem to bother him at all despite his condition. Jill began to wonder if he was actually as a good a liar as Jack had implied.

"We need to talk," she said her voice hard and serious. No pleasantries this time around.

"Well, then by all means. Come on in," he said pleasantly stepping aside to allow her to enter. Just before stepping inside Jill turned her head and saw a flash of what she could determine was a person in jeans and a T-shirt in the nearby wood. Plain-clothes or not she knew the stance. Cop. So Jack had called in reinforcements just in case. "Fuckin' Jack," she muttered to herself as she entered the foyer.

Jack took a sip of his coffee and looked over at the Emery's and Detective Winsler. "First of all, I want to thank you for taking the time to come in this morning. I understand this is a difficult time for both of you." He was met with silence. "The purpose of this meeting as I'm sure Detective Winsler explained to you is to discuss your relationship with Carmen De Santo. We have reason to believe that she tutored your son, Mark. Is that correct?"

Tom looked over at Detective Winsler as if he needed approval before he answered the question and Annie continued to look down at her hands clasped in her lap. Detective Winsler nodded at Tom.

Tom cleared his throat. "Yes. Carmen De Santo tutored Mark."

Jack took another sip of coffee and said casually, "I spoke with you a few days ago and you told me you didn't know Carmen De Santo. Was there any reason why you didn't want me to know about the relationship?"

Tom's eyes sparked. Jack could sense a fire beneath the surface of this man. "I never met Carmen De Santo. Annie knew her. I told you Annie knew her but she couldn't speak with you because she had a migraine." Detective Winsler patted him comfortingly on his arm.

Jack looked over at Annie. "Annie, how often did Carmen come over to tutor Mark?"

Annie looked up. Her eyes were wide and startled as if she were a deer caught in headlights. Perhaps she had been told she wouldn't have to speak with him directly.

"Carmen came over once a week," Tom answered for her.

"I'd like to hear this from Annie. As you said you did not know Carmen directly and Annie did so I really need Annie to answer for herself," Jack stated simply. He tried to keep the edge out of his voice. If he botched this with his temper Jill would never forgive him.

Tom shifted in his seat his agitation apparent, but he said nothing.

"Annie?" Jack offered.

Annie looked down at her lap quickly, then looked back up at Jack. Her eyes darted towards her husband as she answered. "Yes. Like Tom said, once per week." Her voice was a thin sound just above a whisper.

"How long did she stay?"

"About two hours."

"What was your impression of her? What did you think of her?"

Annie's eyes darted to Tom again. "She was a very nice lady. Mark learned a lot with her."

"Did Mark like her?"

"Yes."

"I understand Carmen stopped tutoring your son a couple months before her death. Why did she stop tutoring him?"

There was silence. Annie's eyes were wider than ever and she began to twist the skirt of her dress between her fingers. She looked down, then back up at Jack. Her eyes were glassy with tears. "There was an … issue with her. I had to tell her to stop tutoring Mark."

Jack looked over at Tom. Tom's eyes had glazed over to produce a cold stare. His jaw was tight with a combination of tension and rage. "What was the issue?" Jack asked.

Annie's eyes glistened all the more and she physically turned to look at her husband and Detective Winsler. Her eyes were searching both of them for answers. Finally one silent tear slipped down her cheek.

Jack stood up. "A word with you, Detective Winsler." He walked to the door.

Detective Winsler followed him out into the hall. Jack closed the door and turned to him. Through the glass partition just aside the door he could see Annie and Tom engaging in rapid conversation. "I think I should speak to Annie privately."

"Out of the question," Detective Winsler responded. He stood straighter as if to make himself more important or perhaps more imposing.

"Look, Annie isn't going to say anything with Tom right there. For whatever reason she seems to need his approval to talk to me and quite frankly I don't have time for it. I just need a few answers so I can do my job. I'm not here to deal with marital issues. I'll get more from Annie on her own. And then we can get that much closer to buttoning up the case. I won't have it any other way."

"So, you're going to play the Fed card, aren't you?"" Detective Winsler said slowly and condescendingly. "I get it. You trump me. I hear you loud and clear, sir."

Jack felt a fire of anger rise from his abdomen and up his throat. It was all he could do to swallow it down. "No. This is my case. And this is what I need to do my job. Got it?"

Detective Winsler only looked at him. "Very well." With that he stormed back into the conference room. It was all Jack could do not to punch the wall.

Nero led Jill into the kitchen. Draped on one of the kitchen table chairs was a robe, which he swiftly threw on and belted. Jill couldn't help but notice that the kitchen was thoroughly bathed in sunlight. The smell of coffee and cinnamon filled the air. But she couldn't get distracted. This was business after all. "Please. Sit down," Nero welcomed her.

"Actually, Nero, we need to talk. This is pretty serious stuff."

Nero looked at her softly as he poured himself a cup of coffee. He laced it with what looked like cream and put it on the table nearest to her. He did not seem at all worried about anything she had to report.

"We know about you and Carmen," she said stoically. "We traced the emails on her computer to this address. We know you were far more than her friend and her brother-in-law."

Nero poured his coffee as she spoke, then turned to her with a sly smile. "What took you so long, Agent?" He leaned against the counter and cradled his coffee in his bejeweled hands as he spoke.

"Did you kill Carmen De Santo?" Jill said with an edge to her voice. His inability to take any of this seriously was really starting to get on her nerves.

"She came to you in a dream, didn't she?" His eyes locked with hers.

"Did you kill Carmen De Santo?" Jill asked again with equal force.

Nero grinned. "Call your dogs off, Agent. We're going to take a ride."

Jack found himself alone with Annie Emery, who continued to look down at her hands still resting on her lap. "Look, I know your husband can't be an easy man to deal with so I hope you feel comfortable with me. You only need to answer my questions honestly and this will all be over. I promise."

She looked up at him her eyes slightly swollen from her previous tears. She bit her lip, but said nothing. Jack looked her over carefully. He could see no bruises on her face. None on her arms. Yet she had all the mannerisms of someone who had been "beaten down" for years, if not physically certainly psychologically.

"We left off talking about why Carmen De Santo was no longer tutoring your son. You said there was an issue. What was the issue?" Jack asked. He kept his voice soft so that he would not intimidate her.

"She accused my husband of abusing our son," her voice shook as she talked. "I was upset and shocked. We couldn't have her over again after that."

"Well, was it true? Did your husband ever abuse your son?" Jack asked.

Annie's eyes widened. It seemed as if no one had even asked her that question, or at least not nearly as directly. "No," she said simply. "Tom has a temper but he does not hurt anyone." She did not look at him when she said this and her eyes shifted quickly to the left. She was lying. He knew it. No more Mr. Nice Guy.

Jill knew this could potentially be the worst mistake she had ever made. She agreed to drive to an undisclosed location with a potential killer. Potential, she had to remind herself. She had insisted they use her government-issued car so that they could be traced if necessary, and prior to hopping in the driver's seat she had walked over to where Jack's police officer was positioned and asked him to return to the station. He didn't seem happy but he had little choice but to comply with her request.

"So where exactly are we going?" Jill asked.

Nero sat in the passenger seat looking straight ahead. "You will see. You must be patient."

Jill followed his instruction as they drove and couldn't help but think that Nero seemed almost larger-than-life to be involved in something as banal as driving as a passenger in a car. He seemed to be someone who should be able to instantly transport himself there. When they got to the forest just outside of where Carmen's body was found he asked her to pull over and park. Jill got chills up her spine. She wasn't sure if this was good or if this were bad. He could show her everything he did the night of Carmen's murder and then in the quiet of the woods shoot her dead or slit her throat. Jill was armed, but that didn't mean very much these days. Everyone was armed.

Jill got out of the car and let him lead the way. This way she was behind him and would have at least a moment to react should he attack. The forest had already changed since the last time she had been there. Some leaves were beginning to change color to a pale yellow. A tinge of red had affected a couple of bushes. The air was cooler. Autumn was on its way. The further Jill followed Nero into the woods the more relaxed she became. She still wasn't sure if she was using the best judgment, but she certainly felt a little better about it.

They entered a clearing and Jill recognized it as the clearing where Carmen's body had been found. Nero walked out into the center. Jill hung back a bit. The clearing was also eerily familiar. Her dreams. This was the clearing where Carmen did her Magick in her dreams. Another rush of chills coursed through Jill's body. Suddenly she felt that she was very near the answers.

"This is where Carmen always came to do her Magick. It was her special place. She felt protected and she had blessed it as her sacred space," Nero began. He ran a hand over his face and his eyes were deep, brown pools of pain. Jill slowly walked closer to him. "It kills me. She must have been followed, that's what I've been thinking. Maybe someone was watching her for a while. I don't know. After she left my place she must have driven here and someone snuck up on her. But to be murdered in your sacred space." There were tears in Nero's eyes. "It doesn't make sense."

"How long were you and Carmen romantically involved?" Jill asked quietly. This was not a killer. This was a man mourning the loss of his lover. His companion. His friend.

"About a year or so. We had grown close and Armand was never home anymore. He was always away on business. Carmen and I took a trip to Omaha, Nebraska. Armand was supposed to come but canceled at the last minute. It was during this trip our love began to bloom. Being away from Lake Shore was the release we both needed." He looked up at the clouds for a minute, then over at Jill. "I know she was supposed to be as a sister to me, but I could never see her that way. She was special, a beautiful, mystical being. She became my everything."

"Do you think Armand knew? Or found out? Do you think he may have followed her here?" Jill asked softly.

"With all the money in the world anyone would lie for you. I have never trusted Armand. He is my brother but he is ruthless in business. If he had found out about us he would have gone crazy. He would have taken out his worst on the first person he came across. If that were Carmen he could have killed her. If he found her here in her sacred space that, too, would have infuriated him."

"Did he ever approach you?" Jill asked.

"No. He has been most pleasant to me. That perplexes me. The only person in the world I could imagine possibly killing Carmen in a rage would be Armand, however he never said a word to me. He never treated me any differently. I'm at a loss. I truly am." He looked down as a few tears coursed down his cheeks.

"You do realize you're a suspect right?" Jill stated. It needed to be said. "A primary one."

The silence that followed was deafening. Nero looked up at the sky his jaw clenched. When he looked back at her there were tears in his eyes and a sadness so hollow Jill was taken aback.

Jack leaned forward resting his elbows on the stretch of table between them. "No little comments? About your appearance, perhaps? Or the house? Or Mark? Nothing?" Annie was silent. "No little pushes here and there? A nudge? The occasional slap? I mean, really, there's nothing wrong with that, right?"

Annie simply looked at him. There were tears in her eyes again. "No. Nothing, Agent Pellingworth."

"So, are you trying to tell me you and Tom have never argued? That Tom was never angry with Mark?"

Annie began to play with her hands and she looked down at them. When she looked up she said, "Look, my marriage to Tom isn't perfect. No one's marriage is perfect. Tom is a bit of a hothead. He gets upset, he leaves, he comes back and he's fine. He doesn't hit us and he doesn't insult us." She looked down at her hands again.

Jack left it at that. He knew she was lying. Of course, she was. It could mean certain death when an abused woman spoke to the authorities about the abuse. And if Tom had threatened her she would be even more remiss to speak up. Thing is, Jack wasn't here to pry into Tom and Annie's personal life. He was here to find answers to Carmen's death. Plain and simple.

"Ok. Well, let's move on here. So, Carmen confronted you directly?"

Annie looked relieved at the change in conversation. She looked up at Jack again. "When she came to tutor Mark again...after she accused Tom...I told her that we no longer wanted to have her tutor here."

"How did she react?" Jack asked.

"She seemed almost shocked, maybe a little sad. She told me to call her if I needed anything. Even if I just needed to talk to her. I remember she looked behind me, I assumed looking for Mark, but he was out back. And that was all. She left."

"Did you ever see her again?"

"Tom thought he saw her the day that Mark broke his arm. At the hospital. But I never saw her again and she didn't come here to visit."

"Did Carmen De Santo have any enemies that you know of in Lake Shore?"

"No. I can't think of anyone. She pretty much kept to herself, but she was also involved in the community to some degree. She definitely wanted to help people. She meant well," As she said this last sentence her voice began to shake and tears began to fill her eyes again.

"Is everything ok? What is making you upset?" Jack asked. He grabbed a tissue from the dispenser and handed it to her.

"It's just that she was such a nice person." A tear snuck down her cheek. She wiped it away, then blew her nose. "She didn't mean anything by it. She didn't deserve to die." With that Annie put her hand over her mouth and let the tears fall freely. Her eyes searched Jack's for something.

Jill was not sure what to expect next. It could be anything. She brushed her arm against her gun to make sure it was still there. This could be a moment of confession or something entirely new.

Nero's voice jolted her back to reality. "I loved her. I really, really loved her. She was everything to me. I would never have hurt a hair on her head. She was absolutely lovely." He paused and looked over at her. "Have you ever been in love, Agent?"

"Once or twice," Jill answered.

"Then you know. It is like nothing else in this world. I had become convinced that Carmen was my soul mate. So, I couldn't understand how it had come that I had met her through my brother. It tore us both apart at times. We both felt so passionately for each other and yet there was this other element." Nero's eyes seemed to bleed with pain. "And now she is dead. I'll never see her again. I'll never touch her. I'll never hear her voice. She will haunt me forever. She will be in my dreams and in my thoughts and in my rituals. She will be everywhere and nowhere at once. She will be my ghost. And I shall never have her." There was a moment of quiet. "I guess I never really did."

"Did you kill her, Nero?" Jill asked quietly.

"No," he said simply. "And my heart will burn until the truth is revealed. There are times when I'm not sure if I want to know who killed her. I worry that the reality of it will kill me. But we must know. It is the only way to bring closure to us all."

Jill looked over at the ruined man Nero had become right before her eyes. She remembered the first time she met him with his wicked grin and virulent attitude. He was both a terrific liar and actor, or he was telling the truth.

"Are you worried about Mark?" Jack asked Annie.

Annie blew her nose and nodded her head. She was quiet. Jack could tell her the truth, which was that there was very little chance her son was still alive, especially with a killer on the loose. Or he could watch her quietly and say nothing. The choice was his.

"I know Detective Winsler is doing all he can to find Mark. Since Mark was discovered missing the day Carmen's body was found in the woods, there may be clues in Carmen's death to Mark's disappearance. In a way you could be helping us find your son."

Annie who had been looking down looked up at him. Her eyes were red with her tears, and her eyes were wide with terror and fear. Her lips trembled and her words were hollow. "You must help us, Agent. You must."

Nero De Santo walked away from Jill further out into the meadow. Jill followed him at a discreet distance. She had a feeling that Nero had not allowed himself to completely mourn the loss of Carmen. After a couple of moments of silence she said, "Carmen came here often didn't she?"

"All the time," Nero said gently. "She loved this place. It was her sacred space."

"What does that mean?" Jill asked. This was a tragedy like none other she had ever encountered. And it would only get worse when she had to confront Armand De Santo about this.

"Wiccans need to develop a space that is blessed and peaceful for when they do ritual and Sabbats. The Witch generally spends quite a bit of time locating the perfect place, then calling on the Gods and Goddesses to bless the space. This is thus called Sacred Space and it is highly protected by the Gods. This way the Witch can do her Magick without having to constantly monitor the space for evil influences. It is unfathomable that she was murdered here in this very space."

Jill wasn't sure if she should proceed with what she was about to tell him, but decided that she could trust him enough since his love for Carmen was so great. And if this meant getting more information out of Nero than it was well worth it. "We didn't release this, but it appeared as if Carmen had been pursued and was running towards this space prior to her attack. She wasn't just found here. She was also murdered here."

Nero lifted his face up to the heavens and withdrew a deep breath. "All along I thought that perhaps she had been seen here or perhaps followed. That she was surprised. It has been my intuition. I knew she had to have been murdered here because this space is too far removed for anyone to go so far as to dump her body and then leave it in plain sight in a meadow. But to be pursued, chased here. I can only imagine she was running for refuge. She had to have had hope the Gods would protect her in this space or at the very least give her the knowledge of how to protect herself." He paused and put both of his hands to his mouth clasping them as if he were about to pray. "It is unquestionably cruel."

Jill remained silent. Nero had given her a little bit more information into Carmen's psyche. She must have believed whole-heartedly in her religion in order to run to the space when being pursued by someone who meant her harm.

Just then her phone rang. On the second ring she said, "Simko."

"Jill, it's Jack." His voice was hardened and clipped. Jill looked at her watch certain she had spent too long out in the woods with Nero. Time seemed to be inconsequential when she was with him. It was still early.

"What is it?" she asked.

"Meet me at the Emery's house. Pronto." He hung up.

Jill felt a shiver go down her spine. She looked over at Nero. "Where is Tom and Annie Emery's house from here?"

"Is something wrong?" he asked.

"I'm not sure yet. Where are they located?"

"A couple streets up from here," he answered.

"I need to be there right now."

"Come along. I'll show you," Nero said sauntering back to the wooded area. "It will only take a few minutes."

Jill pulled up in front of Mark and Tom Emery's house, which as Nero had stated was only a couple of minutes up from the woods. Lights from two police cruisers resonated red and blue. She saw Detective Winsler, Lieutenant Copeland, and Jack standing just outside the Emery's barn. Jill rushed out of the vehicle and ran down the driveway to meet them.

"What's going on?" she asked her eyes wide. "Jack?"

Jack was looking at something behind her. His face was hard as stone. "He can't be here," he said.

Only then did Jill remember Nero De Santo. She looked back at him.

"Not to worry, Agents! I can walk home from here. It is a pleasant, Autumn day and I would be happy to enjoy the beauty of it," Nero said waving his hand at them and turning around to walk up the road. Jill watched him for a minute.

"Jill," Jack said shaking her out of her reverie. She whipped around to look at him. She seemed stunned. As Jack had expected she was completely enamored with Nero. "Something has happened and it is absolutely insane!"

"Here at the Emery's? I thought you were all meeting at the station."

"We were. Then the absolutely most insane thing happened. During our conversation Tom seemed to be a controlling presence for Annie. I spoke with her alone. It did not take her long to completely crumble before my eyes." Jack took Jill's arm and moved away from the Detective and Lieutenant. "I was not kind."

Annie had looked at him her eyes wide, tears streaming, and her entire body trembling. Jack could see beads of sweat on her brow. If she had information of any kind he needed it. Now. "Help you? What happened?"

Annie looked down but her hands were trembling beyond her control. "The night Carmen died..." She started.

"You saw Carmen the night she died?" Jack jumped in. "And you never told us?"

"No!" Her eyes went wide again and she shook her head almost violently. "No! Agent, no!"

"What do you know, Annie? What do you know?" He had gone from sympathetic to accusatory in the blink of an eye. He could see he was confusing Annie, who may have gotten used to him as a confidante. She began to squeeze her left arm with her right hand.

"Please, Agent Pellingworth. Please," she begged. The tears were streaming freely now and her eyes were round saucers. "Let me finish. Please."

Jack was silent. He looked at her sternly. Then he said, "If you have information that you are holding back from us so help me..."

"Please, Agent!" she begged. Her body trembled more than ever and a couple beads of sweat slid down her brow to her temple. "Please! The night Carmen died, Mark was hit by a car!" Her voice was louder than either she or Jack had expected. Her eyes grew wide again as she relived the moment.

"He was playing in the woods across the street. I called him in for dinner. He ran without looking, and......and......and....." She let out a loud sob and buried her face in her hands. Jack was silent. She had broken. Jack let her sob for a moment. He needed a moment himself. He wasn't sure what this kind of revelation meant for his case. His mind was spinning. What did it mean for Detective Winsler's case? And exactly where did Mark Emery go? What the Hell was going on here?

Annie's voice softer than before broke his reverie. "The car just kept going. Up the street and away. It slowed down but no one ever got out. It just kept going. I ran to him. I ran as fast as I could. And he wasn't moving. He didn't move a muscle. He was broken and bleeding. Oh God!" The agony in Annie's voice pierced through Jack's heart. As a Special Agent you had to harden yourself to circumstances like this so that you could remain impartial. There were days like this one that were harder than others.

Jack gave her another minute. "Then what happened?" he said softly.

Annie looked up at him. She was strangely calm after her initial release. "I picked him up, ran for the house and yelled for Tom. We brought him into the living room and put him down on an old carpet remnant so that we wouldn't get blood on anything. Tom kept checking his pulse, but it was clear. He was already dead. We were both scared to death. I asked Tom what we should do. Tom told me to pour myself some wine, go upstairs, and he'd take care of everything."

Jack tried to remain calm, but inside his heart had started to beat faster. He was not at all sure he believed the hit-and-run story. It was quite possible that Tom could have beaten Mark to death or perhaps stabbed him or worse. "Is that what you did?" he asked calmly.

Fresh tears sprouted from Annie's eyes. She began to tremble again. "I had to leave. I couldn't face it. I drank wine upstairs until I passed out in bed. When I woke up the next day in the afternoon, I heard about Mark's missing persons report on the news. I also heard about Carmen. It was all too much for me. When I asked Tom why Mark was in the paper he told me he had come to a decision on what to do. From that point forward I've spent as much time as possible in bed."

Jack sat back. This was just too much. If Tom had been beating his family it was quite possible he had accidentally murdered his son. Annie's inability to face facts was disconcerting, but whatever the case they needed the body. "What did Tom do, Annie? What did he do with Mark?" His voice was slow and controlled.

Annie just looked down at her hands tears once again forming in her eyes.

"Where's Mark now, Annie?" he asked softly. "In the barn. Tom put him in the barn." Her voice was very soft and she looked exhausted like she may collapse.

"May we go there to get him? We need to take a look at him. Please." Again his voice was soft and giving.

"Yes. Of course."

Jill looked at Jack her eyes wide in shock. "So, we're here to uncover Mark Emery," she surmised. "Oh my God. This town is so fucked up. Where are the Emery's now?"

"In custody. Annie has been given a pill and she's resting. Tom is in holding. He has been told there has been a delay and he will be questioned momentarily. He asked to speak to Annie but we told him she is not well. We don't have a lot of time here."

"All right, Agents!" Detective Winsler called over to them. "Are you ready?"

Clouds had morphed the sun lending an eerie, dark glow to the Emery's front lawn. The doors of the barn stood before them like the locked gates to Hell. Jack and Jill joined Detective Winsler and Lieutenant Copeland and started walking to the barn doors.

"She promised the doors would be unlocked," Jack said.

All four officers stood staring at the doors. "Are we ready for this, men?" Lieutenant Copeland asked. Jack and Jill fell back as Detective Winsler made the approach and put his hand on the barn door. He took a deep breath and opened the door quickly and with one gesture as if he were pulling off a band-aid. He entered followed closely by the other three.

The barn was relatively neat and smelled of sawdust. There was a walkway in the center with each section containing the usual storage items.

"What we're looking for is a large carpet remnant. It is dark maroon in color," Detective Winsler announced as if the rest of them had just come upon the scene. Jack rolled his eyes. They sectioned off the barn each office designated to an area and began the search. Jill began moving old yard furniture and boxes in the search of her section. She was meticulous but couldn't help but wonder in the back of her mind why they couldn't smell the body. This far decomposed an in the extreme heat the body would have smelled just awful. They should have been able to smell it even outside the barn. But this barn smelled of sawdust, a smell that was almost clean. When she was half way through her section she wondered over to Jack.

"How's it going?" she asked him.

Jack looked up at her. "Needle in a haystack," he muttered. "The boy isn't here. I know it. You'd be able to smell him a mile away."

Jill smiled. "My thoughts exactly."

"But let's play nice right now. Detective Winsler owes us big time. We may need him to find Carmen's killer. You never know."

Jill nodded, then returned to her section to search. Just shy of three hours later all four investigators met at the central aisle again. No luck. No one had found anything. Not even one scrap of a carpet remnant.

Detective Winsler looked discouraged. He looked over at Jack and Jill. "First of all, I want to thank you so much for taking the time to come here with us today. At this point, we have no choice but to get a warrant to search the premises. This is only because we need to be thorough and we need to put faith in our witness. One thing is clear. Annie Emery is not telling the entire truth."

"If I may," Jack interjected. Detective Winsler only nodded. "Annie Emery was extremely agitated when I spoke with her. If she's lying she's a pretty good one. I have the distinct feeling that the boy is dead and that his body is here somewhere. The Emery's have been too closely watched for the body to have gone far. Now, did a car accident actually occur? I'm not so sure. Was Tom the only one involved and Annie just played along? Again, who knows?"

Lieutenant Copeland interrupted at that moment. "Are you trying to say you believe Carmen De Santo's ramblings about abuse here? Are you saying the Emery's murdered their son? After all we did to investigate this family? After we found nothing?" His voice was louder than expected in the empty barn his face redder than the barn doors.

Jill could feel Jack tense. "Look, Lieutenant Copeland. What Jack is saying is that we need to consider all possibilities. Right now we only have Annie's side of things. Anything could have happened that night. We need to be open to that. To anything. Not just a car accident." She looked around at everyone. "Ultimately we need to find that body. That body will tell us everything. This is serious stuff now, guys. We can't mess this up."

The barn was silent for a moment.

"Time to get a warrant," Detective Winsler pronounced.

CHAPTER TWENTY-ONE

After a call in to the Bureau it was determined that Jack and Jill would do whatever they could to assist the Lake Shore police department in their efforts to locate Mark Emery's body. Although Jack tended to feel they were spinning their wheels, Jill agreed that the connection to Carmen De Santo warranted their presence during the investigation. Unfortunately, this did not include the interrogation of Tom Emery. Jack had wanted a piece of that, as well, but had to resign himself to the fact that this was not actually their case at all. Detective Winsler had full right to run it the way he saw fit.

Jack and Jill spent the afternoon discussing Nero De Santo while waiting for the search warrant to come through. Jill explained his deep love for Carmen and his willingness to cooperate with them. "I'm just not so sure we should discuss this with Armand. Quite frankly, even though he is also a primary suspect we don't have much to link him to Carmen that night. I'm just not so sure if it's our place," Jill stated sipping her ice tea.

"Honestly, I think you're getting too close to this case," Jack said simply. "We can't let anything slip by us at this point. Carmen was cheating on her husband with his own brother. Are you kidding me?! If Armand found out about that he could very well have flipped out."

"But he was at a function that night. Out of state. There are multiple witnesses. He certainly wasn't there and he couldn't have killed her," Jill rebutted.

"He could have had someone else kill her," Jack said. "We have to be open to that possibility."

"We need more proof. I don't think we should confront him about any of this until we have more proof that he could have hired out," Jill stated shaking her head vehemently.

"That would mean pulling his phone and Internet records, something we haven't had to do yet," Jack stated simply. He would much rather just talk to Armand directly and get as much information out of him as possible. It was starting to annoy him that this case was taking so long.

"Then that's what we'll need to do. I don't want to be the one to tear this family apart if Armand never knew about Nero and Carmen. You don't get over something like that."

Jack pinched the bridge of his nose. "And that's what makes me believe you've gotten too close to this case, Jill. You're getting too emotionally involved. You need to back off a little."

Jill looked at him for a moment her eyebrows pulling together. "Well, excuse me for adding a human element here," she said her voice shaking a bit.

Jack's phone rang. He nodded, said that they'd be there, then hung up. He threw his phone on the table, then looked over at Jill. "We got the warrant. Back to business."

Maybe she was getting too close to this case. It was hard not to. They had been on this case longer and more intensively than they usually were. Renault had taken up so much of their time that the human element had begun to fade. Renault was a monster and when you're searching for monsters humanity is non-existent. This case was refreshing. There were real people living real lives in a normal, everyday way. This could happen to anyone. Jill shivered as she and Jack drove silently to the Emery's house. It was later that afternoon and the sun was slanting in a way that made the trees look dazzling. Twilight would be upon them in just a couple hours. They didn't have much time left in the day.

Tom and Annie Emery were being held in custody. Tom had refused to speak with Detective Winsler. His silence spoke volumes. Detective Winsler had tried to explain to him that any information could possibly help him out in the long run. All Tom did was stare at him vacantly with his mouth firmly shut. Annie had awoken with a scream for her son. She had been unreasonable in her anguish and transported to the closest hospital psychiatric unit for analysis.

Jack and Jill pulled up to the house in silence. They had agreed to disagree, but even in that there was a tension that neither of them felt very comfortable expressing. Police lights swirled around them in blue and red, and both Lieutenant Copeland and Detective Winsler were present, as well as a few fellow investigators. As she stepped out of the car Jill could smell it. They were getting towards the end of a journey here. Although it most definitely wasn't their own. She looked over at Jack. He glanced at her a similar look on his face. As they approached the group they could hear Detective Winsler assigning sections to the search party. They were looking for a body. Plain and simple. There may or may not be a carpet remnant involved anymore. This could be inside the house or outside on the grounds. Anything at all was possible. Usually in these cases there was a sense of excitement. Call it the thrill of the chase, the quest for answers. This time around the mood was somber. There was a deep sadness for the passing of such a young child in such a terrible way.

The search began. At first Jack and Jill took the perimeter of the house searching for any areas where the earth had been recently shoveled or moved in any way. Two search parties worked inside the house one working top to bottom, another working bottom to top. Yet another search group worked on the outer edge of the property moving in towards Jack and Jill. As Jill searched around flowerbeds and brush her flashlight illuminating every nook and cranny she thought about Nero De Santo. His sadness had been beyond comprehension for her and she did not know what to do with these feelings. Had she been a Federal Agent for too long now that even she couldn't understand what it would be like to feel such grief to such a degree? She also began to think of Annie Emery locked away in a psychiatric unit drugs keeping her asleep so that she did not have to relive the moment when her son was killed. And she thought of her own daughter. What would she ever do if she lost that precious child? What would her daughter do if something happened to her? At this very moment standing on the precipice life seemed very fragile.

The sky was beginning to get dark. The K-9 unit had arrived approximately an hour prior and they were working out further in the woods pushing in towards the house. Flashlights were everywhere and two light stands had been brought onto the scene. They put out enough brilliance to make the sun blush. Jack threw on a sweatshirt as the air had gotten progressively chilly and continued to work in the back yard. He remembered how he had visited here once before and had been curious about the back yard, but had not gotten the opportunity to look around since Tom appeared from behind him and had gotten his attention. He also remembered he had smelled an odd, foul odor, which now he thoroughly believed had been Mark Emery's body. For the life of him he could not understand what made people do what they did. Why would a husband even think to hide the body of his dead son after a hit-and-run driver struck him? Why in the world would anyone panic to the point that they would go to such extremes? Jack thought of Tom's cold, steel eyes and he knew. Abuse. If the child were beaten to death the parents would absolutely want to hide it. Annie Emery, scared insane, would have wanted to cover for Tom, but would need to relieve her psyche even just slightly. The best of both worlds, perhaps? Perhaps not. It did not solve the problem that her only son was dead, her husband may have killed him, and the only person in the world who had reached out to help her was also dead. The world worked in mysterious ways. They just needed the body. The body would tell them more than they knew right now. That was for damn sure.

"Come on, Mark," Jack muttered under his breath. "Where are you?"

Jack glanced over at Jill who frowned in concentration and pushed around a few rocks to look around underneath. He decided that after this case she might need a vacation. Heck, both of them may need a little break. Jill had become more involved in this case than she was willing to admit. Her dreams. Her conversations with Nero De Santo. The dazed look on her face from time to time. Her visions. What had happened to them in the past couple of weeks? Well, one thing was for sure. Lake Shore was a very strange, strange place.

There was a loud sound at the back corner of the property as a few of the investigators yelled for others to gather around. One of the K-9 dogs began to bark. Jack looked up and the wind began to stir ever so slightly. He saw dark figures with flashlights rushing across the lawn. Jack felt his heart skip a bit and a cool sensation flooded his bloodstream. They found something. He just knew it.

Jill's eyes met Jack's. In a moment they were both running in the direction of the activity. Flashlights bounced in awkward angles against tree trunks and shrubbery as they ran. The small section of the property was quite crowded by the time Jack and Jill reached it. Jack pushed his way through until he was directly in front. This was no time for hesitation. This was a time for answers.

In front of him was a small area of ground that had been partially unearthed. One of the investigators held a small shovel and continued to dig. A dog on patrol sat next to the three-foot hole intently staring down into it. The investigator holding the dog matched his canine brother's intensity while looking into the hole. In the center of the hole was what looked like a bundle still slightly covered with soil. Another investigator began to help dig out the dirt around the bundle creating more and more space in order to remove it.

All around there was silence. Not a breath. Not a heartbeat. There was only a feeling of deep sadness. It was as if it were universally understood that this was Mark Emery and that for all intents and purposes it appeared as if Annie Emery's story was correct. Well, at least the part where her son was dead. For a small town this may just be too much to bear. Children were supposed to have happy, cheerful lives where things went their way every day and they could live the bliss that could no longer be attained in adulthood. This seemed to happen less and less nowadays.

The man digging in the hole yelled up to a fellow investigator. Jill watched as the second man jumped into the small hole and took one end of the bundle. The two men began to hoist the bundle upward until they were able to move a couple steps to the right and place the bundle on solid ground again. The smell of the earth was strong all around them. A chill began to encircle them as if whispering to them, "It is him. It is him." Jill looked around for a second certain that someone had just whispered in her ear. She pulled her jacket around her. The chill went right through to the bone.

The bundle was a maroon carpet remnant. Detective Winsler called for the high intensity light stands to be moved to the location. The smell of cigarette smoke mixed with the smell of earth as the lights were moved closer. For now everyone just looked at the bundle. Once the lights were positioned, two investigators and Detective Winsler began unraveling the carpet remnant. Jack stepped forward.

"I think that that should go directly to the M.E. As is," Jack called out.

Detective Winsler stopped what he was doing and looked over at him. "We need to determine there is even a body in here first," he said simply. He continued to help in the unraveling. Jill began to smell the sweet, maple-syrup smell of decay.

"We know there's a body in there. For Christ's sake, I can smell it! There can't be any potential disruption of the body," Jack said angrily. Jill could see that his face was red in anger, which could only mean he was about to lose his control completely.

Detective Winsler stopped again and looked at Jack. "Thank you for your help, Agent," he said softly.

Jill stepped next to Jack and put her hand on him. She could feel his arm trembling. "We're here to help, Jack. This is not our case," she whispered softly. Jack let out a deep breath. His jaw was deeply set and his eyes were piercing. He didn't know if that was a dismissal from Detective Winsler, but he had not gone this far to be left in the dust.

Detective Winsler and fellow investigators continued unraveling the carpet, then abruptly stopped. Jill saw Lieutenant Copeland suddenly turn his back to the scene and bend forward. At first she thought he was being sick, which was understandable considering the circumstances, but then she realized that tears were streaming down his face. She left the scene and walked over to him. She put her hand on his arm to console him. He took deep breaths to control his tears, then stood up straight and looked over at Jill.

"This is truly awful," he said to her. "Little Mark Emery was such a wonderful child. How could this have happened?" Jill was silent. There were no words to answer that question. "And you do this every day, don't you?"

"Some cases are harder than others," Jill said simply. "This is a pretty hard case."

The chill of the cool air swirled all around them. Jack made his way over to Jill. His face was no longer the angry bit of stone it was just a few minutes ago. "They have recovered the body of a child about eight years old. The body will need to be positively identified." He looked over at Lieutenant Copeland whose face was white as a ghost, then looked back at Jill. "The body will be moved to the M.E. for immediate examination."

"Do we follow?" she asked.

"Detective Winsler will inform us if help is needed. For now, I say we get some dinner and hit the hay. Tomorrow is another day and Carmen De Santo's killer is still out there.

CHAPTER TWENTY-TWO

Jill called her daughter the second she got to her hotel room that night. The sound of her sweet voice instantly warmed Jill's heart. She went to the bed feeling like there was some semblance of humanity left in the world. She also decided that after this case a sabbatical was in order. She needed time to spend with her daughter and just be a mom for a while. There was something so richly rewarding and amazing in that simplicity. Jill went to sleep with a smile on her face.

The sound of her phone ringing pierced through Jill's sense of tranquility. She instantly had a bad feeling. She picked up the phone and looked at it. Jack. "Yeah," she breathed.

"M.E. just called. He said we need to be there stat," Jack said without introduction.

"Jack, this isn't even our case," she complained. All she wanted was to go back to sleep to a sense of peace and the warmth of her daughter's voice.

"It is now," he said and hung up the phone.

Jack and Jill drove swiftly to Dr. McKinley's morgue. Jill was still in the dark about what was important enough to drag them out of bed at 3 o'clock in the morning, but Jack promised that Dr. McKinley had stated that he found something on Mark Emery that may help in the Carmen De Santo case. Dr. McKinley's office smelled of coffee when he sat them down. He was still in his scrubs and only perched on his seat as he looked over at them.

"This better be good," Jack half-joked.

Dr. McKinley nodded vigorously. "We found a large gouge on the side of Mark Emery's torso to the right of his sternum. At first I thought it might be part of a bumper of a car. On closer inspection and a little surgery it became more obvious what it was." He paused.

"What was it?" Jack asked.

"See for yourself." Dr. McKinley pushed a photograph across the table at them. Jack and Jill looked at it closely. Sure enough right where Dr. McKinley said it would be was an incision near what looked like a large wound with dark bruising all around it. On the table directly next to the torso was a small figure that looked like a small horse.

"Looks like a horse," Jill said.

"All indications confirm that he was hit by a car; exsanguination the cause of death. There was a perforation in his aorta from the impact," Dr. McKinley stated.

"And this horse?" Jack asked. "You must have a theory."

Suddenly Jill looked at him her eyes wide and her face a bit pale. "Jack. Jack, it's a Mustang. It's a Mustang emblem."

Jack and Jill both looked down at the photograph and then back at each other. "Oh my God," Jill breathed. "Carmen De Santo hit Mark Emery. It was her car." The silence that followed was deafening as both Jack and Jill contemplated what they had just learned.

"I went back into Carmen De Santo's case files. She had to have hit the boy with her car less than an hour before her own death. The boy would have been nearly killed on impact and I have quoted his death as approximately one hour prior to Carmen De Santo's death," Dr. McKinley interjected.

"If Carmen De Santo killed Mark Emery by hitting him with her car, then who killed her? Oh, this is so weird," Jill nearly whispered.

"Annie Emery," Jack breathed. "We need to talk to Annie Emery."

The psychiatric ward of the R.C. Bellows Medical Center located about thirty minutes north of Lake Shore was quiet at eight o'clock that morning. Jill had to wonder if the medication dose was just higher in the morning or if the more erratic behavior was reserved for the nocturnal hours. Clearly, she had watched too much television growing up. Jack and Jill were led down a long, white hall and into an equally sterile, white conference room. There was only a desk, three chairs, and an observation window. They had been told that all notes had to be kept in their heads as pens and pencils were not allowed into the facility. Although Annie Emery's condition was not considered suicidal, there were enough people here that were.

Jack and Jill sat on two seats next to each other and waited. The silence in the room was unnerving somehow. "Did you ever see that movie, Session 9?" Jack asked.

Jill turned to him. "Can't say I have."

"It's a horror movie released back in 2001. They filmed it in the old Danvers State Insane Asylum up on the North Shore. It was by far one of the creepiest movies I have ever seen. Danvers State was abandoned at the time of the filming and the crew were convinced it was inhabited by evil spirits." Jack shivered. "Unbelievably creepy."

"What made you think of that?" Jill asked.

"Ever since seeing the film, psychiatric units give me the heebie jeebies."

At that moment the door opened and a nurse walked in. She was wearing pale-blue scrubs and smiled kindly at the two agents. She left the door partially open and approached the table where they were sitting. "Hi. I'm Patricia. I'm Annie's nurse right now." She spoke slow and clearly as if speaking to children. "Annie had a tough night last night. She woke numerous times screaming and needed a pill to sleep so she's tired this morning. She may be a little slower than usual but I do hope you get some answers." She smiled kindly again, then turned away to retrieve her patient. Patricia returned to the room pushing Annie Emery who sat in a wheel chair.

Jack shivered again. Annie sat in the chair and stared at both agents, but she looked as if she were a million miles away. Her eyes were slightly red and swollen and she had a cut on her lower lip. Her skin was quite pale and without the disguise of makeup there were severe, dark circles under both eyes. She looked both a young child and an old woman all at the same time. Patricia told them she could be called at any time by pressing the yellow button on the wall and that the interview would also be observed through the mirror. Precautions.

When Patricia left the room she shut the door tightly. Jill assumed it was locked. So here they were locked in a room with a mentally ill patient. Lovely. Annie kept staring at the wall. Jill looked over at Jack, who shrugged. "Hi, Annie," Jill began. "Do you remember me? I'm Agent Simko. Jill, if you'd rather." Annie continued to stare. "We're here to ask you a couple questions. These will be tough questions, but I know you can handle it. I know you're strong." Annie continued to stare. Jill looked over at Jack, who shrugged his shoulders. "Annie, some things have happened since we last talked to you. It has to do with Mark. And it also has to do with Carmen De Santo. I know this is hard, but you may have some information that can help us."

Annie blinked her eyelids rapidly a few times.

"You helped us out so much. We found Mark. He can now go in peace. When we found Mark we also found something else." She paused. Annie just stared making no attempt at movement. "Did Carmen De Santo hit Mark with her car? Her red Mustang?"

There was silence, then Annie sucked in her breath deeply so that it sounded as if she were wheezing. Her hands gripped the armrests on her wheelchair and she turned her attention to Jack. Her eyes blinked wildly. Then she let the breath out slowly her arms gradually releasing their grip and her eyes beginning to blink slowly again. Her mouth frowned and she nodded.

"Is that a yes, Annie?" Jack asked her softly.

"Yes," she hissed. "Carmen….." She dropped her chin to her chest at that moment and began to breathe deeply in and out. Jill could only imagine the impact of such grief. Annie looked up at Jack her eyes silently pleading. "She didn't mean it. She really didn't mean it. She was so, so….so kind to Mark. So kind."

Both agents remained silent. Annie began to shiver then began shaking her head "no" over and over again. Her lower lip trembled. "So kind. She didn't mean it. Mark was running away from the house. Tom had hit him again. This time on his face and neck and Mark just ran away. In a flash he was out the door and out into the street."

"What happened after Carmen hit Mark with her car?" Jill asked her softly.

Annie's lower lip trembled violently. Tears began to pour from her eyes. "Mark dropped. She stopped, got out of her car and ran over to him. She got there before I did. She was holding him like a baby when I got there."

Carmen looked up at Annie her eyes wild, her red hair in a disarray. To Annie she looked like a mystical mermaid come to earth. Her skin was paler than ever and there were dark circles under her eyes. "Oh God, Annie!" she shrieked in agony. "Oh God. Look what I've done." There were tears in her eyes as Annie knelt beside her and touched her son's hand. It was unresponsive.

Carmen immediately put Mark down on the ground and began checking his throat and then his wrists for a pulse. She put her ear up to his mouth. No pulse. No breath. She looked over at Annie wildly and began to shiver even though the evening was quite warm.

"God, I'm so sorry, Annie. We need to call the police. Someone. He still may be ok. I don't know. Oh God, Annie."

She grabbed Annie's hand. Hers was ice cold. Her eyes were wild. Annie heard Tom approaching. His voice was harsh. "What exactly is going on here?!" he yelled.

Carmen had stood up at that moment her eyes wild with grief and now with a touch of fear. "I'm so sorry. He came out of nowhere."

"You!!" Tom cursed. "You with your going to the police and telling them all your lies. You....you witch!!" He was screaming at this point his face red, tendons bulging in his neck.

"Please. Get help for Mark. There may be help yet. Please!" Carmen begged. Annie had stood at her knees and pulled Mark into her arms. Her baby now. She kept kissing Mark's slack forehead over and over again. The dark corners of grief were beginning to seep in. She looked up and could see Carmen begging her eyes wild and her hands out. Tom was taken steps closer to her and was screaming. Annie couldn't hear anything they said.

Carmen turned around and ran. In a second she was a white dress shimmering like a ghost in the night. Escaping into the night. Tom was running after her. Then they were both gone. Annie looked down at Mark and lay next to him cuddling him into her own body. The darkness was seeping deeper. Deeper still.

She could have been there seconds or minutes or days or even years when she heard Tom returned. He simply said, "I've taken care of it." Tom lifted her up. She could smell blood and there it was all over him. The darkness was seeping deeper still. He placed her on the bed and that's when the darkness covered her completely.

And now they knew, too. Jack looked over at Jill. Case closed. Well, sort of. They'd need to speak with Tom Emery. This case could not be built on the words of an insane woman. Jill stood up after Annie told them everything and gave her a hug. "I'm so sorry you've had to go through all of this. I truly am." There were tears in her eyes. One mom to another. "No one should ever have to go through that."

"Tell Carmen I forgive her. Please tell her," Annie said. For a moment her blue eyes were wide and clear, then they glazed over and began staring at the wall again.

On the way to the station to speak to Tom Emery, Jill could not stop thinking about her own daughter. She had a desperate need to hold her tight and never let her go. Her heart and arms ached for it. She remained quiet considering what agony Annie Emery had been through. For some reason her pain seemed so much worse than the unfortunate situation Carmen De Santo had found herself in that night.

"I'm not so sure Annie Emery's testimony will stand up in court," Jack stated.

"We can only hope," Jill breathed. "She was sane when it all happened. This has to be a temporary high degree of grief. It's not necessarily insanity. Once the case is in court she may be treated enough to make an honest, sane testimony."

"Do you think Tom will confess?" Jack asked.

"We can hope, but I highly doubt it."

"I'm going to go brutal on him," Jack.

"Watch out, Jack. This guy is pretty dangerous. I believe he's been beating his family for years and he's killed Carmen De Santo in a vicious way. He could strike out at you, too."

"I hope he does."

Lieutenant Copeland was in a grim state when they met him at the station to brief him on their meeting with Annie Emery. He looked at them with sad eyes red and puffy as if he had been crying. "This is a tough case," he admitted. "This town is so small and so close. For this to happen to two of our citizens at the hand of one man is terrifying. You just don't know about people do you? I just thought that Tom was a hot head and reclusive, but I never thought he could be a murderer."

"Lieutenant, he is clearly ill and completely lost it when Carmen, the same woman who had called him out for abuse, hit his child with her car. It may have even seemed insulting to him," Jill said softly. "However scary and hard to understand sometimes these things happen. They happen in big cities and in small towns like these. They happen every day." She patted his arm. "It's our job to protect as many people as we can to get these people off the streets and away from innocent civilians. Our job is vital."

"I feel like I could have stopped this from happening. If only I had looked even closer into Tom Emery and the family. I just didn't think it was possible. I wanted to think the best about them," Lieutenant Copeland said glumly.

"No one could have stopped this," Jill said. "Sometimes things just happen. You can't blame yourself. You did more than a lot of people would have done."

Lieutenant Copeland nodded, then straightened his shoulders. "Tom Emery is waiting for you," he said. "I'll be watching from the window. Good luck."

"I'll accompany you," Jill said. "Jack needs to do this alone. It's a tactic we often use for some men who don't respect women. Jack will get more out of him then I will ever be able to."

Jill followed the Lieutenant to the small back room while Jack approached the door to the interrogation room. He put his hand on the doorknob and took a deep breath. He entered the room in what he liked to call his "tough guy" mode. Shoulders back, face firm and solid, jaw clenched.

Tom Emery sat at the table a cup of water beside him his hands folded in front of him. Jack closed the door with a thud. Only then did Tom look over at him his eyes hard and cold. It was all Jack could do not to deck this man who had hidden his dead or dying son and killed an innocent woman desperate to help his family. Jack sat down across from him and glared at him.

"Well, you've been pretty busy now haven't you, Tom," Jack sneered. Tom simply stared at him without blinking. "Everything's pretty convenient for you now, huh? Your boy isn't a bother anymore, and neither is that red-headed bitch who kept meddling with your family." Tom just continued to stare at him. "Thing is, you're in a world of shit right now. That little redhead's dad is Senator Ricci and he's calling for the chair. Child murderers are despised in prison and to top it all off I'm pretty sure Senator Ricci has all the connections to make sure you are treated less than adequate in prison," Jack hissed.

Tom continued to glare at him, but this time his jaw clenched hard. Jack had the sense he was holding himself back something fierce. "Small-town boy killing a pretty, young, happy socialite. Yikes. I can only imagine what will become of you. You should've thought about that before you lost your temper. But then again, I guess it would have happened sooner or later, right?" Tom's lip twitched.

"Aren't you going to speak up for yourself, man? Aren't you going to say that I'm wrong, that I have the wrong man, and that you never killed your son and Carmen De Santo. Or are you just going to sit there and stare at me? Like an idiot." Jack's voice was hard and condescending. He glared at Tom Emery.

Tom's eyes flashed and both hands clenched into fists. "I didn't kill my son," he growled. "That fucking bitch did."

"And so you hunted her down, stabbed her and nearly beheaded her, and torched her car right? That woman, who really only wanted to save your family from the likes of you," Jack growled back. He placed his palms on the table and leaned forward at that moment.

Tom's eyes continued to flash at him but he said nothing and his fists eased a bit. Jack continued. "You are a monster. You do realize that right.

Do you have anything to say for yourself?" He leaned forward a little bit more.

Tom only looked at him, then he smirked ever so slightly and in a tight voice he said, "Not unless I have my lawyer present."

Interrogation closed.

Jack met Jill and Lieutenant Copeland in the back room once Tom Emery was placed back in custody awaiting his attorney's presence for further interrogation. It had already been a long day without much sleep the night before so Jack called the Bureau who concurred that local authorities should continue with the interrogation. They did their job. They had found their man. This meant that they were off the Carmen De Santo case. The only question was whether or not they were back on the Renault case.

"Well, Lieutenant," Jack sighed. "This was simply awful. I am happy we were able to help you, but it may have been a lot easier if it had just been another Renault case."

"Lieutenant, we'd like the opportunity to visit with Armand De Santo to break the news to him personally," Jill said. "Would you have any objections?"

Lieutenant Copeland looked tired, and yet he had so much more to do that day. And it wouldn't be easy, that was for sure. "No, of course not," he said. "I hope he is able to take this news. Everything has been so hard on him."

Jack and Jill both said their goodbyes and headed out of the station. They decided they would take the rest of the afternoon off and would visit Armand De Santo after checking out of the hotel on their way back home. Jill couldn't believe home was only a day away. She sighed in relief as they headed back to the hotel that afternoon. Jack mentioned an early dinner, but she decided to pass so she could get to bed early. The sooner to bed, the sooner to morning and thus home to her daughter. It didn't get any better than that. Besides there was someone else she wanted to visit before they left Lake Shore.

VALERIE R. KACIAN

CHAPTER TWENTY-THREE

Her heart beat furiously in her chest. Her mind was spinning. The events of the last few minutes had left her in a state of complete confusion. Her white dress swirled around her as she ran into the darkness led only by the glorious moon up above.

He had literally come out of nowhere. Her head had been dizzy with fever and all she had wanted was to get home, take Nero's poultice, and sleep it all away. For the life of her she couldn't understand why she had gone out when she could barely see straight, but Nero's poultices were the only things that could make her better at a time like this. She had seen a blur across her windshield and had felt and heard the thud of something hard, but giving. Worried she had hit a deer she had stopped her car immediately and ran out. When she saw a young boy huddled on the ground her stomach had turned and she had almost gagged. Instead with the world spinning around her she had dropped to the ground and pulled him into her arms. Her eyes instantly swelled with tears and her mind couldn't quite comprehend what had just happened. When she looked up and saw Annie Emery running toward her there was only one explanation. In that instant an agony flooded her so great she almost lost consciousness. She had pleaded with Annie, who looked dazed and as distraught as she was. She had pleaded with Tom, who looked murderous his eyes glazed over in anger and suspicion. He had screamed at her until she was certain he would strike her. He blamed her for bringing shame to his family and now for hurting his son. She had continued to plead her mind suddenly clear with her fear until the ice in her blood told her to run and to run fast. So, she had. She ran into the night desperate to be away from Tom, from Annie, from Mark, from everything. She needed the Goddess. Goddess would bless. Goddess would bring answers and make her feel better.

He had followed her. She hadn't expected that. As she ran down the street, then into the woods she could hear him. She needed the Goddess. If only she could get to her Sacred Space. If only. Her mind whirled as tree branches grabbed at her hair, her face and her clothing. She stumbled a couple of times and wished she knew of a place to hide. Soon enough the clearing was in front of her. She fell to her knees and looked up at the moon chanting a prayer to her Goddess. Tom Emery tore through the branches and screamed at her as she knelt. It was only a second later that she felt the coolness of the Goddess and an urgent need to run again. To hide. She knew exactly where to hide now. The Goddess would help her through this after all. As she got up she stumbled on her dress and fell to her knees and chest.

In that instant Tom was upon her pulling at her feet dragging her closer to him. She screamed. The Goddess told her to fight. Fight with everything she had. Carmen turned herself around and struggled to free her feet of Tom's grasp. He was strong and she was afraid of breaking her ankle, and thus ruining her chance of escape. Suddenly her right foot broke free and she began thrashing and kicking with her foot to free herself again. As soon as Tom let go of her feet she scrambled up again and began to run in the opposite direction, but the world kept tilting around her in her fever and she found herself once more on the ground on her stomach. She scratched at the dirt desperately trying to get to her feet again. Everything was still spinning. Spinning.

Tom turned her around roughly and straddled her. Her breath was coming in gasps now and her vision was beginning to blur. He was saying something she could not hear and his eyes sparked hellfire. That was when she saw the glisten of the blade and her heart began to beat so fast that she could barely catch a breath. She struggled but could not free herself of this man. Her mind screamed at her wildly to run and to get away, but she couldn't.

The first time the knife stabbed she only felt warmth and a strange sensation of opening up inside. She screamed as loud as she could desperate to alert someone. Please. Help. I'm going to die. Then the warmth spread again and again and she screamed out in agony as the opening up began to bring her closer to death. Suddenly she felt very calm. She felt the coolness of the Goddess all around her and the voice told her not to struggle. It told her all would be well. Carmen could see the splendor of the bright moon above her, and she let the light pour into her until she felt as if she were completely filled with it. And She had been right. The Goddess had made everything better.

Jill sat up her entire body soaked with sweat tears pouring down her eyes. The dream had been so real she almost felt like she could touch it. She looked around the dark hotel room and sobbed. "I'm so sorry, Carmen. I'm so sorry."

VALERIE R. KACIAN

CHAPTER TWENTY-FOUR

Jack and Jill ate breakfast in the hotel restaurant for the last time, then checked out and hopped into the sedan on their way to Armand De Santo's house. The day was perfect, crisp, Autumn air with a hot, warm sun above. No clouds in the sky.

"Hard to believe it's over, huh?" Jack asked.

"I know. This has been such a strange case," Jill breathed. She could not forget her dream from the night before and the degree of sadness she had felt for the passing of this woman.

It was not long before they pulled up to the spacious circular drive of the De Santo estate and rang the doorbell. Bea had been expecting them and they were directed to the library again. She set down pastries that looked too good to resist and steaming, hot coffee. While Jack and Jill sipped their coffee, Armand De Santo entered the room. He motioned for them to keep seated and poured a cup of coffee for himself. He sat down, crossed his legs, and looked at them grimly.

"So, this is all," he breathed. "I've already been told whom you have in custody. I knew Carmen was tutoring Mark Emery, but I had no idea about her concern for him. It makes me sick to think that it came to this." His lower lip quivered and he had to take another sip of coffee to hide it. When he put his cup down he looked up at them his eyes glazed with tears. "Carmen was a wonderful woman. She was open and caring, and I'm not sure I had ever given her exactly what she needed. I wish I could have had more time with her to show her just how much I cared for her." He shook his head. "It never should have turned out like this. Never. I must thank both of you, however. At least we all have some closure now and this town

271

can rest. What will happen in the weeks to come I have no way of knowing. I can only hope that the sun will continue to shine here at Lake Shore."

Jack and Jill graciously accepted Armand's gratitude and after a few minutes left the De Santo household for the final time. As they drove down the driveway Jill said softly, "I have one other person I would like to visit."

Jack nodded. "You know this is rather unprecedented." Then he grinned and Jill smiled back at him.

They pulled up to the small house and walked through the garden to the front porch. The garden was beginning to turn over for and thus omitted an earthy scent under the heavy gaze of the sunshine. Jill knocked at the door, then waited. After a second knock there was no answer.

"Mustn't be here," Jill said.

"We should've known he wasn't. I don't think we've ever had to knock here," Jack chuckled.

Jill grinned. "I think I know where he might be."

They got back into the car and proceeded down the same road Carmen De Santo must have driven on her way back home. As they passed the Emery's house, Jill shivered. Without anyone home the place looked even more dilapidated and Jill could almost imagine the ghost of Mark Emery stalking the premises. Jill looked away quickly. A little ways up Jack parked the car and Jill got out. Jack told her he would sit and wait for her. He had a feeling this was more of a private exchange anyhow. Jill walked down the path Carmen had to have run down on the night of her death. Again a chill went up her spine. It was cooler in the woods without the sun so Jill pulled her light jacket closer to her, crossed her arms and continued until she reached the clearing. When she broke free of the trees she stopped her breath hardly coming at all. The sadness was palpable here, but there was also something else. Hope. Jill took a deep breath of the hope she could smell all around and looked to the center of the clearing. There stood Nero De Santo staring up at the heavens.

"Are you looking for her up there?" she called out to him. "Because it you are you are wrong."

Nero turned his head to look at her.

"She is everywhere. You need not look up. She is all around us."

Nero just continued to look at her his eyes twinkling. Jill could indeed see why Carmen would not have been able to control herself around this man. He was beyond anything she had ever known. "Very well put," he encouraged her. "But I was looking at that hawk up there." He looked back up and pointed to the sky.

Jill looked up and saw the outline of the hawk hanging for a moment, then switching directions in flight. She smiled. Such hope in little moments.

"And what brings you out to this fine wood this morning?" he asked.

"To see you," she said quietly. He looked at her one eyebrow raised. "I assume you heard the news."

"Karma," Nero said softly. "I'm trying not to be angry because then I may do something I later regret. I put my trust in Karma. She will prevail and make sure that justice is served." His eyes were suddenly hard and angry. It was not only that he had to grieve, but the discovery of her murderer could ignite a distinct and chilling anger. It so often did. Nero took a deep breath. "So, I have come here to let Karma do her bidding and to soak in the sweet memory of Carmen. Being here makes things bearable."

"I hope that this place will also eventually make you happy," Jill mused. "You can be with Carmen here. In spirit, anyway."

He looked at her a moment his eyes sparkling again. "Are you sure you are an investigator, my dear? Or do I hear a high priestess calling?"

Jill laughed. And time would heal all wounds.

She spent a little more time with him to say goodbye to Carmen and all she had been and all that she was. Then she headed back through the wood to Jack in the sedan and a life before Carmen. Somewhere inside of her something had changed. For the better, and forever.

PROLOGUE

Jill smiled at Amanda and gave her a warm hug. She just couldn't get enough of her little girl these days. After returning from Lake Shore, Jill had decided to take a month off to spend some time with her family. Although the Bureau wasn't so happy about this, Jack had convinced them he would continue his pursuit of Renault on his own until Jill was ready to return to the investigation. Bailey had insisted he work with Jack on the case, but he had already made a couple of mistakes, which at this stage in the game was unforgivable so Jack maintained the case alone.

The timer on the oven began to buzz. Jill pulled herself away from Amanda and opened the stove. As she began to take the chocolate chip cookies out of the oven her front doorbell rang. Jill quickly put down the hot pan and called over to Amanda that she would get the door.

She rushed to the door wiping her hands on her jeans as she went. She couldn't remember the last time she had been so happy. Jill opened the door to see that her front porch was empty. She looked left and right on the street and saw no one. She looked down. On her welcome mat there was a small stack of two books.

She bent down and picked them up. One book was entitled, "Wicca for Dummies" and one small, black book was entitled, "Wanton Pleasures of a Desperately Deserving Woman." Jill flipped through this book and saw the writings and drawings of Carmen De Santo from her grimoire.

Jill grinned and breathed the sweet air in deeply. "Thank you, Carmen," she whispered.

ABOUT THE AUTHOR

The Ghosts of Carmen De Santo is Valerie R. Kacian's first published novel. She lives with her husband, two children, and two mischievous puppies in the greater Boston area. When she is not writing she can be found reading, running, spending time with family, or studying human nature.

www.ingramcontent.com/pod-product-compliance
Lightning Source LLC
Chambersburg PA
CBHW060304260626
47160CB00007B/2500

* 9 7 8 0 9 8 8 3 0 2 4 2 6 *